Vordan's Inn

-Isles

Pirate King's
Keep

Lycon's Peak

Map

Supply
Post

Lagoon
Island

ANERIA

Kalligan's Map

DAUGHTER OF
THE SIREN QUEEN

Daughter of the Siren Queen

TRICIA LEVENSELLER

FEIWEL AND FRIENDS • NEW YORK

3\18
Brr

Y
Lev

A Feiwel and Friends Book
An imprint of Macmillan Publishing Group, LLC
175 Fifth Avenue, New York, NY 10010

Our books may be purchased in bulk for promotional, educational, or
business use. Please contact your local bookseller or the Macmillan Corporate
and Premium Sales Department at (800) 221-7945 ext. 5442 or by e-mail at
MacmillanSpecialMarkets@macmillan.com.

Library of Congress Control Number: 2017944810

ISBN 978-1-250-09601-2 (hardcover) / ISBN 978-1-250-09602-9 (ebook)

Book design by Liz Dresner

Feiwel and Friends logo designed by Filomena Tuosto

First edition, 2018

10 9 8 7 6 5 4 3 2

fiercereads.com

For Mom,
because you said I could write a book
instead of getting a summer job.
I love you.

"AND THAT WAS WITHOUT
EVEN A SINGLE DROP OF RUM."

—CAPTAIN JACK SPARROW
Pirates of the Caribbean: At World's End

Chapter 1

THE SOUND OF MY knife slitting across a throat feels much too loud in the darkness.

I catch the pirate before his corpse hits the ground and gently lower him the rest of the way. He is only the first of Theris's—no, Vordan's, I remind myself—crew who will die tonight.

My own crew is spread out across the cobblestone streets, dispatching Vordan's men one by one. I cannot see them, but I trust all of them to do their parts tonight.

It's taken me two months to track down the pirate lord and gather enough intel to infiltrate his holding. Vordan thought to make himself safe from me by traveling inland. We're miles from the nearest port, and though I don't have a way to replenish my abilities, I came fully stocked.

My source inside gave me all the details I needed. Vordan and his crew are living in the Old Bear Inn. I can see it now up ahead, a four-story structure with a near-flat roof and painted green walls. The main entrance is composed of an impressive archway, a large sign depicting a sleeping bear jutting out from its top.

Vordan's crew of pirates have transformed themselves into a gang of land thieves, preying on the inhabitants of Charden, the largest of the Seventeen Isles. He bought the inn and pays the wages of all the staff, keeping it as his own personal stronghold. It would seem he has no fear of living in plain sight. The men in his employ number near one hundred, and there isn't a united force stationed on this island large enough to dispose of them.

But I don't need to dispose of them. All I need is to get in and then get Vordan and his map piece out without alerting the rest of his men. His questioning and inevitable torture will happen once we're back on my ship.

I slide down the street, keeping close to the roughly constructed townhome on my right. The city is asleep at this hour. I haven't spotted a soul moving about, save Vordan's men on watch.

A tinkling sound stops me dead in my tracks. I hold my breath as I peer around the next corner, into the gap between this home and the next. But there is only a street urchin—a young boy perhaps eight or nine years of age—searching through a pile of glass bottles.

I'm surprised when he turns his head in my direction. I've

been as silent as the dead, but I suppose to survive on the streets, one must sense when a threat may be nearby.

I put my finger to my lips, then toss a coin at the boy, who catches it without taking his eyes off me. I give him a wink before crossing the gap to the next home.

Here, I wait, watching my breath fog out in front of me in the slim moonlight. Though I could use the heat, I don't dare risk the sound of my hands rubbing together. There is nothing for me to do now except to hold perfectly still.

Finally, an owl hoot comes. Then another. And another. I wait until I hear all seven of them—signaling that each crossing street and guarded rooftop has been cleared.

I watch the windows of the large inn in front of me. There's not a single candle lit, nor a silhouette of movement behind the glass. I take my chance and scurry up to the inn.

A rope already hangs down from the roof. Sorinda has beaten me here. I hoist myself up floor after floor, avoiding the windows, until my boots steady on the stone tiles of the roof. Sorinda is just putting her sword away, four of Vordan's men dead at her feet. There is nothing she excels at more than killing.

Without saying a word, she helps me to pull up the rope and reattach it so it dangles on the west side of the rooftop. Vordan's window is on the top floor, third window from the right.

Ready? I mouth.

She nods.

Holding my knife against a sleeping Vordan's throat fills me with the sweetest feeling of justice. I move my free hand to cover his mouth.

His eyes fly open, and I press the knife in a little deeper, just enough to slice the skin but not enough to make him bleed.

"Call out for help, and I slit your throat," I whisper. I remove my free hand from his mouth.

"Alosa," he says, a bitter acknowledgment.

"Vordan." He's just as I remember. A man with unremarkable looks: brown hair and eyes, an average build, average height. Nothing to make him stand out in a crowd, which is how he likes it.

"You figured it out," he says, obviously referring to his identity, which he'd initially lied about. When I was a prisoner on the *Night Farer*, he had pretended to be one of my father's men and had gone by the name Theris.

"Where's the map?" I ask.

"Not here."

Sorinda, who stands as a silent sentinel behind me, begins moving about the room. I hear her rustling through the drawers of the dresser, then picking at the floorboards.

"I have no use for you if you don't tell me where it is," I say. "I will end your life. Right here. In this room. Your men will find your body in the morning."

He smiles then. "You need me alive, Alosa. Otherwise I'd already be dead."

"If I have to ask you one more time, I'll start singing,"

4

I warn. "What should I make you do first? Break your legs? Draw pictures on the walls in your own blood?"

He swallows. "My men outnumber yours three to one. I'm not going anywhere, and that voice of yours will do you little good when you can only control three at a time."

"Your men won't be able to do much fighting when they're asleep in their beds. My girls are already locking them in their rooms."

His eyes narrow.

"Pity you didn't catch my spy in your ranks, and it's a shame you didn't notice her switching out all the locks on the doors. Yes, they lock from the outside now."

"They've been alerted. My men on watch—"

"Are all dead. The four men on this roof. The five in the streets. The three on the butcher's roof, the tanner's, and the supply store."

His mouth widens so I can see his teeth. "Six," he says.

My breathing stops for a beat.

"I had six on the streets," he clarifies.

What? No. We would've known—

A bell tolls so loudly it will wake the entire town.

I swear under my breath.

"The little boy," I say, just as Vordan reaches underneath his pillow. For the dagger I've already removed. "Time to go, Sorinda."

Get up. I direct the words at Vordan, but they are not an ordinary command spoken with an ordinary voice. The words are sung, full of magic passed on to me by my siren mother.

And all men who hear them have no choice but to obey.

Vordan rises from his bed at once, plants his feet on the floor.

Where is the map?

His hand goes to his throat and pulls out a leather cord hidden beneath his shirt. On the end is a glass vial, no bigger than my thumb, stoppered with a cork. And rolled up inside is the final map piece. With it, my father and I will finally travel to the siren island and claim its treasure.

My body is already alive with song, my senses heightened. I can hear the men moving below, shrugging on their boots and running for their doors.

I pull the vial at Vordan's neck. The cord snaps, and I place the entire necklace in the pocket of the ebony corset I wear.

I make Vordan go out the door first. He's barefoot, of course, and wears only a loose flannel shirt and cotton trousers. The man who locked me in a cage does not get the comfort of shoes and a coat.

Sorinda is right behind me as I step into the hallway. Below, I hear Vordan's men throwing the weight of their bodies against their locked doors, trying to respond to the warning bell. Damn that bell!

My girls haven't reached the upper floors yet. Men from this floor and the one below spill into the hallway. It doesn't take them long to spot their captain.

I sing a series of words to Vordan in no more than a whisper.

He shouts, "Outside, you fools! It's the land king's men. They approach from the south! Go and meet them."

Many start to move, heeding their captain's call, but one man shouts, "No, look behind him! It's the siren bitch!"

That man, I decide, dies first.

Vordan must have warned them against a situation like this, because the men draw their cutlasses and charge.

Blast it all.

I expand the song, placing two more of Vordan's men under my spell, then send them in front of us to battle the oncoming men.

The narrowness of the hallway works to our advantage. The inn is rectangular, with rooms lining the edge of one side of the hallway and a railing on the other. Over the railing one can see clear down to the first floor. A stairwell zigzags up to each floor, the only way up or down except for the windows and the long drop to the bottom.

I step in line with the three men under my spell to fight the first wave. I ram my shoulder into the pirate who dared to call me "the siren bitch," sending him over the railing. He screams until he's cut off with a loud crunch. I don't pause to look—I'm already thrusting my sword through the belly of the next pirate. He collapses to the floor, and I walk over his twitching body to reach the next man.

Vordan's pirates have no qualms against cutting down their own men, but they won't touch their captain. As soon as one of the spares goes down, I enchant the next closest man, having him fill the gap, keeping three under my control at all times.

Sorinda is at our backs, facing the two men who came out

of the rooms on the very end, and I don't worry about checking over my shoulder. They won't get through her.

Soon Vordan's men realize that if they kill their own men, they will be the next victims to fall under my spell. They retreat, running down the stairs, likely hoping to change the battleground to the open first floor of the inn. But my girls, the ones who were locking doors, meet them on the second floor. Ten women, personally trained by me, led by Mandsy, my ship's doctor and second mate, prevent them from taking the stairs.

We've got them fighting on two sides now.

"Snap out of it, Captain!" the unusually tall man fighting me now shouts over to Vordan. "Tell us what to do!" After parrying his last jab, I send my elbow into the underside of his chin. His head snaps back, and I cut off his grunt by raking my cutlass across his throat.

Their numbers are dwindling, but those who were locked in their rooms have started hacking through their doors with their cutlasses and joining the fight.

Men begin jumping over the railing of the second floor, crashing onto the tables and chairs of the eating area below. Some fall only to break limbs and twist ankles, but many manage the fall and attempt to attack my girls from behind.

Oh, no you don't.

I jump over the railing, land on my feet easily, and tackle the four men approaching my girls. I dare a glance upward as I find my footing, and see that Sorinda has dispatched the men once at my back and has now taken my spot.

"Sorinda! Get down here," I yell, pausing my singing just long enough to get the words out.

I cut at the hamstrings of one of the men I felled. The next gets the point of my dagger jammed into the base of his spine. The other two are rounding on me, finally finding their feet.

The smaller of the two meets my eyes, recognizes who I am, and makes a run for it out the main entrance, just past the stairs.

"I've got him," Sorinda, having reached the main floor, says, and darts past me.

The last man in my path throws down his sword. "I surrender," he says. I hit him on the head with the pommel of my sword. He crumples in a heap at my feet.

There are maybe forty men left, trying to force their way down past my crew. Vordan and two of his men remain at the back of the line, still under my spell, fighting against their own crew.

But my powers are running out. We need to get out of here. I glance around the room, noting the unlit lanterns hanging all along the walls, contemplating the oil resting inside.

Jump, I command Vordan. He doesn't hesitate. He throws himself over the railing. He lands with one of his legs bent awkwardly beneath him, just as I'd intended.

I release Vordan and the two pirates at the back of the line from my spell, and instead focus the rest of my efforts on the three right in front of my crew.

Hold the line, I command. They rotate instantly, turning their swords on their own men. To my girls, I shout, "Unload the extra gunpowder for your pistols onto the stairs."

Mandsy steps back, pulls the powder pouch from near her holster, and throws it onto the step just below the men under my spell. The rest of the girls follow suit, nine more bags of powder dropping to the floor.

"Go get Vordan! Get him to the carriage."

Vordan swears at the top of his lungs now that he has his senses. My girls pick him clean off his feet, since his leg is useless, and carry him through the exit. I'm right behind them, pulling my pistol from my side and aiming at that pile of gunpowder.

I fire.

The blast presses at my back, pushing me faster. Smoke fills my nostrils and a surge of heat envelops me. I lurch forward, but catch my footing and hurry on. Looking over my shoulder, I take in the destruction. The inn still stands, but it's burning apart from the inside. The wall surrounding the main entrance now lies in tatters around the road. The pirates still inside are burning husks on the ground.

I make a turn down the next street, racing toward the rendezvous point. Sorinda materializes out of the darkness and runs silently next to me.

"In and out without anyone being the wiser," she says, deadpan.

"Plans change. Besides, I had all of Vordan's men piled together in one location. How could I resist blowing it up? He has nothing now."

"Except a broken leg."

I smile. Sorinda rarely bothers with humor. "Yes, except that."

We round another corner and reach the carriage. Wallov and Deros sit at the reins. They were the only men on my crew until Enwen and Kearan joined, but I left the latter two on the *Ava-lee* to guard the ship under Niridia's watch. Wallov and Deros are my brig guards. They jump from their seat and open the carriage doors. A cage rests on the floor inside. Deros pulls out a key and unlocks it, letting the opening swing wide.

"Wallov, show our guest inside," I say.

"Gladly."

"You can't put me in there," Vordan says. "Alosa, I—"

He's cut off by Sorinda's fist slamming into his gut. She gags him and ties his hands behind his back. Only then does Wallov thrust him inside the cage. It's rather small, meant for a dog or some sort of livestock, but we manage to squeeze Vordan inside.

I step up to the carriage door and look inside. On the seats rest two wooden chests, their locks broken.

"Did you get it all, then?" I ask.

"Aye," Wallov says. "Athella's information was spot on. Vordan's gold was in the cellar underneath the false floor."

"And just where is our informant?"

"Here, Captain!" Athella steps out from among the group behind Mandsy. She's still in disguise, her hair hidden beneath a tricorne, fake facial hair stuck to her chin. She's put face paint over her brows to widen and darken them. Lines around her cheeks make them look more elongated. Blocks in her shoes give her the necessary extra height, and she wears a bulky vest under her shirt to fill out the men's clothing.

She pulls the masculine accoutrements from her body and wipes her face until she looks like herself once more. What's left is a reed-thin girl with hair that falls to her shoulders in a smooth, black sheet. Athella is the ship's designated spy and most renowned lockpick.

I turn back to Vordan, who's staring bug-eyed at the young girl he thought was a member of his crew. He swivels his gaze to me, eyes sizzling with hate.

"How does it feel to be the one locked in the cage?" I ask.

He pulls at his bound hands, trying to free himself, and my mind is pulled back to that time two months ago when Vordan stuck me in a cage and forced me to show him all the abilities I possess, using Riden to make me comply.

Riden . . .

He, too, is back on my ship, healing from the gunshot wounds Vordan gave him. I'll have to finally take the time to visit him once we get back, but for now—

I slam the carriage door in Vordan's face.

Chapter 2

I DON'T KNOW HOW landfolk do it.

Ships don't leave your thighs sore. They don't leave foul-smelling piles on the ground. Horses, I decide, are disgusting, and I'm relieved to be rid of them when we finally reach Port Renwoll a week later.

My ship, the *Ava-lee*, is docked in the harbor, waiting for me. She's the most beautiful vessel ever built. She belonged to the land king's fleet before I commandeered her. I left her the natural color of the oak she's made of, but I dyed the sails royal blue. The *Ava-lee* bears three masts; the middle is square-rigged, while the other two have lateen sails. With no forecastle and only a small aftercastle, she fits all thirty-three of us snugly.

She may be small, but she's also the fastest ship in existence.

"They're back!" a voice chirps from clear up in the crow's nest. That'll be little Roslyn, Wallov's daughter and the ship's lookout. She's the youngest member of the crew at six years old.

Wallov knew Roslyn's mother all of one night. Nine months later she died giving birth to a baby girl. Wallov assumed responsibility for his child, even though he hadn't a clue what to do with her. He was sixteen at the time. Previously, he'd been a sailor on a fishing boat, but he was forced to give it up once he had a daughter to care for. He didn't know how he was going to feed the two of them until he met me.

"Captain on board!" Niridia shouts as I step on deck. As my first mate, she's been captaining the ship in my absence.

Roslyn's already lowered herself onto the deck. She throws herself at me, wrapping her arms around my legs. Her head barely reaches my waist.

"You were gone too long," she says. "Next time, take me with you."

"There was fighting to be done on this trip, Roslyn. Besides, I needed you here watching after my ship."

"But I can fight, Captain. Papa's been teaching me." She reaches behind her too-big britches and pulls out a small dagger.

"Roslyn, you're six years old. Give it ten more, then we'll see."

Her eyes scrunch up in a glare. Then she lunges for me.

She's quick, I'll give her that, but I still dodge her blade effortlessly. Without pausing, she swings back around and swipes at me. I leap backward, then kick the dagger out of her reach. She crosses her arms defiantly.

"All right," I say, "we'll check again in eight years. Satisfied?"

She smiles, then rushes in to give me another hug.

"You'd think I didn't exist," Wallov says to Deros from somewhere behind me.

Roslyn, hearing him, lets go and runs to him. "I was getting to you, Papa."

I survey everyone else on board. I left twelve behind to guard the ship. They're all on deck now, save our two newest recruits.

"Was there any trouble?" I ask Niridia.

"It was downright boring. And you?"

"We saw some action. Nothing we couldn't handle. And we brought back some prizes." I pull out the makeshift necklace by the cord, displaying the map for everyone to see. I have a copy of the first two map pieces already, and while we sail back to the keep, I'll have Mandsy create a replica of the new one. Father will lead the journey to the Isla de Canta, but I want to be prepared should we get separated or tragedy befall his ship. It would be foolish to have only one copy of such valuable items.

Over by the port side, Teniri, the ship's purser, peers over toward the carriage and asks, "What else? Anything of the sparkling, gold variety, Captain?"

Mandsy and the girls make their way up the gangplank. It takes four of them to lift each chest. Deros and Wallov have already deposited our prisoner, cage and all, onto the deck of the ship. Vordan lies there, gagged and ignored, as the girls all circle around the chests. Until everyone is divvied out their fair share, no one is permitted to touch the gold except Teniri. She's the oldest on the ship at twenty-six. Though she's still plenty young, she has a gray streak of hair on the back of her head that she tries to hide in a braid. Anyone who dares to mention it gets a swift kick to the gut.

She raises the lids of both chests at once, revealing a hefty amount of gold and silver coins, and some priceless gems and stones.

"All right," I say. "You've had your chance to look at it. Let's get it stored safely and be on our way."

"What about him?" Wallov asks. He kicks the cage, and Vordan wrinkles his nose at him, not bothering to attempt yelling through the gag.

"I'd have you put him in the brig, but I need to stock up tonight. Better be the infirmary, then. Keep him in the cage."

"Captain," Niridia says. "The infirmary is already occupied by a prisoner."

I hadn't forgotten. I would never forget *him*.

"He will be relocated," I say.

"To where?"

"I'll handle it. See that everything else gets put in its proper place. Where's Kearan?"

"I'll give you one guess."

I huff out a breath of air. "Get him out of my rum supply and to the helm. We're leaving now." Far, far away from the stench of horse. I need a bath.

After my previous navigator lost her life during the battle on the *Night Farer*, I stole Kearan from Riden's ship. He's a useless drunk most of the time, but he's also the finest helms-man I've ever seen. Though I'd never tell him that.

I turn toward the infirmary and stare at the door.

I haven't laid eyes on Riden in two months. Instead, I put him in Mandsy's care, trusting her to help his legs heal and see that he gets food every day. Were it anyone else, the idea of leaving her alone with him would make my blood boil. But Mandsy's never shown an inch of interest toward men or women. She's just not made that way.

So, as the ship's doctor, I ordered her to take care of him and give me updates: when she took out his stitches, when he started walking on his bad leg again.

"He asks for you, Captain," she would say before we left to capture Vordan, but I was never ready to see him.

When I was locked in that cage, Vordan threatened Riden in an attempt to control me.

And it worked.

Riden had been my interrogator while I was a prisoner on the *Night Farer*. He was a means to an end. A distraction from the tedium of searching a ship from top to bottom—albeit a very attractive distraction who also happens to be a good kisser. It was all fun. Just play.

At least I thought so. Vordan's words to Riden from the island still haunt me. *There is at least one thing she cares about more than her own justice. You.*

The thought of talking to Riden, even if it means I can lord his prisoner status over him, is unsettling.

Because he knows I let another man control me for the sake

of him. He knows that I care about him. But *I'm* not ready to know I care about him. So how could I face him?

But now, I have no choice. We need this room for Vordan. Riden is going to join Kearan and Enwen on the deck. I can't avoid him any longer.

The door swings open much too quickly, and I find Riden in the corner, stretching out his bad leg. His hair has grown some, its brown lengths reaching just past his shoulders. A couple days' worth of stubble clings to his chin, since he's only permitted to shave when he bathes. He's not any less fit than I remember, so he's been making good use of his time stuck in here.

The changes only make him look more roguish. Dangerous. Almost irresistibly handsome.

He'll need to shave first thing when he leaves the room. Otherwise the girls won't be able to focus on their work.

He looks up as I close the door behind me, but he doesn't say anything, merely surveys me from head to toe, not even caring that he's staring at me far longer than is necessary.

A spark of heat flickers low in my belly. I try to expel it by coughing.

He smiles. "You took your time coming to see me, Alosa."

"I've been busy."

"Busy catching up with your intended?"

I had a short list of all the things I was going to say to him, about why we're relocating him, or even keeping him on the ship in the first place. But it all flees my mind at his words.

"My intended?" I ask.

"That blond fellow with the curly tresses. Looks a bit like a girl."

At my confused look, he adds, "The one who helped overpower the strength of the *Night Farer* with your father."

"Oh, you mean Tylon? He looks nothing like a girl." Though I'd pay a fortune to have Riden say otherwise in front of him.

"So he is your intended, then?" He asks it casually enough. A smile still rests on his lips, but one mental switch and I can see he's swirling with a dark green. Jealousy in its deepest, rawest form.

He glares at me. "Don't do that to me. Turn it off."

I back up, startled by his cold look and outburst, before I compose myself. "I forgot you notice when I'm using it."

"That hardly matters." The smile comes back. "I thought you hated using your abilities. Aren't they supposed to make you feel sick to your stomach? You must care a lot about what I think."

I don't like where he's turning the conversation, so I divert it back. "Tylon is not my intended. We're *pirates*." Marriage isn't really something we do.

"What would you call him, then? Your lover?"

I snort. Tylon wishes, but I would never let the slimy eel touch me.

Riden doesn't need to know that, though. I'm beyond amused by his accusation. I'd much rather see how this plays out than deny it.

"Sure," I lie, "lover works."

This time he can't hide behind indifference. His eyes flash a dangerous black, and his fists clench slightly. I pretend not to notice.

"Am I to understand, then, that the two of you have an open relationship?"

When I don't respond, he adds, "He doesn't care that you spent the better part of a month sleeping in my bed?"

He and I both know that sleeping is all we did in that bed. Well, that and a few kisses.

"I had a job to do, Riden. Getting close to you was part of it."

"I see. And just how many men have you gotten close to in order to do your job?"

I don't like his tone one bit. Riden needs to be reminded who he's speaking to.

"I have your brother locked in the deepest, darkest cell in the pirate king's keep," I say. "He's paying for everything he did—and tried to do—to me. One gesture from me, and I could have his head. It is only by your request that I haven't killed him yet, but that's not good enough anymore."

Riden straightens. I have his attention now.

"What are you saying?"

"Keeping prisoners is expensive. They have to be fed and cleaned up after. My father rarely holds prisoners for an extended amount of time. Either they give him what he wants or they're killed. We don't need anything from Draxen. He's useless to me. You, however, are not."

"What do you want from me?"

"I've just captured Vordan and his map piece—the final piece my father needs before we set sail for the Isla de Canta. When the fleet departs, you will be joining my crew for the journey."

Riden's gaze narrows. "Why would you possibly need me? Surely His Royal Blackheartedness has enough pirates in his fleet."

He most certainly does. More than he could possibly need. And I've got some of the most skilled sailors and fighters in all of Maneria aboard the *Ava-lee*. We don't *need* Riden, but I can't set him free. How would that look to my father? I can't lock him up at the keep because there's no reason to keep him alive. Father will kill him and Draxen both. The only reason Draxen isn't dead yet is because I told my father I need him alive to get Riden to cooperate. So now that Riden is better, I'm down to my last option. He has to come with me. He has to be part of the crew. But how do I possibly explain that to Riden without making it seem like I've gone soft on him?

I tell myself I'm doing this because I owe him. He saved me. He took two bullets for me. I may have brought him back from nearly drowning, but that was my fault to begin with. We are not even, not yet. That is the only reason why I'm keeping him alive.

If I think it enough times, maybe it'll be true.

Finally, I say, "I don't know what we'll come up against on the voyage. I might need some extra muscle. With Kearan and Enwen, the men on this ship number four. Enwen is so scrawny that I'm pretty sure Niridia can lift more than he can. And the only lifting Kearan does is when he puts a bottle to his lips. I'm not about to recruit some random person off the keep, because I need people I can trust."

"And you trust me?" he asks with one raised brow.

"I don't need to. I know you'll do anything to protect your brother. I can count on your full cooperation as long as he's locked up. And besides, you owe me for saving his pathetic life in the first place."

He pauses for a moment, probably to think it over. "Will I continue to be kept under lock and key?"

"Only if you do something stupid. You'll be free to roam the ship as much as any sailor. Any attempt at escape, though, and I'll send word to the men left guarding the keep that Draxen's head is to be removed from his body."

Riden turns his face away from me.

"What?" I ask.

"I'd forgotten how ruthless you can be."

I take a step toward him and pierce him with my gaze. "You haven't seen ruthless from me yet."

"And I pray I never will. I'll come with you to the island on two conditions."

"You want to bargain with me? I hold all the cards."

Riden stands in one fluid motion. "Going with you is pointless if you're going to kill Draxen as soon as we get back. I want your word he'll be freed once I help you journey to the island and back."

"And I suppose the second stipulation is your own freedom?"

"No."

I blink, take a step closer. "What do you mean 'no'? You hold

Draxen's life in higher regard than your own? He's a disgusting worm. He deserves to squirm below ground."

"He's my brother. And you're a hypocrite." Riden takes his own step forward.

"What is that supposed to mean?"

"Your father is the most despicable man to roam the sea. Tell me you wouldn't do anything for him."

I advance farther, a mere foot from him now, deciding whether or not to clobber him with my fists. In the end, I take a step back and breathe in calmly. "What is your second condition?"

"You will not use your siren abilities on me ever again. Even if it's just to know what I'm feeling."

"What if your life were in danger and I could save you with my voice? Would you prefer I let you die?" For some reason, I feel the need to defend myself. And my abilities. To him. Why to him? His opinion of me shouldn't matter. *Doesn't* matter.

"I've survived this long without you, and I will continue to do so."

"Ah, but you've never sailed with me before. Danger is always nigh for my crew."

"With you in their midst, how could it not be?" He says this quietly to himself, but I still catch it.

"Will you sail with me or not?" I ask.

"Do you agree to my terms?"

I look heavenward. I'll have the whole voyage to figure out what to do with Riden and Draxen when we get back. For now, I can agree to this.

Riden holds out his hand to seal our bargain. I extend my own, anticipating a firm squeeze.

What I do not expect is the tingle of heat that shoots up my arm from where we touch. Though I tell my hand to let go, it doesn't listen, and my feet seem rooted to the spot.

I look up from our clasped hands, and my eyes land on the stubble along his jaw. I wonder what it would feel like rubbing against my chin and cheeks as he kissed me.

I blink repeatedly. *What the—Was I just staring at his mouth? Did he notice?*

I look up. Riden's eyes capture my own, glinting with mischief. He is the first to speak. "This is sure to be an exciting voyage. The two of us stuck together on one ship." His thumb draws circles on the back of my hand, and my breathing hitches. It appears my lungs, too, have forgotten how to function properly.

Riden starts to draw closer, and my mind finally remembers something.

He's my prisoner. Anything he does will be an act to further his goal to free himself and his brother. I cannot trust any of it. After all, did I not try to use physical closeness with Riden to further my own goals when I was the prisoner and he the captor?

His pretty face will not earn him privileges on this ship. Nor will I allow him to use it to get closer to me.

I tell my limbs to stop misbehaving and finally step away from him.

I have gone two months without his kisses. I can go the rest of my life without them as well.

"It is a very large ship," I say at last, even though it's a lie. And then, because I want to see him squirm, I offer him the most seductive smile I have, and wet my lips with my tongue ever so slightly.

The way his eyes move down to my mouth—and the bounce of the nob of his throat as he audibly swallows—is more than enough reward.

Yes, I am the one in control.

I turn to open the door and extend one hand toward the deck, an invitation for Riden to precede me onto the ship.

He walks perfectly out the door, no limp in his step. Good.

I watch him as he descends the companionway, surveying the crew as they go about their chores. His eyes take in the clouds, roam over the sea, and I feel bad for keeping him cooped up for two whole months.

"Admiring the view, are we, Captain?" a voice asks. Lotiya and Deshel, sisters I picked up from the island of Jinda two years ago, take up position on either side of me. "He looks delicious," Deshel adds.

"From behind, anyway," Lotiya says. "Can't judge the man properly until we see the front."

"Not to mention *naked*."

Giggling ensues.

Riden looks over his shoulders, partly amused yet a little uncomfortable. He heard them. I'm certainly glad I'm not prone to blushing. For I've seen Riden's front. And him naked. The sisters' talk immediately brings the image to the surface of my mind.

I glare at the two of them. "We have a new recruit," I shout for the whole crew to hear. "Meet Riden."

Many of the girls look up from their tasks. A couple drop down out of the rigging now that the ship is under way. I see a lot of curiosity in their faces. And some interest in others.

"Riden!" I shout, remembering something. He looks up again. "Go below and shave. You look haggard."

He raises a brow, but doesn't dare to disobey the first order I give him after our deal. He treads belowdecks. Lotiya and Deshel try to follow.

"Get back to your posts," I shout at them. They sigh in resignation and scatter.

"Haggard?" Niridia asks. She's at the helm. Kearan, it would seem, hasn't arrived yet. I join her. "That man is handsome as hell."

"Troublesome as hell is more like it," I say. "I don't know what I'm going to do with him."

"I could tell you what I'd like to do with him."

"Niridia," I warn.

"A jest, Captain."

I know. Niridia hasn't been able to stomach the touch of a man after what she went through before I found her, but that doesn't keep her from teasing. As my best friend, it's her job. She's able to jump back and forth between the roles of friend and first mate effortlessly, knowing when each is appropriate. I love her for it.

"We're keeping him, then?" she asks.

"Yes."

"Hmm" is all she says. She's the overly cautious type, the most responsible out of everyone on the ship. She always has something to say.

"What?"

"Just remember he's Jeskor's son. Your families are rivals. Have you wondered if being on this ship is exactly where he wants to be?"

"Just like when I was a 'prisoner' on his ship?" I intended to get captured—all because I had a map to find on Riden's brother's ship.

"Exactly."

"Riden's not like that. He doesn't have his own ambitions. The only thing that drives him is his brother."

Niridia blows a golden wisp of hair out of her blue eyes. "I wouldn't say it's the *only* thing, Captain." She looks at me pointedly.

To change the subject, I ask, "Where is Kearan?"

Niridia waves toward the bow, and I'm surprised now that I didn't spot him sooner. Kearan is massive. His bulk is tucked into his usual dark coat, a jacket full of pockets where he houses all his flasks. The man drinks like a parched fish.

But now it looks as though he's had a few too many. He's pressed against the starboard side, the contents of his stomach depositing into the sea below.

I'm trying to think of a suitable punishment for him when Niridia and I spot Sorinda materializing out of the shadows near the foremast. Her raven-colored hair is just a shade darker than her skin. It's held up with a band, the ends reaching just past her shoulders. Sorinda never bothers with a tricorne. She spends most of her time in the dark and has no need to keep the sun out of her eyes. Instead of a cutlass, she carries a rapier at her side, favoring speed to strength.

Right now, however, she holds the end of a rope.

"What is she doing?" Niridia asks.

I'd tasked Sorinda with keeping an eye on Kearan when he first joined the ship. She hated it, though her job turned out to be easy since Kearan couldn't take his eyes off her. She's threatened to cut out his eyes multiple times, but I've expressly forbidden it. He can't navigate my ship without them.

Now that we're back from our mission, it looks like Sorinda has picked up right where she left off. Tolerating Kearan.

She ties the end of the rope she's holding around Kearan's waist. He doesn't even notice, merely fidgets with another wave of sickness. Since he's already halfway over the edge, it takes Sorinda very little effort to push him the rest of the way. There's a quick shriek followed by a loud splash.

And Sorinda—my dark, quiet assassin—smiles. It's a beautiful thing, but so fleeting. She composes herself before peering over the edge, the only outward sign of her preening over her victory.

Coughing and swearing ensues on Kearan's end, but Sorinda molds back into shadow without another word.

Sometimes it's so easy to forget Kearan is only a few years older than Sorinda and I are. Carrying on like a drunk will age a man considerably.

"See to it that someone helps him out of there, will you?" I ask Niridia. "He and the rest of the men need their ears covered. I'm going to stock up."

"Now?" she asks carefully. She knows exactly how much I hate this particular part of being half siren.

"It needs to be now. I haven't any song left after the fight on Charden, and I'll need it if I'm to properly interrogate Vordan." I smile then, thinking of the fun the two of us will have.

My methods of interrogation have been known to make men lose their minds.

Chapter 3

ONLY ONE CELL IN the brig has cushions: my cell.

Fluffy red plush covers the floor and props against the wooden wall. I remove my boots and leave them far out of reach of the bars. Then I unlace my corset and set it atop my boots. I step inside the cell, wearing naught but leggings and a simple long-sleeved blouse. I can't wear buttons or laces or hairpins. Not in here.

I shut myself in and lock the door. With the tightest grip I can make, I yank at the bars. I know they haven't grown any less sturdy, but I always fear I might break out. I have to check each time, just to reassure myself the metal won't bend under my fingers.

Mandsy comes down with a bucket of water. She places it

just on the other side of the cell, so I can reach it through the bars. Then she collects my boots and corset. I hand her the key.

"All the men have their ears covered, Captain," she says. "They know the drill."

"What about the new recruits?"

"Well, Kearan is probably too drunk to be roused even by your abilities, but Sorinda made sure his ears were properly covered anyway. Enwen took enough wax for three men's ears, saying you could never be too careful." She laughs. "I like that one especially. He's a funny sort of fellow."

"And Riden?"

"He took it calmly, no questions asked."

"You explained to him what I was doing?"

"Yes, Captain."

I want to ask more. What expression did he have on his face? Did he seem disgusted?

He made a point of telling me I was never to use my abilities on him. Is he sickened by what I am? But then I remember I shouldn't care. I *don't* care.

My fingers tingle as my gaze flits to the bucket of water. Though I dread what it does to my mind, my body revels in being so close. Without another thought, I plunge my fingers into the bucket and pull the water into me.

Everything becomes heightened instantly. The creaking of the wood, the sloshing water outside the ship, a woman's whistling from up top, boots on the deck, coughing, laughing. I can sense the breaths of all the people around me—puppets for me to play with.

Like plucking a string on an instrument, my voice tugs at the string of a human's consciousness. *Come to me.*

The human before me smiles. "Won't be following that order, Captain. I'll just take this stuff up top, then."

A human girl. I hiss at her. She's incapable of joining in the fun. Her back turns to me, and my blood boils inside me. *How dare she dismiss me!* I lunge at the bars, banging and tugging, but they will not move. They've trapped me. The disgusting humans. I can sense them moving above. I sing out to one after another, trying to find an ear to free me, but none answer my call.

Some of the power leaves me. My body itches with need. I look around quickly, and my eyes land on a bucket of water. My fingers sink in, gathering it to me, and I sigh from the pleasure of it. Far below me, I can sense the sea life. Water rushes across gills, curls over tentacles, bubbles up from the sandy bottom. A startled fish changes direction at the approach of the ship. A dolphin prepares to breach the surface. A whale hums far in the distance.

And I am queen over them all.

This cage will not hold me long, and when I'm free, I will have the men on this ship dance for me until their feet bleed.

There's a quiet groaning of hinges, a whisper of feet. A face peeks around the corner.

It's one of the men. I smile at him coyly, showing just a hint of teeth. Not enough to show him the predator I am. With one curled finger, I beckon him forward. He listens, but takes no more than a couple of steps, distancing us by several feet.

He's a handsome fellow with silky-looking brown hair. I can picture perfectly how it would look submerged underwater, the strands being brushed by the waves as his corpse bumps onto the shore.

There is a spark of fear in those rich brown eyes. They're dotted with gold. Fascinating. If I could just reach one with the tip of my nail, I could pluck it out and . . .

Those eyes firm up with determination. Is he resolved to be unafraid? Well, let me help the poor fool. I round out my mouth and let a few low notes drop from my lips. It's a slow, sensual rhythm that should bring him to me faster than he can blink.

But the man doesn't move. He points to his ears. Ah, yes. The humans think they're safe if they cannot hear me. Doesn't he know I can do more than sing?

Very carefully, I roll my sleeves up past my elbows, showing off more skin. I run my fingers slowly through my hair, letting the strands fall around my shoulders. The man is riveted, watching my every move.

At last I lean back on the cushions, arching my breasts upward, and stroke the cushions next to me lovingly in invitation.

He turns right around and walks away from me, never giving me a second look. I half scream, half sing at him to return, but of course he cannot hear a thing. All it does is force me to take in more of the water.

I stretch and yawn after waking the next morning. Niridia is waiting for me outside the cell with breakfast and boots.

"Sleep well?"

"Like the dead."

Satisfied that I'm my usual self, she opens the cell and thrusts the tray of food at me. While I busy myself with bread and eggs, Niridia reaches for the bucket.

"Had a rough night, did we?"

"What do you mean?" I ask, wiping crumbs from my face.

"There's not a drop left."

The siren in me will eventually give up calling on my crew with her song. There's usually plenty of water left in the bucket. But last night was different.

It comes back to me quickly.

"Riden," I growl.

"What?"

"The fool came down here last night." I stuff the rest of my breakfast in my mouth and shove my feet into the boots as I walk.

"Stars help him," Niridia mutters from behind me.

I'm up top in an instant, scanning the faces around me. I spot Mandsy in a corner, folding some clothing she's likely just finished mending.

"Where is he?" I snap.

Riden was her charge until he finished healing. She knows exactly who I mean by *he*.

She points near the stowed rowboats, where Lotiya and

Deshel have cornered Riden. That only makes my temper flare further.

"Allemos!" I shout. I don't think I've ever called him by his surname before, but I'm so furious I can't stand to let his first name come out of my mouth.

He looks up from the sisters, relief spreading across his features. Until he sees my face.

"Get your arse over here now!"

The girls giggle as he passes, staring at that arse as he moves.

When he finally reaches me, it's impossible to keep my voice calm. "Draxen may have been lenient with you not following orders, but *I* do not tolerate it."

He doesn't look worried as he stands there. The wind blows across his hair, pressing the strands against his neck. I'm far too furious to become distracted by the slope of his neck.

"Have I done something?" he asks. The rest of the crew pretend to be focused on their chores, but I can tell they're all listening.

"You were told to stay above deck last night, yet you deliberately disobeyed and ventured to the brig."

He looks around at the others. "And just who claims to have seen me disobeying orders?"

"*I* saw you." Idiot.

His eyes widen momentarily. "I didn't realize you remembered things from when you're all . . . different."

"Whether you thought you'd be caught or not is irrelevant.

You're my prisoner. Disobeying orders isn't an option for you. Need I remind you that your brother's head does not need to remain attached to his neck?"

His nostrils flare, but he reins in his own temper and steps closer, speaking low so only I can hear. "I was only curious. I wanted to see you when you're all wild. I didn't take the wax out. I was careful."

I speak just as loudly as before so everyone can hear. "I don't care. You put everyone on this ship at risk with your curiosity."

"Everyone was perfectly safe."

I think of the lewd way in which I held myself, how I tried to beckon him closer by using my body as an incentive. I hate the siren.

"Do you know what would have happened if you had taken just three more steps? Let me tell you, since you excel at underestimating me. I would have been able to reach you through the bars. I'd have pulled your arm through. I'd have snapped it clean out of its socket. Then I'd have whittled at your finger bones until I'd fashioned them into lockpicks. Do you want to know what would have happened to you once I was out of the cell?"

His face has frozen. He manages a single shake of his head.

"I cannot control the siren. She is a monster, which is why we take precautions."

"I didn't realize—" He cuts off, and his voice turns firm, as if he can salvage this. "I wouldn't have gone any closer. Your siren self does not interest me."

"Niridia," I practically shout, "lock him down in the brig. Riden needs some time to think. Have the lads put Vordan down there as well. Separate cells." Riden hates Vordan as much as I do. He might try something.

"Aye, Captain," she says.

I turn from them both and head for my quarters. I need to change.

∞

When I reemerge, I'm no less furious with Riden. This ship is too small, I decide. I could have ordered him put back in the infirmary, but that's less of a punishment. It's only comfy living quarters. No, it's the brig for the cocky bastard.

I am making a beeline for the hatch leading belowdecks, when I have to pause to let Enwen exit first. He's so tall, he has some difficulty angling himself out of the hatch. With small eyes, hollow cheeks, and a perfect nose, he resembles a tree trunk.

"Enwen, where have you been?"

"Helping Teniri in the treasury, Captain. There was a lot of gold to count through."

I narrow my eyes at him. "Turn out your pockets."

"No need. Teniri already searched me before I left. You can ask her yourself. I wouldn't steal from my new crew. Unlike back on Draxen's ship, I actually enjoy living on the *Ava-lee*."

"Then why did you stay with Draxen?"

"Who else is going to keep an eye on Kearan?"

"Some job you're doing. Why don't you keep him out of my cellar? I'm sick of seeing him throwing up over the side of my ship."

"I was meaning his emotional well-being, Captain."

"You can't be serious. Kearan has the emotional depth of a clam."

"Well, a man can try, can't he? I wouldn't be doing my job as his friend if I didn't try."

"How many times do I have to tell you?" Kearan shouts from the other end of the ship. "We are not friends!"

"Yes, we are!" Enwen shouts back.

"Stop yelling," I tell Enwen. "Sort it out yourselves. I have work to do."

"Captain, wait!" A different voice this time. Little Roslyn's. She intercepts me before I get a foot through the hatch. "I need to talk to you about having a celebration."

"A celebration?"

"For getting the map and stealing the pirate lord's treasure! Niridia said we couldn't last night because you had to lock yourself in the brig for the night to let the siren out."

"That's true. And right now I have a prisoner to interrogate. How about tonight?"

"That works for me," she says. As though she might have had an important appointment scheduled. "Can I help with the prisoner?"

"No."

She crosses her arms, ready to argue.

"Have you practiced your letters today?"

She throws her head back and sighs angrily.

"No interrogating prisoners when you haven't performed your own chores." Not that I'd let her help anyway. She doesn't need to witness me torturing a man. "And no celebrating if you haven't practiced."

"Oh, all right," she says, stomping off.

Wallov and Deros are playing cards in the brig when I get down there. Vordan has finally been let out of the cage, only to be placed into one of the brig cells instead. He's unbound and ungagged, his back to us. Riden is two cells over, seated on the floor with his arms atop his knees. He doesn't look at me.

Good.

"Your daughter is getting awfully cheeky, Wallov," I say.

"Can't imagine where she gets it from, Captain," he says.

"I hope you're not suggesting she's getting it from me."

"Wouldn't dream of it," he says. But his tone is too light to be sincere. I smile at him.

"You two are relieved for now," I say. "I'll keep an eye on the brig rats."

They both scoot out of their chairs, starting for the stairs. "And see to it, Wallov, that Roslyn is actually practicing her writing and not threatening people with that dagger."

"Isn't it a beautiful piece of work, Captain? Won it off Deros in one of our games."

Deros folds his massive arms. "I lost on purpose so the lass would have a way to protect herself."

"Take it up top, lads," I say.

I wait a few beats until the hatch slams closed behind them.

Vordan has risen, standing on one leg—the one that didn't break during his fall at the inn—and turned to face me already.

He jerks his head toward the cell on the opposite side of the brig from him and Riden, the one filled with plush cushions. "I'd have preferred that one, but I take it that one is yours." He smiles at his own cleverness. "What is it like having to be locked up on your own ship?" he continues. "I can't imagine it—"

I cut him off with a deep, low note. Vordan holds a knife in his hand. He glances at it in fear before thrusting it down into his own leg, the one that isn't broken. He screams before changing the sound into an angry grunt. It's a rather pathetic attempt at maintaining his composure.

I halt the song, and Vordan comes out of the hallucination. He looks down at his leg, sees that it is whole, that his hand holds no knife, and fixes me with a filthy stare. His breathing has quickened. Even though his mind now knows he's not injured, it takes time to recover from the echo of pain.

"This is a dream come true for you," I say. "Looks like you'll get to experience the full brunt of my abilities after all."

His face pales, and the satisfaction I get from it is a soothing balm to my senses.

"Now, then," I say, "I want to know all of the spies you have in my father's fleet. I want their names and which vessels they sail on."

"I don't—"

Another note flows out of my mouth. A puddle of water appears at Vordan's feet, and I make him stick his face right into the water and hold it there for half a minute. I let him pull his head up for a few seconds to breathe and then stick him under the imaginary puddle for a full minute. Though his mind is fully alert as to what's happening, I have taken his control over his own limbs. They obey me now.

When he comes up for air this time, I release him from the song.

He flops over onto his back, feeling the dry ground. No water. He hasn't the strength to stand as he sucks down as much air as his lungs will allow and coughs it back out.

I dare a glance in Riden's direction. He is watching everything, his face carefully blank. I'm not about to go back on our bargain to sense what he's feeling, though I'd desperately like to.

"I could, of course, force you to be truthful with me," I say, returning my attention to Vordan, "but I want nothing more than for you to suffer before you die. So by all means, Vordan, continue refusing me the information I want."

Once he's breathing a bit more easily, he stands, hopping pitifully as he finds a balance with the broken leg.

"On the *Deadman's Blade*, you'll find a pirate going by the name of Honsero. He's my man. Klain sails with the *Black Rage*." He pauses to catch his breath before listing several more ships and pirates, and even giving me the names of some who are stationed within my father's keep.

When he finishes talking, I utter a higher note, something piercing and throttling. I ask him if he's spoken the truth and if he's omitted any names. While under my influence, he confirms his earlier testimony.

My power slips away the more I sing. It feels similar to the way hunger creeps up on a person between meals, leaving them small and empty. It's infuriating how fleeting my abilities are.

When he returns once more to his senses, Vordan says, "You killed every man I had at the inn with me. For all I know, you killed the little boy who gave you up, too."

I didn't. I don't slaughter children. Especially when they have no fault save choosing the wrong man to accept food from. But I remain silent. Let Vordan think I'm so cruel.

"And now you know about all of the rest. You've taken everything. When you and I could have been so great together."

"No, Vordan. I could have made you great. You are not the sort of man who could ever achieve greatness on his own. You are ordinary, and you've accomplished nothing."

He laughs, a quiet sound meant for himself as he rakes his fingers through his hair.

"You're right," he says at last. "I have only one card left to play, Alosa. A bit of information to exchange for my life."

"There is nothing you know that I want."

"Not even if it's a secret your father keeps from you?"

I keep my face still, refusing to react to anything he says. He has nothing left but lies now.

"I overheard many conversations between you and Riden back on the *Night Farer*," he continues, smirking in Riden's direction. "Do you remember the talk the two of you had about secrets? You were trying so desperately to learn where Jeskor had hidden the map, preying on Riden for any information he might have. You even told him some lie about hidden floorboards in your father's rooms where he keeps secret information. As if by telling him something of your father, he might tell you something of his."

Vordan smiles at the memory, and I can't believe I hadn't noticed him sneaking about more.

"But you and I both know," Vordan says, "that your father has a secret study in his keep."

Yes, I do know. It's my father's private room. The one place in the keep where only he is permitted to enter. I spent much of my childhood trying to find a way in, curiosity getting the better of me, and suffered dearly for it.

Vordan says, "I sent my best spy at the keep inside, Alosa. Would you like to know what he found?"

I open my mouth to tell him no. Lies will not get him anywhere. He cannot manipulate me. Not anymore. I am not his prisoner. He has not won this time.

But none of that comes out. Instead, I ask, "What?"

A grin takes over his face, and I get the urge to punch him. That physical manifestation of him thinking he's gotten the upper hand on me.

"Will you free me if I tell you?"

"I can get it out of you with my powers or without them, Vordan. Your choice."

He grits his teeth. "Fine, but don't you forget it was I who found out for you."

I'm about to open my mouth and start singing, but he cuts me off.

"Have you not always found it odd that your father is unaffected by your abilities? Do you know why?"

"Because his blood runs through my veins. That connection protects him."

"Is *that* what he told you?"

"It's the truth," I bite out through clenched teeth.

"Wrong." Vordan seems to savor the word as it leaves his lips. "He found something on that island where he met your mother. A weapon. A device that protects him from the sirens. A device that lets him control them, should he find them again. A device that lets him control *you*. He's been manipulating you since you were born."

His words are ludicrous. I've been defying my father since I learned to control my own limbs. I don't always listen. That's why my whole body is covered in scars.

As if sensing my doubt, Vordan adds, "Think about it. Think about all he's done to you. The way he's beaten you. Tortured you. The way he hurt you just to prove a point. He's been crueler to you than any other person alive, and yet you still serve him. You always go back to him. You always, ultimately, carry out his orders. Does that sound like something you would willingly do? You may try to rationalize it, Alosa. He's your father. He's only ever tried to make you strong. To make you a survivor. But do those sound like your own thoughts in your head? Or his thoughts bringing you back to him yet again?"

My blood turns cold. Air vanishes, and my vision blurs. No. It can't be.

"You're lying," I snap once I find my voice.

"Am I?" he asks. "See for yourself."

I do. I call forth a song so swept up in emotion, I can hardly breathe out the notes. But even as I listen to Vordan's truthful response, his story doesn't change. He's telling the truth. Or at least what he believes is the truth.

His spy is deceiving him.

He has to be wrong.

I flee from the brig, needing space from the two men within more than I've needed anything.

I wish I had simply killed Vordan and not bothered to question him. His words follow me wherever I go.

He's been manipulating you since you were born.

I cannot doubt my father over one sentence spoken by his enemy. I *won't*.

And yet I cannot forget the words. Because they did not change even when I used the power of my voice to demand the truth from him. There is an uncomfortable tightness in my gut that I must ignore. Because if I were to examine it, to admit what the name of that feeling is—it could ruin everything I know. Everything I've worked for my whole life.

So I suffer silently, not daring to pull out that doubt and investigate it.

Journeying back to the keep will take a month. That should be plenty of time for the sensation to be extinguished. For me to remember exactly where my loyalties lie.

I tamp down those needling thoughts as I push myself through the rest of the day. I'd forgotten entirely about the promise I made to Roslyn about having a celebration, but it would seem Roslyn took matters into her own hands, because the revelry starts without my having to say so.

Out on the main deck, Haeli, one of my riggers, pulls out a lute and begins playing a jaunty tune. Lotiya and Deshel dance together, arm in arm. Other girls clap along or join in the dancing. Wallov and Deros take turns twirling the girls about. Enwen soon joins the fun, but Kearan sits alone in the corner with his drink.

Roslyn, noticing this, takes a break from the dancing and tiptoes over to him.

"What do you want?" Kearan asks.

I can tell by the way she tips her head that she's surprised he heard her. "I watch you from above sometimes. You pull out that flask a lot. Does rum really taste so good?"

Kearan turns to her then with strangely sober eyes. "Doesn't need to taste good. Only needs to be strong."

"Can I try some?"

Kearan shrugs and offers the flask. Before I can step forward, Sorinda is there, yanking the flask from his grasp. She upends it on his head.

Kearan sputters, "Damn it, woman! Do you delight in anything other than soaking me?"

"Idiot," she says. "You don't give drink to a child."

"I wasn't going to! As soon as it was near her nose she would have handed it back."

"You couldn't have known that."

"You can't stand to come within five feet of me because the drink is so strong."

"I can't stand to be near you for many reasons."

They go on like that, lashing out at each other. If Kearan could manage to keep up with her, I'm sure it would come to blows. Roslyn wisely shrinks back from the two of them and returns to the dancing.

"Quite a pair those two," Niridia says, stepping up beside me.

"I've never seen anyone get under her skin like that," I say.

"It's probably a first for her. I wonder how long it will be before she realizes she fancies him back."

I let out a guffaw. "Sorinda? Fancy Kearan? I don't think so."

Niridia shrugs. "He wouldn't be so bad if he cleaned himself up a bit."

"And stopped drinking."

"And shaved."

"Worked out a bit."

"And had someone right his nose."

We both laugh. I hadn't realized how much I needed it.

"All right," she concedes. "I suppose he doesn't have a chance." We turn to observe the dancers together, and Niridia adds, "You know, it wouldn't hurt to have one more man out here to share among the girls."

And just like that my thoughts return to the brig. To what Vordan said.

"Has Riden suffered enough?" she asks.

I want to say no. To leave him in there until we reach the

47

keep. But that would be me being selfish because he overheard what Vordan said and not me punishing him for what he'd done. I was only going to leave him in there for the day anyway.

"You may let him out," I say, "but warn him that if he disobeys orders again, he'll stay in there until we reach the keep."

"Understood."

She watches my face for a beat longer. "Is something wrong?"

I force a smile onto my face. "It's nothing." And then, because I know she won't leave it alone without an explanation, I add, "Seeing Vordan again reminded me of what he did to me on that island. That's all. I'll be fine."

Her eyes fill with understanding. "Try to enjoy the celebration. Dancing always cheers you up. We could talk about it later, if you'd like."

I nod encouragingly, and as soon as she disappears I let the smile fall from my face. I debate going straight to bed, but I don't want to be alone with my thoughts. I'd much rather watch the crew having fun.

I tuck myself into a corner, crossing my legs under me while I sit atop a crate, letting the music replace the uneasiness inside me. Niridia returns with Riden in tow. Lotiya and Deshel are thankfully busy with Wallov and Deros. It's Philoria and Bayla, two of my gunwomen, who reach him and pull him into a twirling dance.

Riden doesn't miss a beat. You'd think he wasn't just thrown in the brig for the day after being severely chastened in front of the whole crew. Not to mention the fact he's only recently recovered from two bullets to the leg. Does nothing get to him?

Nothing save his brother, anyway? I stare at him openly from my hiding spot, watch the way his limbs move to the music, the way he interacts with each of the crew as though they've been lifelong friends. It's almost as if he has enchanting powers of his own.

Golden-brown eyes flit to me, as though he knew I was sitting here the whole time watching. At the next break in between songs, Riden saunters over. I tense, hoping Lotiya and Deshel will spot him leaving and capture him for once.

But no, he reaches me without anyone getting in his way and sits on the crate beside me.

I wait for him to say something. To try to convince me of Vordan's words. Has Riden not attempted to tell me since we first met that my father is corrupt and controlling? I'll bet he smiled at all of Vordan's words, pleased to have someone else confirming them. What had he called me when I told him he was ridiculous for being loyal to his despicable brother?

A hypocrite.

"You keep interesting company," he says.

My mind scrambles as it tries to tie the words to what happened down in the brig with Vordan. "What?" I ask.

"Those sisters."

I follow his line of sight to where Lotiya and Deshel are eyeing him. They take a break from their clapping hands and stomping feet so Lotiya can blow him a kiss while Deshel waves her fingers at him.

Riden shudders uncomfortably.

They're both very beautiful girls. I'm surprised at his reaction.

"They act like a couple of . . ." He trails off.

"Whores?" I finish for him. "That's because they were. At far too young an age, they were forced into that life. I broke them out when I witnessed them fighting off a couple of men who tried to take their services for free after hours. They're good with knives," I add in warning.

"I wasn't going to say whores."

"No?" I ask, relieved to be talking about a neutral topic. "What were you going to say?"

"I honestly don't have words to describe them."

That prompts a little defensiveness in me. I'm glad to feel something different from the uneasiness that hasn't left me all day. "If this arrangement is going to work, you're going to need to remember that we're not only women, we're pirates."

I remember the comments the sisters made earlier about wanting to see Riden naked. I add, "You wouldn't give a second thought to a couple of men aboard your ship behaving in such a way or talking such talk. You do not get to judge us more harshly for being women. It's not fair, and it doesn't make sense. Not to mention I'll throw your arse overboard if I catch you doing it again."

Amusement lights up his face, but I push on as determined as ever. "I have twenty-eight excellent girls aboard this ship, and their pasts have shaped them. Just as yours has shaped you. And every single one of them, down to little Roslyn, deserves your respect."

Riden watches me for a few more moments before looking on at the dancers. "I admire your love for your crew, Alosa, but you don't need to defend them to me. I make no judgments because they're women rather than men. I was surprised, is all. I apologize."

I ignore his apology, yet also warm at it. I'm accustomed to defending my girls. To my father. To the men on his council. To other pirates. Women don't belong on the sea in their eyes.

But Riden is *apologizing*.

I don't know how to handle that.

"And I apologize for disobeying orders before," he says. "I won't go below again when you're replenishing your abilities."

"Good."

"They're . . . kind of terrifying."

I'm not sure whether to bristle or be amused by that.

"Alosa?" Riden asks.

I brace again for the mention of what Vordan said.

"I never did thank you for giving me and Draxen a chance. We would have been dead if you hadn't stepped in with your father. Thank you."

When I don't answer, he asks, "Why did you do it?"

And there's the other thing I'm not thinking about. Why I bother sticking my neck out for Riden and his worthless brother.

I dare to look at him. "I don't know."

He smiles then, a beautiful stretch of his lips—as though he has his own thoughts on why I might have done it.

I turn away to avoid staring at his mouth and listen to Haeli strike up a new song.

"Dance with me."

My neck turns so quickly in Riden's direction that I actually hear it crack. "What?"

"Come on. It'll be fun."

He grabs my arm and hauls me to my feet before I can refuse, which of course I was intending to do.

I'm sure of it.

It's too late now because he's already moving me in circles. To refuse him now would only cause a scene. Besides, the crew is cheering. Wallov, Deros, and Enwen grab new partners and join us. My movements are stiff, hesitant. I can feel my mind and body warring for dominance. There are so many reasons why this is a bad idea. Not to mention I have too many things to worry about to even attempt to enjoy myself.

"Come now, princess," Riden says. "Surely you can do better than that."

I shouldn't let him goad me, but I often can't help responding when I've been issued a challenge. And I do love dancing. My mother is a siren, after all. Music is in my blood.

I feel the music waft over my skin and move to help it along. I caress it with my hands, sashay around it with my hips, tread lightly over it with my feet. I make Riden follow me and my steps, but occasionally he forgets himself, stopping completely and watching me, caught up in my movements. He catches himself and starts to dance again. He's not bad at all. He stomps his feet in time. His twists and turns are sure and even graceful. Each time we come into contact—our hands, our arms, the brush of our knees—the dance grows more exciting, more electric. I am charged like storm clouds—it's ten times stronger than what I feel when I use my siren abilities. And different. Something decidedly human.

I see the way Riden behaves around me: the focus and heat in his eyes, the way his hands linger, the way he positions his body next to mine. Normally, I would know exactly what it means. But then I remember yet again that he is my prisoner. He will say and do anything if he thinks it will help his cause.

The song finishes. Haeli starts up another, but I take my leave. "Go on, then!" I shout to the crew. "Continue into the night, but I'm off to bed." I smile at the happy faces. They're reddened with the joy that comes from a successful plunder.

I head for the stairs, certain I won't actually be able to sleep with all the weight burdening me, but needing to get away nonetheless. I remind myself as I go, *Riden is my captive, Riden is my captive, Riden is my captive.*

Someone grabs my hand and pulls me under the companionway. Out of sight and into shadow.

An equal surge of excitement and dread hits me before I even see his face.

"Alosa," Riden says as he takes my hands in his and presses me gently against the wall.

He leans in, and I ask, "What?" As though he were about to ask me a question instead of saying my name aloud simply for the pleasure of hearing it roll off his tongue.

"You dance beautifully," he says, and I feel his nose sidle up next to mine. My eyes have already closed.

Damn, but he smells good. Like the coconut soap we have

on the ship mixed with an earthy musk that belongs solely to him.

It would be easy to let him kiss me. Maddeningly easy.

But he wants his brother freed. He wants his own freedom. Any intimacy between us is deliberate on Riden's part.

It has to be.

"Good night, Riden," I say, dropping his hands. But as I pass him by, I kiss his cheek.

Once I get to my room, I chide myself for such a childish move.

But what scares me most is that I almost could not help it.

Chapter 4

FROM THE OUTSIDE, there is nothing remarkable about the keep. It looks like any other small island in the groupings located far northeast of Lycon's Peak.

But the king's pirates recognize it for what it is.

The island has many lips and jutting trenches, a maze built of water and land. One must steer a careful course so as not to beach one's ship. The sea flows right into a series of caves that house the separate ships of the fleet. Their numbers range to about fifty now.

Niridia directs us up to the dock. Haeli and the other riggers tie down the sails while Lotiya, Deshel, and Athella secure the docking lines. The gangplank is lowered.

"Send Wallov and Deros to bring up Vordan," I tell Niridia. "And have Mandsy tail Riden like a shark on a blood trail."

"Of all the women on this ship, I wouldn't say Mandsy most resembles a shark," a voice says from behind me.

For the last few days of the journey, Riden was required to stay belowdecks so he wouldn't learn the exact location of the keep. I hadn't expected Mandsy to let him back up top so quickly.

"And I suppose I would have that happy privilege?" I ask him.

"No, it's those vicious sisters. I can't say which one is worse. Deshel thinks my lap is a chair, and Lotiya has her fingers in my hair as if it were a glove for her to don."

It pleases me beyond words to know he's frustrated by their advances. I say, "I thought you enjoyed female companionship. Living on a ship full of women should be a dream come true for you."

He stares at me as though his gaze should hold some deeper meaning, but I don't see it. And he's forbidden me to use my abilities on him.

"I'm not a mind reader, Riden. So spit out whatever it is you want to say."

Eventually, he says, "Their attention is unwanted."

"Then tell them that."

"You don't think I've tried!"

"If you're looking for sympathy, go find Mandsy."

He glares at me. "Sympathy is not what I want from you, Alosa."

Before I can even begin to guess what he means by that, he

storms off. Niridia shows up with Mandsy in tow. I just point in Riden's direction.

Mandsy, her brown hair in two braids over her shoulders, follows him.

"Careful," I shout after her. "He's in a mood."

"I've just the thing for that," Mandsy says.

"And what would that be?"

"Sewing. Nothing like working with your hands to relax your mind."

Mandsy is a godsend. She heals, she sews, and she fights. Knowing where every major organ is located on a person makes her a most efficient fighter. She's patched me and the crew up time and time again. Many of them owe her their lives. I wish I had ten more of her. I'd even take the excessive optimism that comes with her.

"I wouldn't give that one something so pointy as a needle," I say.

"I'll take my chances."

Wallov and Deros both come up top, each gripping one of Vordan's arms firmly. He's wriggling in their grasp, but no single man is a match for their joined strength. Vordan shouldn't even bother, injured as he is.

"You're handing me over to Kalligan?" Vordan asks.

"You're to stay in the keep's dungeon for safekeeping until I decide what to do with you."

"Have you forgotten our little chat already? You need me. I—"

"You can go to the dungeons standing or we can get out the cage again. Your choice."

Wisely, he shuts his mouth.

I dart my eyes to the men on either side of him. "Take him through a side entrance. I don't want to see him again."

"I'm heading out," I tell Niridia. "See to it that everyone cleans up and gets well rested. I want the *Ava-lee* stocked up for sailing again. I doubt it will be long before we're back on the sea. The king will want to move the fleet to the Isla de Canta as soon as possible."

I leap off the side of my ship. Most would prefer to use the gangplank, but the distance doesn't bother me. It takes just a second to reaccustom myself with solid, unmoving ground after weeks at sea.

Several ships float along the separate docks in this particular cave. It's the closest one to the keep's main entrance, so only those in my father's inner circle are permitted to anchor here. Among them are *Hell's Breath*, which belongs to Captain Timoth; *Black Rage*, which belongs to Captain Rasell; and the *Deadman's Blade*, which is captained by Adderan. My face contorts in disgust when I spot *Death's Secret*. If Tylon and his ship weren't so important to my father, I'd whittle holes into the latter when no one was watching—maybe the former, too.

The docks lead to a path down through the cave, which eventually opens up onto the island. From there is a well-trodden trail obscured from the beach by large fir and spruce trees. It's incredible that their roots are strong enough to breach the island's hard surface. The keep is a composition of hollowed-out rock with wooden embellishments.

Several islands over is a long-at-rest volcano. The little

island the pirate king uses as his keep is a series of tunnels, once carved out of rock by steaming lava, a deadly natural force.

Now it houses the deadliest men alive.

I kick a pebble out of my path as I reach the largest tunnel opening, which serves as the keep's main entrance. Dead men dangle by ropes from the top of the tunnel, giving it the appearance of a gaping mouth with scraggly teeth. The ropes are tied to large hooks at the end, hooks that have been inserted into the mouths of traitors. They are hung up like captured fish for all to see what happens to those who meet my father's wrath.

The tunnel forks into multiple paths, which also veer into their own countless directions. The keep is an endless maze to all except those who serve the pirate king.

I'm following a tunnel deeper and deeper into the keep, in search of my father, or at least someone who can tell me his location, when I pause in front of a door.

The door.

He found something on that island where he met your mother. A weapon.

After weeks of distance from Vordan and his lies, I'd begun to relax. But just like that, doubt creeps back in. Unbidden and unwelcome.

The entrance to my father's chambers is just one door over. There's another door inside adjoining the secret study to my father's bedchamber. As one of the select few allowed to visit my father in his private rooms, I see this door regularly.

It's my study, Alosa. Surely you know what a study looks like? he said after I asked him what it looked like inside when I was little. Out of embarrassment, I never asked again.

My thoughts are my own. I am not being controlled. I can't listen to Vordan. I *won't*.

And yet, I press an ear to the door, listening carefully.

I don't know what I expected. To hear ticking? Feel the pulse of anti-siren magic?

Sighing, I move down the hall. I raise my fist and rap on the door to my father's rooms, remembering why I came here in the first place.

No answer.

I'll have to look for him elsewhere. I turn—

My breath leaves me. I'm being shoved backward, and wood slams against my spine. Brilliant blue eyes glare at me.

"Alosa."

I strain at the hands that hold me, but Tylon has me boxed in pretty good. The weight of his body has me firmly planted against the door. Every ligament of his is lined up with mine, our faces far too close for comfort.

If I hadn't been so distracted by my father's secrets, he never would have gotten the drop on me. I should know better than to let down my guard at the keep.

I let out a sound between a growl and a frustrated sigh. "Let. Me. Go."

"It seems the only way to have a conversation alone with you is to ambush you in the halls."

"Most men would take that as a hint and back the hell off."

He manages to get even closer to me. "Why? Why are you

avoiding me? Ever since you returned from the *Night Farer*, you've been distant. You've been different."

I turn my head to the side to get as far away from him as I possibly can. "Different? I can't think of a time when I didn't hate you, and I can assure you that hasn't changed."

A low sound gurgles up from his throat. "You'll come around. It's only a matter of time."

"Yes, how can I not when you attack me in tunnels?"

"I wouldn't have to if you'd let me see you on your ship."

Niridia has explicit orders to dump Tylon into the sea on sight. I'm told he'd been swimming several times before we left to hunt down Vordan.

Using my song on Tylon would be a waste. I finally break an arm free of his hold and use it to push at his chest, sending him staggering backward. I place a solid kick to his stomach.

It lands him on the floor, gasping for breath.

"I know you're not the brightest pirate," I say as I lean over his body, "so I'll say this slowly. You and your advances are unwanted. The next time you touch me, you'll find an iron ball in your stomach instead of my foot."

Buttered fish and salted pork leave a mouthwatering scent on the air. I promise myself there will be time for a hot meal later.

Many of the men are taking lunch in the mess hall. Tables upon tables are heaped with all the best foods. From sliced fruits to warm breads to freshly caught seafood and well-aged rum. Only the best is served in the pirate king's keep. We can afford regular shipments of perishable foods. At the rate my father's going, he could soon buy all of Maneria. Money pours into the keep from all the merchants and land nobles purchasing safety for their ships. Some of the pirates under my father's control never even need to leave the keep. Nor would they want to; anything a man could want can be found here. A floating brothel anchors in one of the caves. Endless food and rum are supplied for all.

I'm used to the stares, glares, or looks of desire that come my way at the keep. Only the ship captains know what I am. I'm a mystery to most. Why would the pirate king bother with claiming a female as his child? Why does he hold me in such high regard? Why am I given the most dangerous and important missions? Some are jealous; some are curious and baffled. Others wish I weren't so capable of defending myself.

I scan the room carefully, looking for my father, but he isn't here. I stop one of the cooks bringing out a tray of rounded breads to add to the tables.

"Has the king been in for his lunch yet, Yalden?"

"No, Captain," he responds. "I've heard he shut himself in the treasury for most of the morning. Must not be out yet."

"Thank—"

Wood smacks against rock as the far doors are split open wide. The room instantly quiets. Everyone reads Kalligan's mood. Even without his fleet, my father is an imposing figure. He's a giant among men, at well over six feet and built like an ox.

Men step away from his path as he stomps to the center of the mess hall, the tables practically trembling from the force of his footsteps. He searches faces as he goes. Stars help whoever he's looking for.

"Praxer!" he finally yells, as he spots a man in spectacles with more shine on his head than hair.

"My king?" Praxer abandons his meal and rises, though he has to be about to wet his breeches.

"I told you there was something wrong with the shipment from Calpoon, did I not?"

"You did, and I went through the inventory twice more. I found the missing chest of coins and added it to the rest of the treasury."

"And did you update the books?" My father's voice turns eerily calm.

The blood flees from Praxer's face.

My father gets nose-to-nose with the man, not bothering to check his voice this time. "Two ships were dispatched last week to punish Lord Farrek for shorting me on money! It'll be a miracle if the frigate reaches them in time to recant the order. What kind of message do *you* think it sends the land nobles if I start *punishing them for paying me*?"

"It won't happen again."

"You're right-handed, are you not?"

The balding man stutters before finding his voice. "Yes, my king, why—"

"Hold him down."

The two men who had been sitting nearest Praxer leap to their feet and restrain him. They're likely his friends, but friendship means nothing when an order is issued by the king.

Kalligan litters the floor with plates of food as he clears the table with one swipe. Those seated nearby freeze for fear of drawing his attention.

With one hand on his head and the other at his back, the first of Praxer's friends shoves him face first against the table. The second extends Praxer's left arm and pins it against the wood.

"No, my king. Please—"

Praxer screams as red sprays the nearby men and tables.

"Fail me again and you'll lose your other hand as well. Look at me!"

Praxer has sunk to the floor. He muffles his screams long enough to meet my father's eyes.

"I have no use for a man without hands. Do you understand?"

"Y-y-yes," he breathes.

Kalligan dries his cutlass on Praxer's shirtsleeve as he surveys the crowd. His eyes land on me. In the beat of a second his right brow lifts slightly. I nod.

"We leave for the Isla de Canta in one month's time," he says to the room. "Let's hope you fools can keep your limbs in the meantime. No more mistakes."

Praxer whines as he rocks back and forth, holding his wrist just above where his left hand was moments earlier.

Kalligan steps over him on his way back toward the door.

"Hello, Father," I say when I've caught up to him. 'Tis no easy feat since his legs outdistance mine considerably. It's a shame I couldn't have inherited a bit more of his height. He towers over me by more than a foot. There isn't a single man I know who doesn't stand in his shadow.

"Your voyage was successful." He says it as fact, not as a question.

"Aye, sir. The sack of filth, Vordan, has been transported to the dungeons."

"And the map?"

I cease walking, and he does the same, facing me. With a tightened fist, I pull the map necklace from my pocket.

His foul mood dispels instantly as he takes it in his hands. "You are the only one I can trust to do things right." One large hand slaps me on the back, and I warm at the sign of affection. It is a big one from him and so rare. "We'll celebrate later tonight. Have one of the cooks send up a 1656, Wenoa stock." Ah, that's a good year. "Have you questioned Vordan yet?"

A pause.

I can't tell him what Vordan's told me. Even if I don't believe it. Which of course I don't. There's no reason to even mention it.

Careful to keep my voice normal, I say, "I have. He sang like a bird. I have a list of names of all the men in our ranks who secretly work for Vordan."

Father watches me carefully. "What's wrong?" he asks.

He is not *controlling you*, I tell myself. Why do I even need to reassure myself?

I hurry to think of something believable to say. "Do you think we'll find my mother? When we reach the Isla de Canta?"

After I get the words out, I realize there is genuine curiosity behind them.

Still, I worry at his reaction. What if he assumes that I think he's not good enough? That I need more than just him? But is it wrong for a girl to want to meet her mother?

"For your sake, I hope we don't. The siren queen is a truly menacing creature, no more than a sea monster feverishly on the lookout for human prey. She'd kill you before you could utter who you are, and even if you did manage to get the words out, I doubt it would make a difference.

"They're not like us, Alosa. You've seen all too well what happens when your siren nature takes over you. Imagine creatures that have only one side. That side."

My blood runs cold. I had so hoped to meet my mother just once, but maybe there are some memories I don't want to make.

"I suggest," Kalligan continues, "you be prepared to kill every siren you meet."

Father calls together a meeting for all the ship captains present at the keep. Over half of them are running jobs throughout Maneria, and he's dispatched yano birds to order their immediate return. Since he knew I was due to arrive any day, he didn't bother to spare a bird to fix poor Praxer's mistake. And honestly, I wouldn't be surprised if Father chose to put on a show of fury and violence just to remind everyone what happens to those who disappoint him.

We set sail in one month for the Isla de Canta, with or without the rest of the fleet. Those captains who don't make it in time will not share in our spoils. I'm certain everyone will make haste.

My belly is full. I've washed and changed. Red hair spills over my shoulders, brushing against an emerald corset. I like to look my best when surrounded by the most important men in the keep, to remind them I'm their princess and will be their queen one day. And I need the extra confidence boost, given all the uncertainty crowding my insides of late.

My eyes are a deep blue. I replenished my abilities again after questioning Vordan on my ship. Though most wouldn't dare to try anything with me or my crew at the risk of upsetting their king, it's foolish to go into territory where I'm surrounded by the most bloodthirsty men in the world and not come fully prepared.

"Shut your mouth, Timoth, or I'll shove my cutlass through it." Father usually calls the meeting to attention with a threat. Though nearly everyone had been talking, singling out one man is enough to quiet the entire room. Especially after Father's display of power yesterday.

I try desperately to ignore the space Tylon occupies. I'm still mad as hell over his ambush yesterday. Arrogant piss pot. As if I'd ever want to associate with him. Tylon is only a few years older than I, and Father adores him (as much as a ruthless pirate can adore anything) because he obeys orders immediately and without question. He's always quick to rat out other pirates at the keep for misconduct, which makes him unpopular with everyone else, but a star in my father's eyes. His biggest flaw, however, is in assuming I will align myself with him. He seems to think I will want to share my birthright with him when Father steps down. That by entangling himself with me, he will become the next pirate king. I'll dagger him in his sleep before that happens. I will become the pirate queen when Father retires, and I will not be sharing power.

"The moment we've all been waiting for is finally here," my father says. He's a large figure at the head of a massive oak table. He stands while the rest of us sit, lest we forget who's in charge. As if he needs to. His sheer size is enough to leave anyone without a doubt as to his status. He keeps his hair and beard short always. Something about not letting it obstruct his line of vision. He once tried to cut my hair to make me a better pirate. I told him where he could stick his scissors, and he jabbed them into my leg instead.

My father certainly has raised me with unconventional methods; sometimes a molten rage surges up when I remember the past. But then I remember the here and now. No one can best me with a blade, save perhaps my father. No one can outdistance me. No one can outlast my stamina. Other pirates fear me. I am proud of all these facts. It is only because of my father that I have achieved them. On top of the skills he gave me are all the good memories I have of him. When he gave me my first sword. The time he stroked my hair and told me I looked like my mother. The jokes and laughter we share when we manage private moments together. These memories are spread out with lots of misery in between, but everyone both loves and resents their parents, don't they?

You may try to rationalize it, Alosa. He's your father. He's only ever tried to make you strong. To make you a survivor. But do those sound like your own thoughts in your head? Or his thoughts bringing you back to him yet again?

I'm not rationalizing. I'm stating facts. Cold. Hard. Facts.

I am under no one's control.

"Vordan's map was the last of the three fragments, the final piece that leads us the rest of the way to the Isla de Canta," Father says, bringing me out of my thoughts. "I've had years to examine the first map, the map that came from my own father and his father before him. It has traveled the Kalligan line for centuries, and we have kept it in pristine condition.

"The second map piece was brought to us by Captain Alosa Kalligan. Jeskor's sons had it hidden on their ship, though they were too stupid to realize it.

"The third has come to us today, once again procured by Captain Alosa."

The eyes in the room swivel to me. Many with jealousy—they wish to be so favored by the king.

"We will set sail in thirty days," Father continues. "We will reach the Isla de Canta, and its treasure will be ours."

"Rah!" cheer the pirates in the room.

"Captains, what is the status of your ships?"

"I've nigh twenty barrels of gunpowder on the *Black Rage*," Captain Rasell says. "Fifty men await my instructions."

Tylon goes next, and I do my best not to frown. "I have five harpoon guns attached to *Death's Secret* and over a hundred individual harpoons that can be thrown from rowboats."

"We'll skewer the beasts!" Captain Adderan proclaims, and

the room goes wild with excitement. For the first time, the thought of traveling to the island makes me sick.

He found something on that island where he met your mother. A weapon. A device that protects him from the sirens. A device that lets him control them.

It goes on like this as twenty pirate captains list their most valuable collections for the trip. The other thirty or so captains are all rushing to the keep to make it in time for the voyage, and some of them will end up staying behind anyway to defend our stronghold while the rest of us sail for treasure.

"Captain Alosa," my father says expectantly.

I swallow my uneasiness and push the image of sirens being harpooned like whales from my mind, vowing that nothing will keep me from traveling to the island. This is too important. And Father has already had to remind me recently that they're inhuman beasts. I know this. I've experienced for myself what happens when I'm submerged underwater.

"I have a crew consisting of twenty-eight women," I say simply.

Adderan snorts. "Women. Good. The men will have company during the voyage." A few others in the room dare to snicker at the comment.

The men may recognize my talents and purpose, even if they don't like them. But other female pirates receive no such esteem.

Father doesn't defend my crew. Nor would I want him to. I can do it all on my own.

The pirate captains and the dungeon master are the only

ones who know about my abilities at the keep, so I don't have to hide them in this room.

I sing a booming note, something that won't go unnoticed by anyone in the vicinity. Adderan rises from his chair and runs face first into the nearest wall. The contact splits open a thin line on his head, but it doesn't render him unconscious. I want him fully awake when I humiliate him.

"While the sirens enchant you all to take your own lives," I say, "my talented *female* crew will be unaffected. We will be the ones who actually reach the treasure and make the journey back home."

The room goes silent. Kalligan's men need to remember these are no ordinary women defending the Isla de Canta.

"Very impressive, Captain Alosa," Tylon says, and I jerk my head in his direction, "but there is a simple remedy to such a problem. I believe you experienced this one while you were Vordan's prisoner."

He pulls something from his pocket, breaks it in two, and molds it into his ears. Wax.

I turn to the man on Tylon's right. "Captain Lormos, kindly prove a point for me and smack Tylon up the side of the head."

Tylon must assume my moving mouth is expelling enchanting notes. He grins condescendingly at his invincibility. But then Lormos, who is especially prone to violence, says, "Gladly," and carries out my request. No singing required.

Tylon grunts and turns to his right, cocking his fist back in retaliation. My father holds out his hands, a simple motion commanding all to stay their violence. Tylon grudgingly complies and pulls the wax from his ears.

"Song is not the only thing you have to worry about," I say. "You will also be unable to communicate with one another, and the sirens can easily get the drop on you then."

"We can have men looking in all directions. Everyone's backs will be covered," Tylon says defensively.

I laugh without humor. "You're being naive. That will cost you lives." If we're lucky, *his*.

"My men will be fine. Don't presume to captain any crew other than your own."

"Don't belittle my crew by insinuating we're only good for breeding!"

"That was Adderan! You're—"

"That's enough." The pirate king's voice cuts across the room. Powerful. Final. I take my eyes from Tylon's enraged face and note that all the captains in the room are staring between the two of us.

"Just get it over with and bed the lass!" Captain Sordil shouts from the back of the room. I slice him in half with my glare. Before I can do more than that, Father continues, commanding everyone's attention once more.

"Captain Alosa has more than made her point," he says, "which is why she and the *Ava-lee* will sail second only to the *Dragon's Skull* on the voyage to the Isla de Canta."

Second?

Because my father's ship will carry a secret weapon that will control the sirens? Or because he needs to keep his place at the head of his fleet?

Silence hits the room at the pronouncement. Then Adderan speaks up. "Are we sure that's wise? Surely the *Deadman's Blade* would be a better choice to have at your back?" His own ship. "It's larger and more—"

"Are you questioning my decision?" Father asks, his voice like a whip.

Adderan immediately recants his words. "Wise choice, sire. The *Ava-lee* should go second."

Kalligan nods. "Good. You can take the rear, Adderan." I grin smugly at Adderan as Father launches into the rest of the details of the voyage, then concludes the meeting. "Alosa, Tylon, stay."

The captains file out of the room, smiling and clapping one another on the backs. It's finally happening. We've waited years to set sail for the unimaginable treasures waiting at the Isla de Canta. Now we can actually count the days.

"This voyage *will* go smoothly," Kalligan says when the last man has left and the door falls back into place, "and I will not have some petty adolescent disagreement get in the way of that. Is that understood?"

"Of course," Tylon says immediately, ever the willing-to-please pawn.

"There is no disagreement," I say. It's more of a blatant abhorrence.

"Whatever it is, it stops now. There will be no more

belittling the other captains during meetings, Alosa. And Tylon, you would do well to listen to the wisdom Captain Alosa has to offer."

Tylon nods. I snort and roll my eyes at the whole scene. Tylon's puppylike obedience is enough to—

Father flies at me, quick as a bolt of lightning. I don't move, knowing whatever comes will be better if I don't resist.

In a flash, I'm backed against the wall. A dagger soars toward me, embedding itself in the wood just to the right of my eye.

"You will not be disrespectful in my presence," Kalligan says. "Else this dagger will move an inch to the left. You don't need both eyes for your voice to work."

I stare into those large, fierce eyes. I've no doubt he means it. And before he tries to do more than scare me, I have to comply.

"Apologies," I say.

See, I defy him all the time. I don't apologize because he controls me. I do it because . . . because . . . I can't finish the thought.

Am I only useful to him so long as I have a voice? Were I mute, would he still love me, still want me to captain a ship in his fleet?

He leaves the dagger in place and exits the room. When I pull away, strands of hair tug from my head, trapped by the dagger, and hang limply against the wall.

Chapter 5

THE DUNGEONS ARE LOCATED deep below the earth. They wind and twist as though formed from the pathway of a monstrous worm. The smell of mold clogs my nostrils, and the dank moisture in the air presses uncomfortably against my skin. Some of the tunnels slide right down into the sea and allow in water. With the tides, some of the cells fill to the brim. An added benefit when it comes to making prisoners talk.

Threck is the keeper of the dungeons. He's a gaunt fellow who perpetually looks like he's climbed his way out of a land dweller's grave. Dirt paints his clothes and skin, and he lets his hair hang about him in matted snarls. But the fact that he's absolutely terrified of me makes him amusing nonetheless.

Right now, however, there is very little that I find amusing.

I pound on the entrance to the dungeons, a large wooden door with a barred window.

"Threck!" I call out. "The king's sent me to question the new prisoner."

A lie.

I sent myself.

The dungeons are massive, but my shout carries in a much-too-loud echo from one tunnel to the next. After the sound dies down, silence is the only thing that bounces back up to me for several moments, and I wonder if he will pretend he didn't hear me. But he's too smart for that. The last thing you want to do is irritate someone who frightens you.

A slow shuffling sound makes its way toward me, growing louder and louder until I can tell the footsteps are just on the other side of the door. The barred window allows me to see to the other side, but Threck must be ducking because I can't see his head.

A key slides under the door, and footsteps retreat in a hurry.

It's difficult to say whether I'm more proud or offended by his reaction to me.

I grab a torch from its sconce on the wall and light it. There is a darkness unlike any other in the keep's dungeon. No natural light can squeeze its way so far below ground. It sucks all the hope from the prisoners trapped in here. I should know—I've been one many times.

Threck doesn't seem to mind it, however. He knows the dungeons so well he traverses them without any light at all.

I slide past row upon row of empty cells. They're never occupied for long. When I reach one of the few cells in use, I pause.

"Draxen."

Jeskor's elder son doesn't move at the sound of his own name. He sits on the stone floor and stares at the wall opposite the cell's entrance. Like his brother, Draxen has changed some. Only his changes are for the worse. His black hair hangs past his shoulders in ratted curls. His shirt is too big for him. It hangs off his bony shoulders and pools on the floor behind him. That'll be from the prisoner diet of cold gruel. But sometimes, if you're lucky, a rat will wander into your cell.

"*Princess,*" he says and spits off into the corner. I can see now he has a rock in his hand that he's throwing up in the air and catching. You've got to pass the time somehow. I would button and unbutton my coat. When my hands weren't shackled above my head, that is.

"Nice weather we're having," I say as I shiver from the cold. How can Draxen stand not to have his coat on? It looks like he's using it as a cushion under his rump.

"What do you want?" he asks.

"Nothing from you. I'm just passing through."

"Then get on with it."

"I didn't realize you were busy."

He turns at the snide remark and chucks the rock at me. I dodge it as best I can in the darkness, but it still skims the side of my arm.

"Stings, that does, you bastard," I say.

"To hell with you and your sorcery."

"Sorcery?"

"You did something to me. And to Riden. You've bewitched

him somehow. And you nearly killed him. So whether you call it sorcery or not, you can go hang by a rope from the tallest tree."

I laugh. It's not a mockery, but a sincere response to his foolishness. "You're furious with *me*? You do remember you kidnapped me? You forced me to witness the most disgusting tortures I've ever seen. You tried to force yourself on me, and your men tried to kill me. All I did was steal a map."

Despite his foul attitude, I dig into my pocket and throw something at him. I make sure it hits him in the back of the head before continuing on.

I hear his hands scramble furiously in the darkness to retrieve what I threw. Then the sound of his chewing is so loud, I hear it for the next twenty feet.

Fresh bread from the kitchens. I don't know what prompted me to bring it for him, but I did.

Now, for the reason I'm really here.

Vordan's cell is tucked into a nasty corner where the tide comes in. Water reaches his ankles. He must be freezing.

Good.

I hate him. I hate that I'm here.

"Alosa," he says when he notices me. Just the tone makes me cringe. The satisfied, self-assured way he manages to say it even when locked behind bars.

"Tell me more," I whisper, even though I know we're alone.

"What? I didn't catch that?"

"Tell. Me. More."

"About what?" he asks, toying with me.

I snap. My voice rushes out like a thunderclap. I burry him under a mountain of snow, let him feel a cold so piercing he'll forget there was ever anything else to feel. I push him from the tallest cliff, let him fall and fall, hurtling down at an impossible speed, knowing he's about to die and there's no way to stop it. I thrust him back into his cell, make the walls rattle as the volcano nearby explodes and blistering heat drowns him. On and on, I throw terror after terror at him.

He's shaking by the time I stop, his breathing shallow.

I tamp down my rage enough to say, "I can still hurt you, Vordan. Tell me what you know or we can keep at this. I'm not feeling particularly patient today, so cut the snark."

It takes him a full minute to find his voice. "You"—deep breath—"you are a monster."

"And you've made the monster angry. Start talking."

"I don't—I don't know anything else."

I open my mouth.

"I swear it!" he shouts.

I cock my head to the side.

"My man didn't take anything out of the king's study. He could only tell me what he saw. Some sort of device and a note in Kalligan's own writing, depicting what it does. You already know I'm not lying about it. I've told the truth while under your abilities."

I'm more frustrated than before. I can't trust my enemy over my own father.

But after what Father did, threatening to take out my eye because my voice would still work without it—

He's only under pressure from the upcoming voyage. He wouldn't really do it.

But have you ever known him to make an idle threat?

How can I question him? After everything he's done for me?

You mean the beatings and imprisonment?

No! He raised me. He trained me. He made me unstoppable.

He made you his loyal pet.

I growl.

"You!" I snap at Vordan. "You put these thoughts in my head."

He raises himself up to his full, unimpressive height, one of his legs bent awkwardly behind him. "I could not create doubt where there wasn't already a seed planted."

That's it.

Enough of this.

There's only one way to get rid of the uncertainty once and for all.

Chapter 6

"YOU WANT ME TO help you break in to your father's study?"

"Yes."

"All right, then," Riden says.

I wait, expecting more. When he doesn't say anything, I ask, "That's it? You don't have any questions for me?" No patronizing words to throw in my face? No conditions or stipulations? No *I-told-you-so*s?

"I overheard your interrogation with Vordan, remember? If it were me, I'd do the same thing."

I realize then that he's not going to lord this over my head. He's not smirking at me the way Vordan did. Not pleased with himself or pleased by my own pain.

He wants to help.

Riden is more confusing than ever.

But I don't have time to think on it.

What we're doing is dangerous. Treasonous. If my father catches us, we're all dead. Which is why I'm bringing only three with me: Athella, because she can get me through any door; Sorinda, because she can cut down anyone in our path; and Riden, because—

I just want him with me.

The four of us leave the ship and enter the keep. We slide along cave wall after cave wall, peering around every bend and turn to make certain it's clear before proceeding. It's getting late, and we can only hope that most pirates have already gone to bed.

When we reach the door, I put Sorinda and Riden on either end of the tunnel as lookouts. Athella gets on her knees to inspect the lock while I stand just behind her. My fingers start to fidget, so I fold my arms.

Athella lets out a low whistle.

"Shh," I say, casting a nervous glance down toward my father's rooms.

"Sorry," she whispers. "It's just that the king *really* doesn't want anyone getting in here. He has one of those fancy new Wenoa locks with a cylindrical keyhole. Most lockpicks haven't figured out how to manufacture the tools necessary to get through these."

"So you can't do it?"

A mischievous grin takes over her face. "Didn't say that, Captain. I'm no average lockpick. It'll just take me a while."

"I don't how much time you'll have."

"Then I'd better get started."

She unrolls her cloth of tools and grabs a hollow, cylindrical piece of metal and inserts it into the hole. Then she grabs a pick and starts poking it around the edges. I thank the stars that I have Athella in my crew. My lockpicking skills are nowhere near as advanced as hers.

"Powerful spring," she mumbles to herself and adjusts her fingers slightly.

I realize I'm holding my breath while she works, so I force myself to let the air out of my lungs. "If you get this open, you can have half of my share of our next plunder."

She laughs. "If? Captain, I'm heartbroken."

"Someone's coming!" Sorinda whispers through the flickering torchlight.

Athella shoves the tools and kit into her corset before standing. "What do we do?"

I haven't had time to soak up more song. I'm practically empty after unleashing myself on Vordan, so we need to be clever in order to get out of this one. And if it's my father approaching, singing will do us no good. As Vordan said, my abilities have never worked on him.

I wave Riden over. He joins us, and I start laughing and walking in the direction of the new footsteps.

Athella and Riden catch on quickly, relaxing their stances. Athella lets out a giggle, and Riden smiles openly. Sorinda falls into line with us, wearing an uncomfortable grimace, but she quickly masks her face with her usual apathy. Sorinda hasn't much practice with playacting. She prefers not being seen altogether, but that is impossible at the moment.

"But the fool was so angry that he challenged me to a duel," I say as though continuing a story.

A few men round the corner, and we continue walking toward them as though we're heading farther into the keep.

"What happened next, Captain?" Athella asks.

"I had no choice but to accept. I embarrassed the poor man in front of his friends."

The footsteps belong to Adderan and a couple of his men. He must have come by to make more apologies to my father, and to give him more assurances of his loyalty.

They give us inappropriate, lingering glances, likely thinking us to be whores requested by the king. That is, until Adderan bothers to look at my face. He grimaces as he recognizes me, then hurries the others along.

I almost wish he'd provoke me. I'd love an excuse to kill him.

We continue walking long after the men pass us. Then, just to be extra cautious, I say loudly, "Hold on, I've forgotten something on the ship."

We turn back down the tunnel until we reach the door once more. Everyone resumes their posts.

"They've moved on," Riden says from his end.

Athella has her tools back out in an instant. This time she's quicker with her hands.

Several minutes pass as she pokes at the lock. Two more times we have to pause at the sound of echoing footsteps, but they're only traveling through some other adjoining tunnel. We don't come into contact with anyone else.

And finally, a low *click* emits from the lock.

"Got you," Athella announces quietly. She places her tools back in their assigned spots before standing. "It's ready for you, Captain."

A chill sweeps down my spine at the pronouncement. I'm really about to do this. I'm trusting a rival pirate lord over my father.

"Athella, take Riden's place and keep watch."

Her lips round in a slight pout.

"You'll see what's inside soon enough. Riden, you're with me."

With Athella and Sorinda keeping watch on either end of the tunnel, I grab one of the torches from the wall and slip into the room with Riden right behind me.

The study looks as though it was carved right out of the rock. The edges break sharply as if a pickax worked at them. The decor is opulent, much like my own tastes. A massive desk is neatly set with quills and parchment. All the drawers are locked. The chair in front of it is padded with feathers, probably goose. Another chair rests against one of the walls, equally soft with black fabric on the seat. A cabinet on the far side holds rums and wines and two glasses. A chaise and bookcase have their own wall. A tapestry depicting sirens and pirates engaged in battle hangs opposite the desk, next to the lone chair.

After placing the torch in a sconce on the wall, I kneel in front of the desk and get to work at the locks on the drawers. The locks are child's play compared to the one on the door. I don't need Athella for them.

"What can I do?" Riden asks as I prod with the tools in my hands.

"For starters, you could be quiet." Harsh, I know. But I'm too on edge right now to be nice.

The top drawer slides open, and I put away my picks.

There are only two items in here: a piece of parchment and a metal rod.

I pull out the rod first. It's hollow, no longer than a foot, and ancient-looking symbols have been pounded into the metal. The supposed siren-controlling device? It doesn't hum or pulse or glow or do anything else mystical. In fact—

I examine a section near one of the openings more closely. I recognize the workmanship. Hakin, one of the keep's smithies made this. It's faint, but there's his signature on the end. He's hidden it within one of the ancient symbols. Anyone unfamiliar with his work would miss it entirely.

Why would Father have this made? There isn't a glass for spying or anything inside of the rod—nothing at all to make it useful. Though you could probably clobber someone with it if you were so inclined.

I pull the parchment out next. I read over my father's handwriting quickly, little phrases jumping out at me.

... *control sirens* ...

. . . wield with care . . .

. . . immunity to enchanting song . . .

Riden reads over my shoulder, but I don't mind. More and more things are becoming clear.

I set the paper down, pick up the device.

And I laugh. "This is all fake. He didn't find it suspicious that my father placed an advanced lock on the main door yet such a flimsy one on the drawers? My father likely planted this for a spy so they would be given false information. And this"—I raise the rod—"it's just a piece of metal. Vordan and his spy are idiots."

My shoulders sag, all the tension leaving me at last. I was a fool for listening to Vordan. For letting him get to me. Of course Father would have something in place for spies wandering through here. Maybe I will venture to those dungeons one last time before we leave so the world can be rid of Vordan forever.

I risked our lives for nothing.

I return the items to the drawer and lock it. I'm about to lead Riden out of here, when my eyes glance over the cabinet of rum once more.

There are *two* glasses. *Two* chairs in the room. And Father is the only one ever seen leaving or entering.

I'm at the tapestry in an instant, pulling it aside and feeling the wall for a switch of some sort.

And I find one.

The wall swings outward, and my breath stops at the sight in front of me. Riden joins me at the opening.

A woman sits on another chaise, staring at a painting of the sea at sunset hung on the wall. She's the most beautiful thing I've ever seen. Her hair is a deep red, twisting around her shoulders as if it were tendrils of flame. Her skin is so fair, as if it has never seen the sun. Her lashes are long and as red as her hair. Her form hides behind a simple dress. And while she looks frail and somewhat sunken, I know she was once strong and beautiful.

She doesn't turn as I step into the room, though I know she hears me. Her eyes close briefly, as though she's irritated by the disturbance.

I feel tears prick at the sides of my eyes, but I don't let them out. Not yet.

I try to speak, but it turns into a cough when the words stick.

She looks at me then, and those green eyes show such surprise, they confirm my suspicions that no one has ever seen her in this room aside from my father.

I try again. "What's your name?" This time the words are clear, but they seem too loud somehow.

"Ava-lee," she says in a voice as beautiful as the rest of her. She brings a hand up to cover her gaping mouth, then lowers it, fingers trembling. "Are you Alosa?"

This time the tears come. I can't stop them, nor do I have a desire to do so.

"Mother?"

She stands in one graceful movement. Before I know it, she's holding me so tightly I can scarcely breathe. The embrace is strange, something I've never quite experienced before, but it is exquisite. Such a simple thing, but it says so much without saying a thing.

A thousand questions fight their way to the front of my mind, desperately trying to be first.

How?

When?

Why?

Why seems the most important.

"Why are you here?" I ask when I can calm my tears.

She steps back to survey me from head to toe. "You're beautiful. You don't look like him at all. Blessed ocean." Tears fall from her own eyes, and she touches them as though she doesn't know what to make of them before focusing on me once more. "Oh, my sweet girl. At last." She crushes me to her again, and I marvel that something so frail can be so strong.

Someone clears his throat from behind us. I panic for a moment, until I remember it's only Riden.

"I'm going to wait back in there," he says, giving us some privacy. I'm sure he'll be able to hear the whole exchange, but it's kind of him anyway.

"Who is that?" my mother asks.

"That's Riden. He's . . . a member of my crew."

"Your crew?"

"I'm the captain of my own ship."

She smiles, but it looks painful on her. "Of course you are. You were always meant to rule. It's in your blood."

A silence fills the space, and I remember then how desperate I am for answers.

"Why are you here?" I ask again.

She brushes a hand over my hair, stroking its lengths while still clutching me to her. It's oddly soothing. "He locked me in here after you were born. It's been over eighteen years. Eighteen years without you or the sea."

"But why?" I pull away from her again, needing to see her face. Suddenly words tumble out of my mouth. "He told me you left me. You didn't want me. You're supposed to be at the Isla de Canta. You're a mindless beast with no humanity." I'm crying again because of what it all means. My father has been lying to me ever since I was born.

She shrinks back at my words. Her voice turns faint. "Please don't think such things of me. I tried to escape this room many times and come to you. I swear it upon the lives of all those I'm sworn to protect."

My heart aches and my face turns downward in shame. "I'm truly sorry for believing him. I don't anymore."

It is a strange thing to be so torn apart from the inside. I'm overjoyed to have found my mother, but that joy is pressed right up against the sting of my father's betrayal.

I dare to look up again. "Why did he put you in here?"

"He's never said so, but I think he didn't want me influencing you. A mother would split your loyalties."

"Then why didn't he kill you?"

She looks away from me for the first time. "You don't want to know."

I'm afraid I already do. "Please, tell me. I think I need to know."

She seems to mull it over for a moment. "You're already a grown woman." Her face falls at missed years. "He wanted more daughters. More sirens to control and manipulate as he's done to you. More power."

Despicable bastard. But I put a hold on cursing his name for a moment.

"Do I have sisters?" The thought is both exciting and horrifying, now that I know what my father is truly capable of.

"No. I have been unable to give him any more children." She looks sad at the thought, and I find that most peculiar.

"Do you want to?"

Her perfect lips turn down in a look of disgust. "With him? I don't want to be touched by him ever again. But I would have liked to have many daughters. I wanted to raise them and teach them. To see them grow. He took that from me." She touches my shoulders gently. "But I'm pleased beyond words to see you now."

Perhaps it should take longer than a few minutes to turn against the man who raised me. To switch sides so easily. But how can I do anything else when I know what he's done to my mother? A mother who is *not* a mindless beast.

A wave of anger washes over me, smothering any loyalty I once had for the pirate king. "I had no idea you were in here. You must know, if I had known, I would have come for you immediately. I'm only in here tonight by accident."

"Don't blame yourself. There's nothing anyone can do. I'm merely a woman when I'm away from the sea."

When the torrent of bitter anger finally clears, resolve takes its place. "Well, I'm not. I'm getting you out of here. Now. Riden!"

He's back in the room in an instant.

"Can you carry her?" I ask.

"Of course."

This is such a dangerous situation—it must be handled carefully, but my mind is pounding, so full it's fit to burst.

My father lied.

My mother isn't a monster.

She's a prisoner.

I have to get her out.

But what if we're caught?

It doesn't matter.

I have to try.

"You will not spend one more night in this room," I promise her.

"What can you do against him? I'll not put you in danger. So long as he doesn't know that you know, you're safe. Get away from here. From him. Don't worry about me."

My aching heart soothes at her words. They remind me of a conversation, or rather an interrogation, between Riden and me.

There are different kinds of fathers. Those who love unconditionally, those who love on condition, and those who never love at all.

My mother doesn't know me, but she is putting my life

before hers. Is that what it should have been like between me and my father?

I scan the room quickly, looking for anything that will help us secret her away. There isn't much. An unmade bed with a feathered mattress. A chaise. Paintings on the walls. Some books on a shelf.

She must have gone mad in here.

I grab one of the blankets from the bed and wrap her in it, taking care to brush all of her hair away from her face and tuck it out of sight under the blanket. I am known for my red hair. If anyone were to see her, it would arouse the wrong kind of curiosity.

"She needs to keep her hair covered," I say to Riden.

He nods, and in one motion, he sweeps her off her feet and holds her easily in his arms.

We'll need to set sail right away. It's fortunate we just restocked all the supplies after our last voyage. Where can we go where the pirate king won't find us? Land? I can't give up the sea. *I'd* go mad.

"Alosa," Riden says.

"Yes?"

"Look at me."

I do.

"We'll get her out of here. She'll be safe. Then we can plan our next move."

It hits me then just how remarkable Riden is being about all of this. Didn't he tell me my father was despicable? That I was a fool for following him? That he didn't truly love me?

But now, when it's all proved correct, he's not menacing or condescending.

He's still helping me.

He's holding my mother so carefully, and the sight gives me the strength to do what I need to do.

"Let's go."

Chapter 7

SORINDA DOESN'T SAY A word when Riden and I exit my father's study. She doesn't even look surprised.

But Athella—

"Who's that, Captain?"

"No time. Sorinda, take Athella and go retrieve Draxen from the dungeons. We're leaving the keep, but tell no one. You must be discreet."

"Have I ever been anything else?" Sorinda asks. Without waiting for an answer, she grabs Athella's arm and leads her away.

"We need to be quick," I tell Riden, "but not suspicious. Walk beside me. Don't speak if we're stopped. Let me handle everything."

He looks at me for a moment, surprise written across his face.

"What?"

"Thank you, for my brother."

"It's nothing."

"It's not nothing. It's everything to me."

His gratitude is overwhelming my already bursting heart. "In that case, you're welcome. Now let's go."

"Lead the way."

We walk at a brisk pace. We haven't taken more than a couple of steps when Riden whispers my name.

"What?"

"When we're out of here, when we're safely away from the king's keep, I want to talk to you about something."

"And what's that?"

"Alosa?" A new voice comes down the tunnel, and it's far too close.

Tylon.

"Go on," I whisper to Riden so quietly I might only be mouthing the words. "I'll distract him. You keep going."

"I don't know where I'm going."

"Just go." I wave one hand frantically.

I rush back the way we came, running right past the study door and halting just before the tunnel bends. Tylon's face appears above mine.

"Are you alone?" he asks, peering over my shoulder. Since he doesn't reach for his sword, I assume Riden listened and kept going.

"Yes, why?"

"It sounded like you were talking to someone. What are you doing here?" He looks curiously at the study door, and my heart plummets. He cannot think I came from there. He'd rat me out to my father in a heartbeat. I need a good lie. And I need it now.

"I was looking for you," I say hurriedly. "And rehearsing what I'd say when I found you."

I reach for the siren in me and pull her out effortlessly. Goose bumps surface on my arms. If Tylon notices, I hope he thinks it's a reaction to him and not from using my abilities. The siren half of me gives me three unique abilities. I can sing to men and make them do whatever I wish so long as I have the power of the sea with me. I can read the emotions of men—they manifest as colors for me to decipher. And last, I can tell what any man wants in a woman, become it, and use it to manipulate him. Since I wasted most of my song on Vordan, it is the latter two of my abilities I pull from now.

My entire focus latches onto Tylon, on his greatest wants and desires. I can see the red of his desire for me. Though I know he's attracted to me, what he really cares about is that I'm the pirate king's daughter. That is what makes me useful to him. Being in my favor serves his own interests. And the only person he's ever cared about is himself.

"Well, you've found me." He folds his arms and steps back to get a better look at me. He's scanning me for deception, trying to spot it in any gesture. One wrong word or movement, and who knows what he'll do.

I need to swallow my nausea and pride in this moment.

Forget what it does to my dignity. This is for my mother. "I don't like arguing with you. What happened today in front of all the captains—it can't happen again."

"I agree."

For some reason, it bothers me more to have him agreeing with me. "And I think you should know, despite what I say and how I act, I don't hate you."

His stiff, suspicious stance relaxes. "I know that."

Sure he does. Arrogant bastard doesn't realize I'm saying the complete opposite of what I feel. "You do?" I ask, adding a hint of playfulness to my tone.

"I can be very likable, if you'll just let me." He peers deeply into my eyes, as though trying to force a connection with me.

"Let you what?"

"Let me show you how great we could be together. Can't you just see the future we'd make? You and I ruling the sea. All in Maneria afraid to leave the safety of land. All the money of the realm pouring into our treasury. With you and your abilities, our legacy will be even greater than Kalligan's."

If he thinks I'd share *my* birthright with him—

No, not now. Forget the braggart. Focus on your mother.

I take a step forward and slide my hands up his arms to his shoulders. "And just what is to be the nature of our relationship?"

The faraway look in his eyes leaves, and he focuses on me. Something new takes hold of him. It is no longer a lust for riches and glory.

He crushes his mouth to mine. All intensity and passion.

The thought of himself becoming the new pirate king has him worked up. And he thinks himself worthy of my attention. He doesn't hope I will kiss him back. He expects it, and I have to if I'm to keep Riden hidden from him.

I cringe as I remember Riden probably heard some of that.

"What's wrong?" Tylon asks against my lips.

"Nothing. Come here." I need to give Riden more time to get away. I grab Tylon by the lapels of his captain's coat and swing him around the next bend of the tunnel, even farther away from Riden and my mother, before pinning him against the wall and kissing him like I mean it. Now that I have him right where I want him, I let the siren go.

My movements are meaningless to me. My mouth moves automatically, leaving my mind free to wander elsewhere. I hope Riden can remember where he's going.

I imagine him carrying my mother all the way to the ship without any trouble befalling them, tucking her away safely in my rooms. Then he'll come find me, maybe smash Tylon on the head because he somehow knows how much I loathe him, even though I told him otherwise.

And then he'll take me in his arms and kiss me. Because he wants it and knows I do, too.

Just a light peck on the lips, but as I try to leave he'll pull me back for more. And I'll be secretly pleased that he wants more.

He'll pin me against some hard surface, place his hands on either side of my waist, and lean down until all the air between us is gone.

I put my hands on his face, feeling the hard planes of his cheeks with my hands. That pleases him. I feel his lips turn into a smile as he continues to kiss me. His lips move to my throat, and I move my hands to his hair.

But instead of the silky locks I'm expecting, I touch loose curls. I open my eyes in a snap and stare at sun-colored hair.

Not Riden.

I'm kissing Tylon.

He's still busy at the base of my neck when I spot an enormous figure rounding the corner over his shoulder.

"Tylon." I slap his shoulder.

He pauses long enough to see that it's my father before adjusting himself, leaning against the wall next to me, and sliding his hand behind my back to rest on my hip. He's holding me against him as though I belong to him. I loathe it.

Tylon grins. "We took your advice and stopped arguing."

Not a muscle in my father's face twitches. "Go stop arguing elsewhere. The tunnels are no place for it."

I turn away as though I'm embarrassed, but the truth is I can't stand to look at my father any longer. Not after knowing what he's done. It's as if he's a different person, when in reality I'm only beginning to understand who he really is.

A monster.

"Then we'll be off," I finally say. I grab the hand at my hip and pull Tylon in the direction of our ships. It's the direction Riden went in. The direction my father just came from. He couldn't have spotted Riden and my mother or else I would have heard a struggle. Oh, but I hope Riden didn't get himself lost.

And stars forbid my father have plans to visit my mother tonight.

I traverse with Tylon down the tunnel, his arm tucked in mine.

He leans his head against mine and asks, "Where are we going?"

"Your rooms."

His breathing hitches, and his steps quicken. Meanwhile, my eyes are scanning every turn and bend in the tunnels for Riden, hoping to spot him before Tylon does.

When I do see him, there's nothing I can do to stop Tylon from noticing, too. Riden leans against the wall, one foot pressed flat against it, his arms crossed casually against his chest.

I open my mouth, unsure of what I'm going to say. Hopefully not what I want to ask him: *What did you do with my mother?*

"Captain," Riden says, "have you finished your business?" So composed. So normal.

"Yes. Where is your cargo?"

"Safe. Just waiting for you so we can get it to the ship."

Tylon looks at Riden closely. "I don't recognize you."

"He's a recent addition," I explain.

Tylon tugs me. "I don't really care. We were on our way somewhere important."

I hope he can't tell my stomach just turned. "Wait, I forgot I need to speak with my father."

"You can speak with him tomorrow," he says, trying to pull me along again.

I force a playful laugh at his insistence. "It can't wait until then. It's about the voyage. He'll want to know right away. It'll only take a second."

He doesn't let me go; instead he stares into my eyes again, as though that will somehow change my mind.

"Go to your rooms," I say. "I'll meet you on your ship."

He leans down to give me one more hearty kiss.

In front of Riden.

But I can't do it again. I. Just. Can't.

I reach for my pistol, and just as Tylon is about to press his lips to mine—I bring it down on his head. He's out before he hits the floor.

"Where is she?" I ask.

"We couldn't go any farther without getting lost. When I heard someone coming, I set her down so she wouldn't be spotted. She's just over here."

I pull Tylon off the floor and throw him over my shoulder. Riden stares for an extra beat at my strength before leading the way. He makes a couple of turns down the tunnel and stops when we come to some stacked water barrels stored along the edges. He stoops behind them, and when he's standing again, he has my mother in his arms once more.

Tylon takes her place.

I finally relax, but it's fleeting. We still have a ways to go before we're out of here.

"Are you all right?" I ask her.

"Yes. Just weak."

"Let's go," I say to Riden.

We hurry. Every echo, every whisper of wind is enough to make my heart stop. We can't be found. It doesn't matter who spots us. We look too conspicuous. Anyone would surely report us to my father. We don't speak, too fearful of who might hear us.

But either the stars are watching out for us or everyone is well asleep, because we meet no one else during the painful march.

We race up the gangplank.

Niridia appears at my side. "Sorinda and Athella have already made it back. Mandsy is seeing to Draxen in the infirmary. I didn't get much out of them except that we need to be ready to sail."

The crew is roused. They await on deck for orders. Some have obviously just been woken—they rub sleep from their eyes. Enwen is still pulling a shirt over his head.

"Listen up," I say. I dare not shout with all the other ships stationed nearby in the cave, but I hope everyone can hear. "The pirate king has deceived me." I point over to where my mother is wrapped up in Riden's arms. "That is my mother. Kalligan has kept her as his prisoner for the last eighteen years. I've only just discovered her by accident."

Everyone swivels their heads in her direction.

"We're leaving, and we're going to do it quickly and quietly. Does anyone have a problem with that?"

Enwen raises his hand, shying away from us.

"What, Enwen?"

"Captain, if that's your mother, that would make her a—a—"

"Siren, yes. Does anyone else have any questions more important than our lives?"

Silence.

"Trim the sails," Niridia barks out. "Raise the gangplank, hoist anchor! Move it!" The easy-going sailor is gone, instantly replaced with the harsh first mate I need her to be. All sea hands race around us to fulfill her orders.

The other docked ships are quiet, no lights lit. I try to assure myself that even if there were anyone keeping watch, they wouldn't think anything of my ship leaving. My father gives me orders without telling anyone else all the time. But uncertainty has my heart pounding.

"Are you cold?"

I turn at the voice.

Riden still holds my mother, and she's visibly trembling in his arms.

"I'm all right," she answers him. Her response is firm despite her shaking limbs. "You're strong, for a human."

"I used to be fast, too. Until I was shot in the leg. Haven't been able to get it back up to strength yet."

"You were shot?" Mother asks. "How?"

"Your daughter got me into trouble."

It must be the oddest thing I've ever seen—witnessing Riden talking with my mother, distracting her from her discomfort.

I will go to her as soon as we're safe. For now, I need to be captain.

Sorinda locates Kearan, who is miraculously sober—well, sober enough to steer—and gets him to the helm.

"Where are we headed to at this hour?"

Yes, where are we going? "For now, the nearest port. Just get us away from here. Like our lives depend on it, Kearan."

He looks down his broken nose at me. "Because they do?"

"When the king discovers I've stolen my mother, he will hunt us down. And if he catches us—"

"Understood."

It truly hits me then. What I've done. We are all going to be hunted by the most feared man in the world. I brought this on all of us by taking her. I just took her and didn't think of my crew.

No, even if I had paused to think, I would have done the same thing. We can't serve him any longer. He's dangerous and vile. He kept her in that room for almost two decades, and I can't even think of the way he used her without my dinner threatening to come back up.

How have I been so blind?

Roslyn wanders up from belowdecks, rubbing her tired eyes. All the noise must have woken her. "What's happening, Captain?"

"Roslyn, you're to go to the crow's nest. I need to know if anyone follows us. And if anyone starts firing on us, you're to go to your post."

Her eyes harden, any signs of exhaustion leaving them. They're the same bright blue as her father's, but Wallov never looks at me like this. "It's not a post. It's a hidey-hole beneath the flooring of the crow's nest."

"Be that as it may, it was designed specifically for you, and if any fighting should break out, you're to go there."

Her hands go to her hips.

"Now is not the time, Roslyn. Can I count on you or not?"

The fight leaves her at those words. "Of course, Captain." She runs to the netting and starts climbing better than any monkey.

The ship finally starts moving, angling toward the cave's exit.

"It's so beautiful," Mother says once the open ocean is in view. Riden still holds on to her. He follows her line of sight to the ocean. I notice now that she takes turns glancing between it and me.

I can't imagine being separated from the ocean for eighteen years.

"Captain!" Roslyn shouts from above. "There's movement on the dock."

I spin and instantly find the beast of a man standing on the dock.

The pirate king.

He must have tried to visit Mother tonight after all.

A shout goes up. More pirates appear. A warning bell sounds: the keep's alarm for if we're ever under attack.

He's waking everyone.

The entire fleet, it seems, will be following after us.

I have a head start, and my ship is faster. We are out of firing range already. There is nothing he can do except follow us by this point. And I know all of his ships aren't stocked for sailing. It may buy us another hour—or even a day.

We need a plan, but nothing is forthcoming, and we're safe for now. So I hurry to my mother, who is still supported by Riden's arms over by the port side.

"Could you set me down?" my mother asks Riden.

"Are you sure? Why don't I take you—"

"No, right here, please. Thank you."

She has both feet on the ground, but she's clutching the railing as though her life depends on it, trembling from head to foot. Only when I take his place by her side, does Riden leave for the infirmary to see his brother.

"You named your ship after me," she manages to say through chattering teeth.

"Let me take you to my rooms."

"No."

"What do you need?" I ask. "Food? Sleep? What can I do to help?"

"Water," she says.

"Of course. I'll get some."

"No, Alosa." She looks sad for a moment. "He let me name you, you know. It was the one thing he did let me do for you. Alosa-lina. We give our children joint names. The first is a unique name—no two sirens have the same first name. The second name is a sung name. It has power. *Lina* means *protector*, and I can see you have already lived up to it."

A shiver shakes her whole body, and she grips the railing more tightly. "My precious daughter. I want to stay here with you. I tried to be strong for you, to give you what your human nature needs, but I can't fight it anymore. The pull is too strong. I need the water. And my sisters need me. They've been too long without a queen. Follow me. I'll lead you home."

Though she's frail and aching, she leans over the railing and lets herself fall. I hear the splash before I fully register what is happening.

"Man overboard!" Roslyn shouts, but I barely hear it.

"No!" I rush over to the edge, peering into the water. She's impossible to miss. Her body seems to glow under the water, taking on a shimmer like fish scales, but she's not covered in scales. Her skin is pearly white. She looks bigger, no longer fragile, but strong and healthy. She circles in place, as though she's . . . stretching, breathing in fresh air for the first time.

From under the water, her face turns upward. I can see her now piercing-blue eyes—no longer green—even from this distance. She smiles at me. Her hand opens and closes, beckoning me to follow. Then she takes off like a shot, swimming at an impossible speed through the water, away from the keep.

Away from me.

Chapter 8

"THAT'S IT?" I SCREAM the words, though I know she can't hear me. "Ava-lee! Get back here!"

Doesn't she know I can't follow her? Surely she knows what happens when I'm in the water? I can't control myself! Can she? Is she the same person who was just talking to me? She's not human. Does she turn into a monster when she's underwater as I do?

She left.

She's gone.

I saved her. I put myself and others at risk for her. And now we've nothing to show for it.

Was it all a ruse? Her pretending that she cared? Was it all just a trick she used to get me to save her? Was the humanity an act?

A tapping at my back makes me flinch, but it is only little Roslyn.

"What happened, Captain? Who was the pretty lady? Do we throw her a rope?"

A voice that doesn't seem to belong to me says, "She was no one. She doesn't need our help anymore. Roslyn, go on back to your station. I need you to tell me if any ships gain on us."

"Aye-aye."

A numbness takes over me as I shut out all thoughts of my parents and what they've done. There is nothing except me and my crew. Nothing that matters except our safety and well-being. We are being hunted. What do we do?

She abandoned *me*.

No—

I tamp down the thought.

Don't think of anything else, Alosa. Your crew is counting on you.

"Kearan!" I say. "Find a suitable port to deposit our extra passengers." Riden and Draxen are not part of my crew. The king isn't hunting them down. There's no reason to drag them into this.

But then you might never see Riden again. . . . A glimmer of feeling tries to sneak through the cracks. I board them up, let nothing but the numbness enter.

In a voice loud enough for all to hear, I say, "I brought the pirate king after us. There's nothing I can do to change that now. But we can survive this."

"What's the plan, Captain?" Niridia asks.

"My father is so feared because he has nearly every man on the sea under his employ. If we're to bring him down, we need to take that away."

"Pirates are loyal only to whoever has the most gold to pay," Mandsy says. "Present company excluded, of course."

"Exactly. We have copies of all three pieces of the map. We're sailing to the Isla de Canta and taking the sirens' treasure for ourselves."

Sorinda, who stands behind Kearan's shoulder, says, "Then starts the reign of the pirate queen."

"Rah!" cheers the crew.

Though I'm certain I have the support of all, I add, "If anyone has a problem with the plan, they can leave when we drop off our prisoners."

A headache starts to pound between my eyes. My carefully built walls will crumble soon. I can't keep them up forever.

"Kearan, keep us steady. Niridia, come get me if a ship follows us out of the keep."

"Aye, Captain." She comes to my side. Quieter, so no one else can hear, she adds, "We should talk about what just happened, Alosa." She calls me this when addressing me as a friend rather than my first mate. I know she means my mother leaving, but I'm barely keeping it together as it is.

"Later," I say, though I've no intention of discussing it. "Right now I need a moment. Alone."

"Do what you need to. I'll see that everything runs smoothly."

She always does.

I finally get a door between me and the rest of the world. And the walls come tumbling down.

My breathing turns to rasping. I grind my teeth and glare at everything in sight. My drapes. My glass-framed pictures. My bed. There's this pressure building inside me, as though I will explode.

I don't know how to let it out. I don't think I've ever been so furious in my whole life.

A knock sounds at the door.

"Get away if you don't want your head bashed in!" I shout. I punch a feather pillow on my bed. It's not enough, though. It doesn't do anything to let out the pressure. I need to hit something hard. Sturdy. Something that'll push back. I want to scream, but the crew will hear that.

I'm so distraught that I don't realize my door has opened and shut until a hand comes down on my shoulder. I spin around and thrust the low part of my palm outward, connecting with—

Riden's chest.

He rubs at the spot but doesn't complain. He won't take his eyes off mine.

"I heard what happened," he says.

"I told you not to come in."

"I didn't listen."

I send an elbow at his gut, but he turns sideways and catches my arm.

"It wasn't an empty warning," I say.

"I know."

"You're an idiot." I swipe his legs out from under him. "You haven't fought against me before."

He takes a few moments to find his feet. I think I knocked the wind from him. "We've fought many times," he rasps.

"Aye, and I was going easy on you."

"Then do your worst now, lass."

I do. At first. I move like an unbreakable current, forcing wave after crushing wave upon him. My legs lash out, my arms strike, even my head connects with him at one point. But he doesn't come at me with his own blows, only tries to deflect me as best he can.

"Fight back, Riden."

"No," he says stubbornly.

"Why not?"

"It wouldn't be right."

"What is that supposed to mean?"

"You're hurt."

"I'm not the one who will wake covered in bruises tomorrow."

"Not visible ones."

I backhand him. It sends him to the ground. As soon as my hand makes contact, I regret the decision. I'm abusing his body. He is not here to be my whipping boy, yet that's exactly how I'm treating him. I can't strike my father. Or my *mother*. The woman who made me feel so loved and then left without a trace.

I hate her for it.

My own ship mocks me with its name. I'm painting over it at the next opportunity.

Riden moves his jaw back and forth with his hand as he rises.

"You're making me feel worse!" I shout at him. "Is that what you wanted?"

"No, I came to comfort you."

"You're doing one hell of a job."

He sets his jaw now. "You're the one making this difficult."

I shake my head once in outrage. "I'm supposed to make it easy for you to comfort me?"

"Let me hold you."

The words startle me so much that at first I don't know how to answer.

Then, "No! I don't need your damned comfort. I want to hit things and scream. I told you what you could do to help. Give me something to fight. Otherwise get out before I kill you."

"You have more self-control than that."

"You don't know me."

My anger cools ever so slightly. These quick exchanges seem to be having some effect on me. For a moment, I let myself try to imagine what it would be like to simply be held by him. What would it feel like? To be caught in an embrace that wasn't meant to do anything but soothe?

"I'm trying to," he says. It takes me a moment to remember what we were talking about.

A new thought strikes me. No, an embrace is too slow. It's not what I want.

I lunge at him. I see him stiffen for the blow as he registers my movement.

But that's not what I want, either.

I place my lips over his so quickly, I think his eyes are still open when I reach him. I can't tell for certain; mine are already closed so I can focus better on eliciting a response from him. My fingers slide into his hair, silky smooth and wonderful, until they reach the back of his head. I put pressure there to seal him in place.

He might be strong enough to resist fighting me, but this . . .

He's helpless against this.

It only takes him a second to get a hand in my hair. The other goes to the side of my face and neck so he can stroke the skin there with his fingertips. I open my mouth to draw in a breath, to draw in him. He uses it as an opportunity to deepen the kiss. His tongue slides in, completely bathing me in sensation. Stars, how did I manage to avoid him for two whole months?

Time wasted.

I grab his back to pull him closer. I need every inch of him touching me now. Right now. Nothing is fast enough. It's the most glorious feeling in the world. This right here. Not having to think. Just feel.

I pull his shirt out from where it's tucked into his breeches. He reaches down, as though to help me take it off, then pauses.

He presses his forehead against mine, breathing so quickly, I wonder how he manages to get words out. "Wait."

"I don't want to wait." My hands are under his shirt now, sliding up his stomach, slowly pulling the cotton up with them. His breathing hitches, and that only makes me pull it up slower, savoring the feel of his smooth skin and loving the way he reacts to everything I do.

"In the tunnels," I say, "you said you wanted to talk about something with me. What was it?" I press a kiss to his neck.

"I wanted to talk about us."

"I can think of something more fun than talking."

He finally grabs my hands with his own. He doesn't pull them away, only holds them in place so he can catch his breath. I tilt my mouth up to his lips again.

"Alosa, stop it."

I open my eyes and look at him. "What's the matter?" I say, irritated.

"I want to stop."

I give him a wicked grin and press my mouth to his ear. "But don't you want to feel my lips here next?" I put more pressure against where he has my hands trapped against his chest.

His entire body shudders, and I lean back, triumphant.

"You don't want me to stop. Now let me take off your shirt."

Riden pauses for a very. Long. Time.

But eventually, he shakes his head.

"What's the matter? Are you tired of standing? Would you rather I kissed you in my bed?"

He releases my hands and steps back several paces until he comes into contact with a painting on the opposite wall. It lands on the floor, the glass shattering, but neither of us looks at it.

"What are you doing now?" I ask.

"You could make a monk break his vows."

"You're no monk."

"No, I'm worse. I—" He takes a deep breath. "You've been abandoned by your mother all over again, and you've just learned your father's been lying to you your entire life. You're vulnerable."

Strangely, I feel like hitting him again. "I'm no weak thing. I know what I want."

"I didn't say you were weak." He pulls his neckline outward, as though he needs more air. "Damn it, Alosa. *I* deserve better than this. You come find me when you're not so emotional."

Emotional? I'm beyond furious and confused now. Maybe a little hurt. But I don't let it show. I cloak my face in indifference.

His face falls and he takes a step forward. "Now I've hurt you. There's nothing wrong with what you're feeling. Take the time to feel it. I'm not rejecting you, Alosa! How could anyone reject you? Just take some time to adjust. Then you can come find me. But right now, you're making me feel like some scoundrel taking advantage of—"

"I'm making *you* feel—well, it should be all about you, shouldn't it?" I ask, my tone dripping with sarcasm.

"No, it shouldn't be *all* about me, but it should have *something* to do with me. When we kiss, I want you thinking about *me* instead of everything that's infuriating you. Until you're ready for that, we won't be kissing."

Something about those words hits deep, and guilt sweeps in. I don't need it on top of everything else! "Right now, *you're* infuriating me. And there won't be any more kissing. Now get out."

I kick his arse on his way through the door.

Chapter 9

DAMNED SIREN BLOOD.

It's the only thing I can think of to explain my behavior yesterday. Surely no human girl would throw herself at some man she doesn't fully trust because her parents disappoint her.

It must be because I'm a creature of the sea. Built for tempting men, killing men, and stealing from men.

At least sleep has done me some good. It gave me time to adjust my expectations and come to terms with my new reality.

If my mother doesn't want to stick around, fine. I'll go to her and rob her blind.

I'm looking through my wardrobe, searching for something that matches my mood, when the door opens and closes.

I panic for a moment, worrying that it might be Riden, but it is only Sorinda.

"Please tell me you don't come bearing bad news," I say.

"No, Captain." She offers me one of her rare smiles. "The king can only come after us with the ships already prepared to sail. The rest will be left to protect the keep. And half the fleet is hurrying to the keep as we speak to prepare for the voyage to the Isla de Canta."

"Yes. What are you getting at?"

"Has the land king not been looking for a way to rid the seas of pirates? What do you think he would do if you sent him the exact location of the pirate king's keep?"

I grin so wide my cheeks hurt. "I think he'd send his armada and do his damned best to blow it to pieces."

"My thoughts, exactly."

"Sorinda, you're brilliant. See it done."

"Aye."

She exits, and I peruse my wardrobe once more. I settle on a silver-gray corset, the color of biting steel as it glints in the sun. Night-black leggings adorn my legs, and I pull polished black boots with silver buckles onto my feet. Matching silver hoops go in my ears.

Now just a hint of paint for my face. Red for my lips. Pink for my cheeks. Silver-gray for my eyelids. The first step to feeling good is looking good, and I look like the royalty I am.

I step up to the edge of the aftercastle and survey everyone below me. Kearan is passed out at the side of ship, empty flask inches from his hand. Sorinda kicks it between two pegs of the railing so it slides over the edge. Then she searches his coat for more flasks to dump.

Most of the crew are absent, still belowdecks sleeping after the late night. A few of the riggers roam the ship, checking to make sure the lines are secure. Some of the younger crew members are cleaning. Radita, the ship's boatswain, is taking a turn at the helm.

"Morning, Captain," Mandsy says from where she sits on a crate off to the side, attending to more sewing.

"Why aren't you watching the brothers?" I don't want to say Riden's name.

"Riden is nursing Draxen back to health. The only time he left his side was last night after Draxen fell asleep. Said he was going to see you."

"And you let him?"

She smiles brightly. "All he wanted was to make you feel better. I thought if anyone could cheer you up, he could."

"You're supposed to keep an eye on the prisoners, not let them waltz into my private quarters!"

She looks apologetic, but I can tell it's faked.

"Are you meddling?" I ask. "Is this some project of yours?"

"Not at all. I merely think he's a better man than you give him credit for."

Apparently, he's more noble than I took him for. Where is the womanizing pirate who only cares for his brother?

"Just do me a favor and keep your charges out of my direct line of sight," I say.

"I'll do what I can."

But as I make for the stairs, I think I hear her add, "But I can only do so much while I'm tending to the mending."

∝

Niridia, Kearan, Sorinda, Enwen, and I huddle around the padded table in the sometimes infirmary / sometimes meeting room, where all three map pieces are splayed out in front of us. Kearan's hair is still dripping water from the bucket Sorinda threw in his face to rouse him. I put a hand to his chest to push him back a step from our only copy of a centuries' old map.

"Where are we dropping off the brothers?" I ask Kearan. He's seen more of Maneria than anyone else I've ever met, despite his young age. He was a hand for hire, went wherever there was a job that needed done. In the three months since he's joined the crew, he's proven to be extremely knowledgeable in navigation—when we can get him sober enough.

Kearan points to a spot on the map, a mere dot of an island. "This is a supply post. The land king stocks it up with food and supplies for his excavating ships. That way they don't have to travel all the way to the Seventeen Isles to restock. We can drop them off there. They can catch a ride on a ship returning to the Isles after depositing its goods."

Losing Riden is a good thing, I tell myself. We don't need the extra mouth to feed. And my father will be so busy coming after me, he'll forget all about the Allemos brothers. There is no reason to put him in danger. Besides, Riden is confusing and infuriating, and he can't be trusted. The ship will be better off without him.

But what about you? asks a little voice in my head.

I ignore it.

"Good," I say. "The supply post won't take us out of the way of our journey." I feared we'd have to stop by the Seventeen Isles before heading for the Isla de Canta. "Niridia, how much food and water do we have on the ship?" I ask.

"Enough for five months at sea."

I examine the map, take a compass to it to measure the distance. "Depending on the wind, we could reach the island in two months' time."

"And what of the king?" Kearan asks. "How long will it take his ships to cross the same distance?"

"With the wind, our ship is faster. He'd reach the island just over two weeks after us, probably."

"Only two weeks?" Enwen interrupts. "That means he's just beyond the horizon right now!"

I nod, and there is a beat of silence as everyone digests my father's proximity—and what will happen if we should lose our lead.

"And without the wind?" Kearan asks.

"Most of the ships in the fleet are equipped with sweep oars. In no wind, he can travel as long as he has men on board with strength to row, while we're locked in place."

"Stars help us if we lose the wind," Enwen says.

"No one is being forced on this journey," I remind him. "You're free to leave with the brothers."

Kearan ignores Enwen's outbursts, keeping his eyes on the map. He points to a few different land masses between here and the Isla de Canta. "These aren't charted on any map I've seen. To think there are more islands in Maneria yet to be discovered!"

We stare at him.

"What?" he asks.

"You're getting excited over something you can't drink," Sorinda says.

"I have interests," he says defensively. "I'm a person."

She shrugs indifferently.

I point to the first large island between here and the Isla de Canta, one with a distinct lagoon. "This must be where my father first met my mother." It's at the very edge of his map, right before where it connects to the Allemos map. I don't know why I bother saying anything. There is no reason why she'd be there now. She'll have gone to the Isla de Canta with the rest of her kind. And there's no reason why I should want to see her.

She clearly doesn't want to see me.

The start of the trip is a bit aggravating with the extra cargo. Draxen is very, well, unlikable. He glares my way whenever he thinks I'm not looking. He spat on the deck once when he saw me, and I kicked him onto his back to wipe the spot up with his shirt. He hasn't tried it again since.

Draxen had such high expectations for himself. Kidnap the pirate king's daughter, obtain the pirate king's map, sail for the island himself. Getting outsmarted by me never occurred to him. He blames me for the loss of his crew and ship.

I hardly see how he thinks himself deserving of such spoils. On top of being a terrible person, he was also a terrible captain.

It's strange watching Draxen and Riden interact. They talk constantly, laughing at what the other has to say. Riden coddles him, trying to force food and blankets on him while Draxen shoos him off. I could almost mistake Draxen for a human being when he's interacting with his brother. But I know the truth. He's a vile man who uses everyone around him to get what he wants, no matter the costs.

Just like my father.

It hurts to think about my father, to fully imagine the scope of his betrayal. I could have grown up knowing my mother. Or, maybe not. Perhaps she would have only abandoned me at a younger age if she could have made her own choices. Maybe she really is the monster Father always said. I don't know what to think about her anymore, what all her actions mean. But my father—he has wronged me past the point of forgiveness. I will dethrone him and take everything he has built up for himself as my own.

At this point, that is the only thing I'm certain of.

I hold on to that resolve, let it carry me across the sea of confusion and bitterness that has become my life.

When we reach the supply post, my mood turns dark, as if someone has doused a flame. I can't explain it.

It certainly has nothing to do with Riden leaving.

I've barely seen him in the time it took us to reach the supply post. He belittled me, humiliated me in my rooms after my mother left. What I offered him was little more than what we'd done aboard the *Night Farer*. Why is he all of the sudden making a big deal over thoughts and feelings? I wanted action. Isn't that what he's always wanted, too?

Regardless, I haven't exactly bothered to seek him out, and he's been too busy trying to put meat back on Draxen's bones to do anything else.

Riden crosses the deck with a much healthier-looking Draxen in tow. He steps through the gap in the railing, preparing to climb down to the waiting rowboat below.

He turns his head in my direction, so I quickly look the other way. To be caught staring, even though I know I'll never see him again, would be even more humiliating.

I should focus on the fact that Riden is the only one I'm losing. Even though I offered escape to anyone who would rather not take on the pirate king, no one in my crew wants to leave. I even took pains to convince Wallov he should take his daughter and run.

He was insulted.

Both of them were.

I should be overjoyed to have the trust and respect of my whole crew, and yet my foul mood will not be dispelled. I try not to let it show as I tell Niridia, "Get us going again."

I scan the ship, displeased by the pace at which everyone is moving. "Get your sea legs moving! We've got a long journey ahead, and the pirate king is on our heels. If you don't pick things up, you can jump ashore now!"

That gets them going. I'm watching their doubled paces

with satisfaction, when my vision is blocked by Mandsy's head. It bears an infuriating smile, a knowing smile.

"Don't you have something to be doing?" I snap.

She only giggles. "Why in such a foul mood, Captain? He hasn't gone anywhere."

"Excuse me?"

"Riden. He's over there chatting with Roslyn."

I lean over the railing, looking in the direction of the shore. Draxen is glaring at the ship from his rowboat, specifically at a spot near the bow of the *Ava-lee*. . . .

Where his brother is in fact still on board, chatting with Roslyn.

"What is going on?" I ask.

"I think he's coming with us," Mandsy says.

I narrow my eyes at her. "Where does he get off thinking he can do things without consulting the *captain* first? And my mood is *not* altered by the comings and goings of that man. Don't you dare insinuate as much again."

She curtsies elegantly before skipping off, probably to weave flowers into crowns or to hug a barnacle or something.

"I'm no passenger," I hear Roslyn say as I approach. "I'm part of the crew." I find her little figure in time to see her pull her dagger from behind her back and press it to Riden's navel. "And I don't care for being talked down to."

Riden's lips twitch as he tries not to smile. "My mistake," he says and takes a step back. "I meant no insult, little lass. Please spare me."

Roslyn considers his plea carefully, as though she's actually debating whether or not to kill him. In reality, I know she's enjoying watching him beg, having someone play along.

"What is your job on the ship?" Riden asks. Though he must have noticed her moving about the *Ava-lee* in all the time he's spent with us, perhaps he never realized Roslyn is part of the hired crew. She gets her cut of the spoils just like everyone else.

Roslyn lowers the knife. "I'm the captain's lookout. I call out danger from up top and navigate us to safety when we're in tricky waters."

"That's a very important job." He's not faking how impressed he is.

My temper fades as I stare at Riden a bit longer. Something in my chest moves as I see him talking with little Roslyn. It's endearing.

I blink twice. No, not endearing. He's as bloody annoying as ever. And he does not dictate who stays and goes on my ship.

"Allemos," I snap in my captain's voice.

The two turn my way. Riden raises a brow at the use of his surname, which I've only ever used once before. When he was in trouble.

"Aye, Captain?" he asks.

"Captain? Who made you part of the crew?"

"You did."

At my confused look, he says, "In exchange for my brother's life."

Well, yes, but that was when his brother needed to stay locked in the keep for appearance's sake. They're both free now. He can't expect me to hold him to that. Does he think me so cold?

"Your debt to me is paid," I say. "You're free to leave."

"Paid how?"

"Through your help freeing the siren."

He pauses for only the space of a breath. "But she got away. Until we find her again, I don't see how I can leave. Just wouldn't be honorable."

I'm about to open my mouth to comment on just how *honorable* I think he is, when he speaks again.

"If it's all the same to you, I'd like to stay."

He wants to be here, I realize. And I can't think of any nefarious reasons for him to wish to stay. His brother is safe. Isn't that what he's always wanted? To stay by his brother's side and make sure spoiled Draxen gets his way?

So then why would he stay? For the treasure?

Warmth blooms in my chest at the next possibility: Could it be for me?

And, the bigger question: Do I *want* it to be for me?

I can't even begin to figure out the answer to that question.

So I lie. "It hardly matters to me one way or the other. But if you choose to stay, you'd better carry your own weight. I'll have no laziness on this ship."

"Of course not, Captain. Where would you like me?"

"Since you enjoy spending so much time with Roslyn, you can join the riggers. Hop to it."

"That's the most dangerous job on the ship," he says. It's less an argument than a statement.

"You start at the bottom and work your way up on my crew."

"Enwen and Kearan didn't."

Roslyn has her dagger back out. "The captain gave you an order, sailor."

"Yes, thank you, Roslyn," I say. "Let's put that dagger away for now. Do I need to have another talk with your father?"

"No, Captain," she says before scurrying up the netting.

Riden looks after her. "She's awfully young to be on a pirate ship."

"Aren't we all?"

There's a spring in my step as I turn for the companionway. We're under way now. Our next stop, the Isla de Canta, where riches and glory await. I find myself humming as I reach the top of the steps, but then I halt.

"Really now, Kearan," I say. He's facedown on the ground. Likely passed out in his own vomit, yet again. This can't continue. I'll have to think of some fitting punishment for him. I couldn't care less what he does in his free time, but when he's on duty, he'd better be ready to perform at his best.

Suddenly his whole body jerks upward, and I take a step back in case he's having some sort of sleeping fit.

"Three," he says on a raspy breath before leaning down to the ground again.

Is he sleep talking? He's been known to do that even with his eyes open. No, wait—"Are you doing *push-ups*?" I ask.

"F-f-four," he says as he rises again.

"Sweet stars, you are. What's gotten into you?"

After five, he lies on the ground and rolls onto his back, breathing heavily. "Just passing the time, is all. We've a long journey ahead of us."

Yes, but he usually passes the time with drink.

He reaches into one of his pockets. Ah, there he is.

But what he pulls out isn't a flask.

It's a canteen. The kind we use on the ship for storing water. He sits up and takes a few sips.

"What's in that?"

He holds the canteen out to me, and I take a sniff. It's water.

"She dumped all of my flasks into the sea while I slept," Kearan says. "Didn't realize she cared so much." He searches across the ship for Sorinda, but she must be belowdecks because he focuses on me once more. "Any more questions, Captain?" His tone sounds bored.

"Are we headed in the right direction?"

"Course, I'm keeping her steady."

"Good," I say before moving on quickly.

Lest Kearan break into song or sprout wings.

As I exit my quarters the next morning, a black-and-yellow bird perches on the railing at the starboard side, a scroll of paper tied to its left foot.

I don't need to guess who sent the letter.

Though it's not addressed to anyone and it bears no signature, I recognize my father's neat writing.

You took something that belongs to me. Return it immediately, and I'll make sure your punishment is swift.

Return *it*, as though my mother were some prized possession and not a living being. Heat snakes up my neck, but it's not because of his careless phrasing. Where's the explanation I'm owed? Is he not going to even attempt to tell me why he lied for years? Why he kept my mother hidden from me? Kalligan is a master at twisting words together. He's not even trying to sway me to his side.

The briefness of the letter can mean only one of two things. Either he's furious to the point where most words have left him, or he knows I can't be reasoned with after what I've learned. Either way, I know the letter is a lie. I don't believe for a second that any punishment he could fathom would be swift.

The yano bird waits patiently, but I have no intention of sending a response. I know silence is the best way to push my father. Let him stew over the loss of his siren.

Over the loss of me.

I wonder which upsets him more.

I was his means of making it to and from the Isla de Canta alive. My female crew and I are the only ones resistant to siren song. Vordan was wrong about Kalligan having a device to protect him. My father and I have always suspected he is immune to my abilities because of the blood we share. But his immunity should only apply to me. Any other siren shouldn't have a problem enchanting him. That makes him vulnerable on the Isla de Canta.

And now that he's lost me, he will have to figure things out on his own.

I shoo the bird with my hands. It squawks as it flies into the air, retreating northeast. It's easy to forget danger is near when one cannot see it, but that bird won't fly long before it lands on the deck of the *Dragon's Skull*.

"Trouble?" asks a voice.

A masculine voice.

Riden's voice.

"Nothing new," I say. "The pirate king wants his siren back."

"And what did you tell him?"

"I didn't deign to respond."

"That ought to cheer him up."

He's trying to make light of the situation. Trying to make light of *our* situation, but I'm not having any of it.

"What do you want, Riden?"

"Right now? Nothing."

He has his hair pulled back in a band at the base of his neck, but a burst of wind pulls a strand free.

I chastise myself for wanting to touch it.

"Why are you on my ship?" Reading my father's note seems to have brought on a bout of distrust.

He watches me carefully, his eyes turning inquisitive. "Is it not obvious?"

"If it were, would I be asking?" I say, irritation coloring my tone.

He smiles as though I've just said the most amusing thing in the world.

It makes me want to hit him.

Since that's not the best idea, I turn around to leave him, but he puts his hand on my arm. Before I can do anything else, he's right there. His chest pressed against my back, his breath warm on my ear.

"I'm here because when I tried to get in that rowboat with my brother, I realized the last thing I wanted was to be away from you." His hand runs up the length of my left arm, which is facing toward the sea. Away from the eyes of the crew. "I'm here for you, Alosa." His fingers flutter against my neck, sending a shiver down my back. "If you can't tell that, I'm not doing a good job of showing you."

His lips graze my earlobe. To anyone else on the ship, it must look as though he's only sharing a secret with me.

Now he wants to touch me? What happened to fleeing to the opposite side of the room? That memory boils back to the surface. I bite out, "You're forgetting. I'm far too emotional for your taste."

I pull out of his grasp and don't look back.

Rejection stings, doesn't it, Riden?

Kearan isn't at the helm when I reach it the next day. Niridia has taken his place.

"Where is he now?" I groan.

She points just below us. I peer over the aftercastle and find Sorinda leaning against the door to the infirmary, her head turned so her ear is pressed into the wood.

"What are you doing?" I ask her.

"Nothing," she says immediately. She disappears below-decks before I can get anything else out of her.

"Kearan's in the infirmary," Niridia explains. "He can't stop shaking and sweating. Mandsy opens the door every once in a while to toss a bucket of his stomach's contents over the side of the ship."

"He's still set on staying off the drinking, then."

I'm impressed.

Chapter 10

I STAND IN ONE of the storage rooms belowdecks, surveying the equipment.

"The *Ava-lee* was already well stocked when we'd arrived back at the keep, Captain," Radita says as she gestures around the packed room. "We didn't take any damage while sailing to pick up Vordan. Though we're not as equipped as I'd like for a voyage this long, we still have plenty of supplies. There's enough canvas to repair each of the sails, stacks of wooden planks should the deck need refurbishing, extra rope if any of the lines start showing signs of wear. I'm checking her every day. So far so good."

Radita spent most of her life training under her grandfather, one of the most famous shipwrights at the land king's disposal.

After the death of her grandfather, she had no way to support herself, since the land king wasn't about to hire a woman to fill the empty position. That's when I found her.

"There's no one I trust more with the ship's upkeep, Radita. Keep up the good work."

"Aye, Captain."

It's been two weeks since we dropped off Draxen at the supply post. The *Ava-lee* has been holding steady under the pressure of strong and favorable winds, carrying us through waters I've never seen before. There are no known lands this far south. The land king paid his dues to my father to allow his ships to explore the area down here, but none have returned with news of land, if they return at all. My ancestors kept their secrets well hidden.

Still, two weeks of good wind means we have a three- or four-day lead on my father, depending on how long it took him to get the fleet moving. It's an acceptable lead, but not enough for me to sleep comfortably at night.

I pass by the opening to the brig on my way back up top and peer inside. Riden sits at a table with Wallov and Deros, playing cards. He seems to have made it his personal mission to make everyone on the ship like him. If he's not gambling with the men, he's up in the crow's nest looking through a telescope with Roslyn or having drinks with the girls. I've even seen him trying to warm up Niridia. She's not the trusting sort, though when you do earn her trust, she's the most loyal friend you'll ever have. I imagine it's only a matter of time before Niridia is all chummy with him as well.

Soon I'll be the only person on the ship who can't stand him.

Kearan is at the helm when I make it to the aftercastle. He's only been back on duty within the last couple of days. Took him some time to recover from his cleansing. It's too soon to tell whether I like the man better sober or not.

"Wind's picking up," he says in greeting. "There's a storm on the horizon. The little one spotted black clouds. We're headed right for them."

Of course we are.

"Keep us steady," I say to him. Then I shout for Niridia. "Get everything tied down and well secured. Storm's ahead."

"All hands to work!" she shouts. "Storm warning. All loose items are to be stowed away!"

All decks are in a flurry of activity as crates and barrels are doubly tied down. Though I stay on the main deck, I know what's happening below me. Trianne, the ship's cook, is securing everything in the kitchens behind cupboards. The cannons are being stowed, dispersed around the ship so their weight doesn't pull us too far to one side. All ports and windows are being closed.

It isn't long before those of us up top can see the black clouds on the horizon.

"The sails?" Niridia asks.

"Not yet." There's not enough distance between us and Kalligan's fleet. Storms usually last no longer than a few hours. Every minute the sails are tied down is another minute the fleet will gain on us.

Night falls, and I order every lantern on the ship lit. No one dares to go to sleep. They're all out on deck. Waiting. Watching.

Most of the night has passed when the storm finally hits. The wind becomes frenzied, and Kearan starts to wrestle with the helm.

"She's the easiest vessel I've ever handled!" He shouts to be heard over the sloshing water and ravenous wind.

"One of the perks of having a smaller ship!" I shout back to him. The sails flap frantically in the wind, no longer doing us any good. They'll only shred if we leave them up.

"Niridia, get those sails down!"

She rushes down the companionway and cups her hands around her mouth. "Riggers, to your posts! Bring down the sails. No one is to climb the masts without a secure line!"

Riden and the others attach ropes to their waists and tie off the other ends to notches near the feet of the masts. The rain comes down hard, making everything slippery almost instantly. The ship turns sharply, the current below sending her in unpredictable directions.

I spin around. "Kearan, relinquish the wheel."

"I can hold her steady, Captain. I'm a seasoned helmsman."

"You don't know the *Ava-lee* like I do. Now move over!"

He scowls but does as I say. Rather than stomping off belowdecks, he hovers behind my shoulder. Another violent jerk starts to move the ship, but I grip the helm and hold her still. Even then, one girl slips from the mast and dangles from her line. The rain is too thick for me to tell who it is. But her hands find the rope, and she pulls herself up. Another girl hurries to her along the beam and helps her to get her feet on solid wood.

"Niridia!" I shout. "All unnecessary crew are to go below-decks!"

"Aye." She races around the deck, shouting to everyone holding on to the railing, masts, and anything else to keep from being tossed into the ocean. Calmly, yet quickly, they head for the hatch. Enwen is the first to reach it. He hauls it open and hands the girls into the hole one by one before traveling down himself.

All the sails are tied down save the topmost square-rig on the mainmast. A larger body that can only be Riden climbs upward with a couple of the girls to secure it.

"Kearan, join the others belowdecks," I say.

"I'm needed, Captain. I'll stay."

I look over my shoulder. "How are you needed?"

"If you should fall, someone else will need to take the helm."

"You no longer care for your own safety, is that it?"

"The only person I trust at the wheel is myself. I *am* watching out for my own neck."

I go back to ignoring him after that. If he's going to start being as difficult about following orders as Riden, then he can get dragged to the ocean's depths and I'll say good riddance.

Wallov comes running out of the trapdoor a second later, rushing for the mainmast. A struggle up at the top drags my attention to it. Riden wrestles in the crow's nest with something.

Another sudden pitch and the ship veers left.

Two bodies, one large and one small, fall from the mast and flail over the edge of the ship, plummeting so quickly, if I were to blink, I'd miss them.

I've left the helm and made it halfway to the port side when the ship starts spinning wildly in a circle, sending me down to my hands and knees. Wallov ends up plastered against the ship where the railing connects to the deck, and the force of the spinning prevents him from standing.

Another sharp twitch and I'm flung onto my back. I crane my neck to see Kearan getting the helm under control once again. I'd leapt for Roslyn and Riden before even thinking of the consequences.

The rope is stretched taut against the lip of the ship. Wallov finally finds his feet and starts pulling at the rope. Once I reach his side, I add my strength to his. We pull little Roslyn's form back on board. She's conscious, but she's groaning so loudly I can hear her over the storm.

"It'll be one hell of a bruise," she says as she rubs at the rope under her arms.

"You watch your language," Wallov says, but he gathers her to him in a crushing hug.

"What happened?" I ask. I grip the side of the railing tightly as my eyes search the roiling sea for Riden.

Roslyn pushes away from her father to face me. "I told him I didn't need his rope! But he wouldn't listen. He untied it from his waist and put it around my own."

"You were supposed to be belowdecks along with everyone else," Wallov says. "What were you doing?"

"I was keeping lookout. It's even more important to have eyes on the sea during a storm. The captain needed me!"

Wallov's face is harder than I've ever seen it in front of his daughter. "Because you disobeyed orders, a man is dead."

Roslyn shivers involuntarily, but I feel my senses clearing.

"He's not dead yet," I say. "Get her belowdecks."

Roslyn hangs her head, ashamed, as Wallov leads her away.

Niridia and the rest of the riggers arrive an instant later. "I'll go in after him," she says as she fiddles with her own rope.

"No," I say. "It's too dangerous." My mind races, knowing every second we delay brings Riden closer to death. "Tie it to me."

"What!"

"Just do it. Use a constrictor knot around my waist. I won't be able to untie it underwater." I don't have to say aloud the next part. *Even in my siren state.* I hand her all my weapons, everything sharp. "I'll have no choice but to return to the ship."

"But you won't be lucid enough to reach him."

"I've done it before." I somehow managed to save us both from Vordan by swimming us to safety.

"How?"

"I don't know, but this is the only way he has a chance."

She looks at me sadly as she finishes tying the rope. I know we're both thinking the same thing.

Riden has no chance at all.

I try to rip the rope free and find it snug. "Be ready to restrain

142

me when I get back to the ship. Have the other men stopper their ears."

Then I dive.

As I fall, I fill my thoughts with Riden. *Don't forget. You are going into the water to save him, nothing more. You will not lose yourself. You will not become the monster.*

I close my eyes as I hit the water, as if that will somehow keep me in control.

Warmth envelops me. The sea enfolds me into the world's most gentle caress. I am one of her own, and she missed me during my long absence. And, oh, how I missed her. I am content to let her push me down, down, down, where I can rest on the ocean's silky bottom.

But there is a disturbance in the water.

I search through the sea's depths. I'd see better if it weren't so dark and the waves so unsettled. As it is, I can still make out a human man. He can't see me; he's too concentrated on his arms and legs. As if he can master the full weight of the ocean with his limbs alone.

I watch him for a moment. If anything, he loses ground instead of gaining it. Sometimes he doesn't even propel himself in the right direction, burying himself deeper under the waves. Soon I grow tired of watching him squirm.

Come here, sad creature, I sing, and the man turns his head in my direction. Though he can't see me, he does his best to obey my beckoning. Every muscle in his body does what it can to bring himself closer to me. He makes better progress than he had before, now that he's not fighting against the direction of the current. But he still moves too slowly for my pleasure. I don't like waiting.

I swim to meet him. I'm almost there, when a force pulls tight against me. I look down and find a rope holding me back.

I tug at it, try to wriggle free, but it is far too tight and unyielding. I could take my nails to it, but the man will likely be dead before then. We won't have nearly as much fun if he's already dead!

Come on, then. Just a little farther!

He manages to get in one more good kick, and I reach him with my fingertips. My lips pull up into a wide smile as I bring him closer.

My, he is pretty. I stroke a finger down his cheek until it reaches his lips.

His eyes strain to see me. He relaxes suddenly as if he's comfortable now that he's with me. No, wait, he's running out of air. That won't do just yet.

I lean down and press my lips to his. I've air left in my lungs from before I jumped. I give it to him.

The touch is electric. My entire body comes alive even more so than before. I still feel the strength of being underwater. I feel the confidence, the power.

And my mind returns to me.

Riden.

I grip his arms and kick to the surface. His face breaks free of the water and gulps down breath after breath of air.

The waves fight against me with everything they've got,

but I don't surrender. I keep Riden above the water where he can breathe. It is beyond strange to be so surrounded by both water and him, as if the two forces are battling each other for residence in my mind. The water encourages the siren, Riden the human.

"Pull us up!" I shout as loud as I can. I'm prepared to sing to Kearan if he hasn't covered his ears yet, but the rope starts yanking us toward the ship, Riden spluttering as we are pulled through the waves.

The cold hits me once I'm out of the water. Riden shivers next to me, but I haven't felt the cold long enough to be affected so deeply by it yet. The extreme temperatures of the ocean don't harm or even register to the siren.

When we reach the ship's edge, several girls pull Riden from my arms and get him onto the deck. Then they grab me. Instead of lowering me lightly onto the floor, I'm practically thrown.

"What the—"

A weight drops on top of me. Ropes. No, a net. I paw at it, trying to break free, but that only entangles me further. Then I'm being dragged.

I focus on my surroundings, wondering who could have possibly boarded us in the storm. But I'm not staring at intruders.

"Niridia?" I say, astonished to find she's one of the girls dragging me. "Get this damned thing off me! What are you doing?"

"Get Riden to Mandsy so she can look him over. And for star's sake get his ears covered."

Oh. She thinks I'm the siren. Of course she does. I went into the water.

"Niridia, I'm fine. It's me."

Haeli and Reona, two of my riggers, look to Niridia questioningly at my lucidity.

"Ignore her. Captain's not herself. She'll be all right by morning." She leans toward Sorinda. "The creature's getting cleverer."

I sigh. "Niridia Zasperon, I'd really rather not spend the night in the brig. It puts me in a mood the next day."

She steps away from the netting and looks at me. "Only the next day, Captain?"

"Very amusing."

She places her hands at her hips. "You would have me put the safety of this crew in jeopardy so you can have a soft bed?"

I hold in a growl. "Fine. Put me in the brig, but I need dry clothes so I don't freeze. And extra blankets."

Niridia chuckles to herself, though I can't hear it over the wind. "All right. Let the captain out. She's fine."

∝

When I can feel my fingers again, I head belowdecks with everyone else. Kearan stays above to keep the ship righted. I promise to relieve him shortly. He brushes off the comment as though he couldn't care either way. He's a lot like Sorinda in that regard.

In a corner of the crew's sleeping quarters, a little girl cries into her father's arms. As soon as she spots me, Roslyn stops her sniveling. She stands tall, pushing out of her father's grasp.

"I will accept whatever punishment you have for me, Captain." She pulls her dagger from its sheath and offers it to me.

I watch her carefully. "Did you hear Niridia call everyone belowdecks?"

"No, Captain, but . . ."

"But?"

"I saw the riggers lowering the sails. I knew the winds were getting dangerous. And I shouldn't have allowed Riden to put his rope on me. It was my choice to stay up in the nest without protection." She doesn't look down; she keeps those blue eyes on me.

"From what I saw, it looked like you put up quite a fight."

"Well, yes, Captain. But I should have been strong enough to fight him off."

I kneel down to her level and hand back the dagger. "As far as I'm concerned, sailor, you did nothing wrong. You are not expected to be anything more than what you are. You didn't deliberately disobey orders, and Riden is alive."

Her eyes light up. "Alive? Truly?"

"Yes. The only one you owe an apology to and a punishment from is your father for scaring him half to death."

"Rest assured," Wallov says, "she'll be punished." He tousles the hair on the top of her head.

Roslyn nods solemnly before asking, "May I go see Riden?"

"Not yet," I say. "He needs to be checked out by Mandsy first. I'm going to find her now for an update, but I wanted you to know he is all right."

She wraps those little arms around me and gives me a squeeze before returning to her father.

I keep a hand on the railing for balance as I ascend the steps. The storm has only worsened, and I worry for the safety of the ship and crew. If we should run aground in this weather . . .

"How's she holding?" I shout to Kearan once I make it up top.

"Not easily, but I've got her."

I nod, tell him I'll be back after I check on Riden, and head for my quarters. Niridia said the girls had carried Riden into the infirmary, a room with a padded table for patients, but the ship was too unsteady for him to be elevated. Eventually he had to be taken to my room. The lush carpets on the floor were the best solution. He can't fall off there.

"For the last *damned* time, Mandsy, I don't want any water! I just spent the last ten minutes coughing it out of my lungs."

"Your body has been through an ordeal. You're exhausted and you should drink something." Mandsy isn't intimidated by any of her patients. Ever. She'd treat a snarling bear if it was injured. She tries to bring the cup back to Riden's lips.

"What I want is to be left alone so I can sleep. Surely sleep is part of your treatment?"

"Yes, but you could be concussed if you hit your head on something underwater. Someone should watch over you."

The ship rocks. Mandsy backs up to catch her balance, but some of the water still tips out of the cup she's holding, and Riden braces himself with his arms from where he lies on the floor. When the ship straightens again, I step all the way into my bedroom.

"Mandsy," I say, "go below and check on Roslyn. Make sure she's all right."

Mandsy treads past me as Riden looks at me in alarm.

"Did she fall into the water, too? Is she—"

"She's fine, thanks to you," I assure him. "I just wanted Mandsy out of here so you would stop being rude."

His worry morphs into a glare. "I said I didn't want *any* company."

"This is *my* room, and I just saved your life. You could show a little gratitude toward all the people who are trying to help you."

He won't look at me now. He finds his feet far more worthy of his fury.

Riden's managed to change into some dry breeches. (I've already dried myself off with my abilities.) A towel hangs around his neck, keeping his hair from dripping onto his bare chest. A dry shirt lies next to him, but he probably doesn't have the energy to pull it on.

"Do you want some help with that?" I ask, pointing to the shirt.

"If you won't leave, then I will." He tries to stand; at least I think that's what he's doing. His legs are twitching.

I rush forward and push against the idiot's shoulders. "What are you doing?"

He bats at my arms with flimsy pressure and tries to stand again.

"Keep your arse on my floor," I say.

"Why don't you *make me?*" he snaps. "You've already broken your promise today. What's once more?"

My mouth drops open. "Is that what this is about?"

He still won't look at me.

"Would you really have preferred that I let you drown?"

"I gave you my conditions for joining your crew. Under no circumstances were you to use your abilities on me."

"You were going to die!"

He snaps his neck in my direction, his eyes finding mine instantly. "Then you should have let me. I practically killed myself trying to *obey* you. I can barely lift my arms, and forget about my legs. I feel as though I've been swimming for years nonstop. Not because I was fighting for my life, but because I was trying to heed the order of a siren."

"You're being a prick. I did nothing wrong."

He mumbles something under his breath. I almost don't call him out on it, but if he's going to insult me, he better have the balls to do it to my face.

"What was that?" I ask.

"You were just like him."

My mind blanks. Him? "Who?"

"Jeskor," he breathes so faintly I almost miss it. His eyes take on a faraway look, reflecting on some former time. Some demon of his past, I realize.

I know all too well what it is like being raised by a pirate. But I don't know fully what life was like for Riden growing up. What did his father do to him?

"What happened?" I ask.

His eyes narrow on me again. "I want to be alone."

"Fine," I snap. I throw the large feather blanket from my bed on top of his head. Maybe he's too weak to adjust it and he'll suffocate, but that's probably too much to hope for.

I leave before I can fantasize more about strangling him.

How dare he scare me to death and then try to guilt me for it! I should dump his arse back into the sea.

"Kearan, go below and tell Mandsy she should stay with Riden if Roslyn checks out all right. Then get some rest. I'll take the helm for a while."

He opens his mouth.

"If you're about to argue with me, I suggest you don't."

Something about my tone makes him go through the hatch without another moment's hesitation.

∝

Two hours pass. The hazy light of dawn finally peeks over the horizon, casting a little light for us to see by. Kearan is taking another turn at the helm while I rest my arms from the battle with the sea. The ship constantly has to be turned into the waves to keep it from capsizing. It's as if the storm is a manifestation of my father's wrath.

A brutal gust of wind strikes the ship, and a *crack* slices the air. I assume it's more thunder until I feel the ship start to tip. I can do nothing but watch as the mainmast snaps just below the second sail. It falls against the side of the ship, slicing through the railing and putting a hole through the deck. It's held together by mere fragments of wood and a few lines of rope.

I run for the trapdoor, open it, and scream, "Niridia, get the crew up here! Now! Before the tension drags us under!"

There's a blur of movement as the crew spills onto the deck, carrying knives and axes. They slice the ropes and hack at the wood weighing us down. Radita directs them so the task can be done in the most efficient way possible.

The broken mast falls into the sea, and the ship sways far to the opposite side. We swing back and forth until the ship rights itself.

Just as slowly as the storm came upon us, now it recedes. The sea rests and the clouds retreat. The sun climbs higher toward its perch in the sky.

Radita lets the crew breathe for a moment before instructing them in cleaning the wreckage. Clumps of sea plants are tangled in the railing. Loose ropes lie everywhere. Wood fragments litter the deck. Radita tells them which pieces of the ship to save and which to toss over the side. Some of the girls start rebuilding the parts of the railing and deck that were lost.

The mizzenmast and foremast still stand, but the rigging hangs limply to the deck, blowing about in calmer winds. The mainmast floats in the water a ways off, and a few girls take the rowboats to try and salvage the sails and crow's nest.

Only then does our new predicament fully hit me.

A sequence of expletives leaves my mouth as I take in the carnage. I don't even feel guilty when Roslyn turns to Niridia to ask what one of the words means.

The ship barely crawls along without the mainmast. We can't unfurl the sail on the foremast yet because the rigging needs fixing. The lateen on the mizzen doesn't do much to push the ship forward. The pirate king will have no trouble catching up to us now.

I can't seem to stop looking at the missing mast. My father betrayed me. My mother betrayed me. Now my own ship has betrayed me.

A feeling of helplessness pokes around the edges of my mind, wanting in, wanting to flood everything else.

Three days.

My father is possibly only three days away.

And our ship is now drastically slower than his.

He'll be upon us in no time.

The thought nearly leaves me breathless with fear. What more could I have done? We had a plan. We were doing fine—but I cannot control the weather. This failing isn't my fault.

Then why do I feel responsible? Did I do something wrong? I discovered my father was not the man I thought him to be. I thought being away from him would be the safest for my crew and me. But by ordering everyone to leave the fleet, I put us in more danger than we've ever been in before.

But you gave everyone a choice, a small, rational voice argues in my head. *You gave them the option to leave. They all chose to stay.*

Still. My. Fault.

A body bumps into me, and I finally look up.

"Sorry, Captain," mumbles Lotiya as she carries a load of planks for repairing the deck.

I take a good look around me, see the men hauling heavier pieces of debris over the ship, see the riggers working on fixing the two sails left standing, watch Roslyn sweep the deck with a broom—the faces of my crew.

They're still alive. The pirate king is not upon us yet.

I'd let despair win too soon. All hope is not lost.

We need a plan.

"Kearan, Niridia! Meet me in my quarters now."

Kearan has a fractured piece of wood thrown over his shoulder. He shrugs it into the sea before following after me, Niridia on his heels.

We go to my desk, bypassing Mandsy and Riden on the floor. I don't spare them a glance.

We're here for the map.

"We need a new mast," I say. We can fashion one ourselves, but we need a tall tree for that. Those aren't to be found in the open ocean, but if we're anywhere near land . . .

"Yes, here!" I point to the island. The one where my parents met. It's not far off.

"We can't just stop," Niridia says. "We've no idea what's out there."

"Would you rather sail around aimlessly until we run out of food?" Kearan asks her. "Or worse. Until the king reaches us?"

"We could replace the mainmast with the mizzen, attach the mainsail to it, and—"

"It's a good idea, Niridia," I interrupt, "but we'll never outrun my father that way. It would speed us up some, but not enough. We've no choice but to stop."

It's in Niridia's nature to be cautious. She always suggests the safest and most practical course of action, but she never fails to follow orders when I say otherwise. She's the reasonableness to my recklessness. And I always need to consider reasonable options, even if I don't always end up taking them.

"Get us here, Kearan," I say. "And let's pray to the stars we can find a suitable trunk ashore."

"Aye, Captain." He leaves us, and I say a silent prayer of thanks that the rudder at least isn't damaged. Then we'd really be in trouble.

∝

I crawl into my room long after nightfall. After two days without sleep, I'm practically sagging from exhaustion.

"Get out," Riden demands.

Oh, *no* he doesn't. I saved him. I worked out saving the ship and the rest of the crew. I've worked too hard and too long. I *will* sleep in my own bed tonight.

I offer him a vulgar gesture in response before stepping over him to reach my bed. "You didn't see it," I say, realizing it's pitch black, "but I just suggested you go—"

"I think I can guess," he says. I hear a shuffling noise, and I realize he's trying to push himself off the floor to leave, just like he did before.

"You're not leaving this room, Riden. Try it, and I'll have Mandsy tie you down."

He growls at me. It's the last thing I hear before falling asleep.

Chapter 11

*Clever, Alosa. Sending the land king after the keep. Oh,
yes, I've heard word. My men are fine. The land king
fled with his tail tucked between his legs. We'll have to
relocate now, thanks to you.*

*Your list of crimes is growing. I don't know if there's
enough skin on your bones for the lashing that's coming
your way.*

*The last yano bird returned rather quickly. If I
didn't know any better, I'd say we were catching up.*

MY FATHER'S LATEST NOTE sends a shiver down my back.

Land could not have come any sooner.

I reach for my telescope and peer toward the line of green

on the horizon. Tall trees stand sentinel over the island. They slope with the rolling hills. Gray clouds hang over the island, and an instant later, the ship passes into a light drizzle.

It is not unlike Lemisa, the closest island to the keep, save the weather is a bit warmer. At last, a bit of luck. Cone-bearing trees are the best to make masts out of, and this island is covered with them. Those closest to the shore are relatively small, but if we traverse inland, where there's sure to be a freshwater source, we'll find taller trees.

"Ladies and gents, we're almost there!" I call out to the crew. Hearty shouts go up in response.

"Begging your pardon, Captain," Enwen says, inching closer to me, "but are we sure going ashore is the best idea? The island could be haunted."

"Sirens roam these waters, Enwen, and you're worried about ghosts?" I ask.

"Ghosts, ghouls, banshees, wraiths—"

"Don't exist," Kearan cuts in from where he steers at the helm.

"Do so."

"Have you ever seen one?"

"No, but there are stories."

"Stories parents tell their children to make them behave," Kearan says. "Nothing more. They're not real."

"You said sirens weren't real once. And now look at our captain!" Enwen looks to me. "Meaning no offense, Captain. You're all right."

"Thanks, Enwen."

"You happened to be right one time," Kearan says. "That does not make the rest of your superstitions real."

"Why's that?"

"Because—" Kearan cuts himself off. "How am I having this conversation? Enwen, go blather to someone who wants to listen."

"You like listening to me."

"I really don't."

"Stop it," I say to the two of them. "We're going ashore. End of discussion. Niridia! Get everyone on the deck."

Though I don't have eyes on her, she answers from below. "Aye, Captain."

In a matter of seconds, everyone is amassed together, the crew eager for change after two days of our slow pace.

Wallov has Roslyn on his shoulders so she can see me from the deck. Lotiya and Deshel have Riden cornered at the edge of the ship, where he's sitting atop a barrel.

He slept for a full day after his accident. Once he could stand on his own, he left my room, left my sight. He won't even look at me now as I give out orders.

"We've no clue what we're going to find on this island," I say, "so everyone needs to be on their guard. What we do know, though, is in the past, my father's men met a group of sirens in the water off this island. Very soon I will order the men to have their ears covered until we're far enough inland that it shouldn't be a problem. Is that understood?"

I pointedly look at each man on the ship. They in turn nod

their heads. Except for Enwen, who seems to have covered his ears before I reached the end of my sentence.

"Though sirens are the only creatures we know exist for sure, we need to understand that there could be many other sorts of magical beings out there. Don't be afraid, only cautious. We're in uncharted waters, but remember, my ancestors reached the siren island just fine, and they couldn't have had half of our talents."

The girls laugh lightly.

"We're here to find us a new mast. I want to be on and off the island as quickly as possible. We stick together. I'll pair the men up with women while their ears need covering. Someone will always be on watch. Radita will take the lead." She'll know the perfect tree for our new mast. "As soon as we have this ship sailing again at full speed, it's on to the Isla de Canta and treasure beyond our wildest dreams!"

"Rah!"

And then I will take everything from my father. It is the greatest punishment I can think of for him, but it doesn't nearly equate to keeping a girl from her mother.

"Allemos," I shout. "Get over here."

I worry he'll defy me in front of the whole crew and I'll have to punish him again, but to my relief, he obeys. He can be furious with me all he wishes, but I am still his captain.

I pull him off to the side so we can have a private conversation.

"You can stay on the ship to guard it while we're gone or you can come help us find a new mast. Those are your choices at this point. Regret it though you might, you're stuck being a member of this crew. It's impossible for you to leave, and I won't have you being an idle passenger the rest of the way."

His face is unreadable. "You're giving me a choice?"

I don't break eye contact. "I think you're an idiot. You're alive because of me, yet you're determined to hate me for it."

His jaw twitches. I know he means to argue, but I press on. "Nevertheless, I did break my promise to you. That is why you have a choice."

He's quiet for a moment. "I don't hate you."

"All evidence to the contrary."

He doesn't have anything to say to that. I think he won't respond at all. Then—

"I'll go," he says. "I'm a member of this crew. My strengths are best put to use obtaining a new mast. I'll see you ashore, Captain."

Captain.

It wasn't enough that his tone was indifferent, accepting of his fate to be stuck on my ship. Now he has to distance himself from me further by refusing to call me by name, as he usually does.

There is so much more I want to say to him. So much I want to demand from him. An apology, for one. Whether his captain, friend, or something more—he should not have spoken to me the way he did the other night. I won't let that slide so easily.

And then answers. What plagues his mind so much that he'd rather die than be saved by my abilities?

Those conversations will have to wait until another time. For now, we have a tree to find.

"You're to pair with me on the island," I say. I don't give him a chance to respond before leaving to help drop anchor.

He can be upset with me all he likes. I won't apologize for saving him.

But if I have to watch Lotiya or Deshel leading him through the island while he cannot hear, I won't be able to focus on the task at hand.

Damn him.

Damn *everything* about him.

The waters are clear as we row toward the shore. The waves aid us, pushing us closer and closer to the island. The men have their ears blocked, even though all signs point to no siren life. We can't take any chances. It's not as though I can sense them. I lived my whole life not knowing my own mother was living on the same isle as I.

If only I had known, I could have spared her years of enslavement.

Would she still have run out on me then?

Would it have stopped you from saving her if you'd known she'd leave you?

No.

Strangely, I'm comforted by the realization, though it doesn't make me any less angry with her.

The island looks . . . normal as we approach. Somehow,

I expected an island tied to the sirens to be more mystical in appearance, though I'm not entirely sure what that would entail.

The boats run aground and we disembark, pulling the rowboats far onto the sand so the waves can't pull them back out to sea. We take in our surroundings as we step from sandy beach to needle-covered forest floor.

A squirrel notices our approach and scurries up the nearest trunk. The wind grabs at the leaves in the trees, shaking them together. Birds pull twigs from the ground to make their nests, and something rustles through the thick grass. Probably a rodent of some sort.

"Break into your pairs," I order.

Mandsy hooks her arm through Enwen's. Athella sidles herself up next to Wallov. Deros gets claimed by Lotiya, and Deshel hovers near Riden. I give her a look that sends her back a step, and grab Riden's hand.

Riden looks at our joined hands, searches my face, looks back down at our hands.

In the rush to avoid Riden touching another woman, I'd grabbed him without thought as to how he would react.

My fingers release their hold before he can pull away, which I'm sure he would have done. I won't look at him after that, but I've got his back should something come rushing out of the shrubbery.

Kearan, who I paired with Sorinda, holds his arm out to her. Sorinda stares at him, unmoving. He doesn't take his arm back; he waits for her to do something. I've never seen Sorinda fail to intimidate a man with a look, but the two are trapped in a battle of wills, with Kearan's arm, which is now more muscled than fatty, extended between the two. All of those push-ups have been doing him good.

"Sorinda," I say, to remind her of her orders while on the island.

She pushes his arm back to his side, but stays near him and keeps her eyes searching the area around them both.

"He's not all that bad, you know," Mandsy says, nudging her shoulder into Sorinda. "Now that he's sobered up, he has interesting things to say."

"No, he doesn't," Sorinda says.

"How would you know? You never stay near him unless following orders."

"And what I hear while following orders is telling enough. He's a bumbling buffoon."

"That's rather rude."

"He can't hear me."

Kearan looks between Sorinda and Mandsy. "Are you talking about me?" he says much too loudly.

Sorinda rolls her eyes.

The rain and light dampen now that they must filter through the trees to reach us. Many trails wind through the undergrowth; whether they were made by animals or something else, it's impossible to tell. Either way, we follow one that takes us away from the sea. I monitor a compass in my hand, so we can find our way back to the ship. Radita stays close by my side, examining trees as we pass, but they're still far too small.

The farther we go, the more entrapped I feel. On the sea, I

can see for miles in any direction. But here, on land in a thick forest, anything could be hiding. A threat could be three feet away, and I would be none the wiser. Why would anyone choose to live in a place like this?

When I judge us a safe distance from the ocean, I motion for the men to pull out their plugs. Enwen takes more goading than the others.

I still won't look at Riden.

Instead I search between the coniferous trees, peering through their branches for hidden dangers.

A figure sidles up next to me.

The one I'm determined not to lock eyes with.

"What was that?" Riden asks.

"What was what?"

"You know what. You grabbed my hand."

"Thought I saw something between the trees. I was protecting you." The lie sounds pathetic even to my own ears.

"I see" is all he says.

The longer we travel without seeing any threats, the more certain I am that something foul is just waiting for us around the next hill. The animal life all but vanishes, as if they're avoiding the center of the island.

After maybe an hour, we come to a clearing. A freshwater spring bubbles up from the ground, giving way to a small stream headed for the sea. A cave opening, likely carved out long ago by the underwater source, rests at the bottom of a rocky rise.

Radita strides over to a tree on the edge of the clearing,

opposite the cave. She examines it carefully. "No signs of decay," she mumbles to herself. Then, "This tall pine is perfect."

"All right," I say. "Ropes out. Get them strung up around the neighboring trees. Riden, Kearan, the saw."

Haeli and Reona, my best riggers, climb two neighboring trees and carefully place the ropes. They'll help support the tree as it falls, giving it a more controlled descent. It will also muffle the sound of it smashing to the ground. We don't need to announce our presence. Lotiya and Deshel are on watch while the rest of us get to work.

Riden and Kearan mark the tree so it will fall at the angle we want. Then the two of them handle the saw. The rest of us wrap ourselves in the ends of the ropes, so we can use our weight to catch the trunk.

The grating sound of metal on wood starts. A bird twitches its head to the side to better view us with one beady eye. After a few seconds, it takes off in flight.

I tell myself it's fleeing away from all the racket we're making and not something coming toward us.

I've posted watches. There's nothing more I can do except help.

My eyes dart from the tree line—

And land on Riden's arms, flexing as they push the saw through the tree.

Damn, but they look good.

"Is there something on Riden's arm?" Niridia asks. It comes out so innocently, but I know better. Oh, she'll pay for that one later.

Riden looks over his shoulder at me.

"Thought I could make him move faster by sheer force of will," I say.

"If you'd like to come saw, I'll gladly switch you places," Riden says.

Three-quarters of the way through sawing, the tree starts to crack on its own, the weight of it bringing it right down toward the ropes. The nearby roped-up trees do most of the work in catching the weight, but we all still get dragged a foot forward in the dirt.

"Cut most of the branches as close to the trunk as possible," Radita says, "but don't nick the trunk. Save a few longer branches as handholds for carrying it back to the ship."

We lower the tree and start hacking with whatever we have. Some brought axes from the ship. Others pull out their cutlasses for the smaller branches. Riden and Kearan take the saw to the lower, bigger branches. The work is painstakingly slow. This pine has innumerable branches, which is a good sign that it's healthy, but more work for us. I keep one eye on the branches I'm cutting, another on the surrounding trees, searching for anything approaching.

I can see the back of Lotiya's head from atop the rocky rise above the cave opening. Deshel is hidden opposite her, probably up in one of the trees on the other side of the clearing, guarding our backs.

Still, this place is too ripe with animal and plant life for me to believe nothing else lives here. It would be the perfect place for a settlement, were the land king to discover this place. And if the sirens migrate to this place, surely it can't be empty? Why else would they come if there weren't men for them to prey on?

I hit a knot in the branch I'm tackling, so I put even more force behind my next blow, and the wood finally cracks. The girls weave around one another to travel from one felled branch to the next. We care not for neat cuts or even nubs. We can make things look pretty later.

Speed is my only concern. On and off the island.

Every mouth groans from the weight of the tree as we carry, drag, push, and pull the trunk to the ship. Several times we have to attach ropes and pulleys to nearby trees to get the trunk over hills. Even with my strength at the fat base of the trunk, the tree proves challenging. We pause several times to catch our breath.

Lotiya and Deshel follow our movements in a wide arc, ready to warn us at the first sign of danger. My entire body is tense, just waiting for a warning call, sure it must be coming any second.

When we reach the beach and the ship is finally in sight, a collective sigh looses into the air. Deshel returns from her position and peers at the spot opposite her own watch, where her sister should be.

"Where's Lotiya?" Deshel asks.

Heads turn, but no one says anything. I know it's not likely that she wandered off on her own. Worry takes root in my chest.

"Lotiya!" Deshel shouts.

"Hush," I tell her. "We'll search for her." I look through the crew. "Sorinda, Mandsy, Riden, and Deros—you're with me.

Niridia, get this trunk to the ship. Radita, do what you can to get my ship going again."

"You don't want me to come with you?" Niridia asks.

"If Lotiya is injured, I'll need Mandsy more." If I'm not with the ship, I always need one of them with it in my stead. I can't take them both.

"Shouldn't I come, too?" Kearan asks.

"No, I need your strength focused on moving the trunk."

Kearan darts a glance in Sorinda's direction so quickly I almost miss it. "What if you run into danger? I could—"

"You're to stay, Kearan. End of discussion."

"I will be joining you," Deshel demands.

"Of course," I say. "Everyone, move out."

The majority of the crew get back to dragging the trunk toward the ship, and my little party of six turns back for the island.

It's easy to retrace our steps. The tree trunk left a clear trail through the forest, turning up dirt and plants as we dragged it in places. In other spots, our feet left deep divots in the ground where the weight of the pine drove us into the forest floor.

We keep the trail to our right, traveling along the path that Lotiya would have taken while on watch. I've brought Deros with us because he has some skill with tracking on land. He and his brother lived together, spending their days hunting in the woods for food, until an accident befell his brother. Another, less-experienced hunter got spooked and shot before realizing it was no beast that was near him. The death hit Deros strongly. He wanted to forget everything that reminded him of his brother. So he looked for work on the sea, hiring on with my crew.

"Here," he says. "I've found her trail."

"It's more than one set of tracks," Sorinda puts in.

"Yes," Deros agrees.

"Someone took her," Mandsy says.

Even I can guess the lines tracing over the needle-covered ground indicate she was dragged.

"There's blood, too," Deshel says, her voice breathier than usual.

Deros moves us at a faster pace through the woods now that we've found the trail, whipping past tree branches, leaping over roots, dodging bushes and brambles.

The trail takes us back to the clearing. The blood droplets end right outside the mouth of the cave.

Chapter 12

THE STENCH OF THE cave is overwhelming. I can't believe we couldn't smell it from outside. It's decaying flesh and human waste all wrapped into one. The airflow is limited, making the scents almost overpowering. Mandsy pulls her blouse over her nose.

The smell is not nearly so disturbing as the bones, however. They cover the floor like a carpet.

I lower one of the torches, which we fashioned out of branches, ripped cloth, and tree sap, to get a better look.

"I recognize deer, mountain cat, and rabbit bones," Deros says.

"These are human," I say, pointing to a pile of skulls.

"I thought we were following human tracks," Riden says. "But this is the lair of some kind of beast."

"I don't understand it, either," Deros says.

"Are we to stand here talking about what we don't understand, or are we going to save my sister?" Deshel asks.

"I can't pick out a trail in this, Captain," Deros says. "I'm sorry."

"I'll take the lead now," I say.

We walk single file, each of us holding a torch for light. Riden is at my back. He is followed by Mandsy, Deros, and Deshel. Sorinda takes up the rear.

We move slowly, doing our best not to make a sound, which is difficult when the bones crunch under our feet.

The cave walls are not smooth like the tunnels at the keep. They're jagged and rough. Everything is wet. Water drips from the roof and trickles down the sides. There must be small openings all along the cave for the rain to get in.

It supports all the insect growth.

Webs dotted with raindrops nestle into the corners. Bugs with far too many legs race across the walls. Worms wriggle on top of the rocky soil at our feet. Crickets fill the space with their chirps.

My skin crawls at the sight. I would brave far worse for anyone in my crew, but did there have to be bugs?

When we come to a fork in the path, I make everyone halt.

"What are you waiting for?" Deshel asks. "Just split us up."

Our group is small as it is, we need to be—

A scream—a sound of pure agony—rips through my senses, making my hair stand on end.

"Lotiya!" Deshel shouts. "I'm coming!"

She takes off like a shot down the right tunnel, and the rest of us can do nothing but follow.

Bones scatter in Deshel's desperate footsteps. She winds around corners, picks random paths when the tunnel forks again and again.

I've almost caught up to her when she halts abruptly.

The tunnel tapers down into a dead end.

"Damn it!" Deshel shrieks. She tries to turn, but I grasp her by the shoulders. Hard.

"Deshel, we will find her, but not like this. You need to stop. Listen. We won't find her this way. All you've done is get us lost."

I grasp her arm. Together, we turn around and start back up the way we came. Another scream chokes out of the tunnels. I squeeze Deshel's arm so tightly she gasps in pain. When I have her attention, I point to one of my ears.

Listen.

Carefully, quietly this time, we follow the sounds, tracking them to their source. Down thin tunnels, up a slight rise, left at two more forks. I'm about to go around another corner, when the screaming cuts off.

Dread rests low in my belly. Screaming is good. Screaming means Lotiya is still alive. But now—

"Wait here," I say to the group. I hand Deshel over to Deros, so she can't disobey orders. Quiet as ever, I duck around the next corner and immediately crouch down low. There's a ledge where my tunnel ends. Below it is a wide cavern, with several tunnels branching out from it in different directions.

A body kneels next to me. Riden. I could smack him right now for not listening to me, but that would alert the men in the cavern ahead of us to our presence.

From our vantage point, the backs of three men are to us. I glance at Riden, who is just as surprised as I am. I was sure we'd find some monster first. Why would there be men in the feeding ground of a vicious beast? Their attire is not unlike ours, save it's quite dirty and worn with rips and tears. They're not natives, then. Perhaps they're men from the land king's fleet who were shipwrecked here during one of their excavations?

Whoever they are, they're huddled over something in front of them, chomping loudly and smacking their lips together. Aside from the men and their meal, there doesn't appear to be anything else in the space except several lit torches that have been staked into the ground along the edges. I size up the room and the exits thoroughly before indicating to Riden that we should back up around the corner.

"What is it?" Sorinda whispers.

"Men. Three of them. No signs of Lotiya."

"We should jump them," Deshel says. "Make them tell us where the creature could have taken Lotiya."

Sorinda pushes off from the wall she'd been leaning against. "And we can threaten to tie them up and leave them for whatever is in this cave if they don't give us answers."

"Let's do it," I say. One by one we silently drop down from

the ledge into the cavern. The men don't stray from their meal as our feet touch the ground. They probably can't hear us over the sounds of their own chomping. Men can be so disgusting, especially when they think no one is looking.

When Sorinda drops down last, I speak forcefully to the men we've stumbled upon.

"Turn around slowly."

Their backs go ramrod straight at my words. They turn, and I expect them to run or draw the swords at their waists or call for help.

Bright red blood runs down their chins. Their eyes are dull, lifeless, as though their bodies are only empty shells. And then, in one of their hands, I spot the remains of an arm with part of Lotiya's shirt still attached to it.

Deshel begins shrieking as the men spring at us. My hand goes to my pistol, cocking it back as I raise it. My gun isn't the only one that fires.

All three of them go down, blood pooling from multiple holes in their chests. The shots echo down the tunnels long after the men fall.

I stare at the bodies for a long time, until a sickly realization comes to me. I know who these men are.

Deshel runs toward her sister's remains. Lotiya's throat has been ripped out. She's missing a leg and an arm and so much blood. It's all over the cave floor.

Animal-like shouts and growls sound down the cave and grow closer, alerted to our presence by the gunshots.

Mandsy goes for Lotiya's body, as though there's something

she can do to help. But it's useless. She's gone. My eyes sting to see what's left of her. Deshel pushes Mandsy aside and grabs her sister's body. She hauls it over her back. "Let's get out of here," she says, a look of steel in her eyes.

She's right. No time to grieve now. I have to get the rest of us out of here alive.

There are four pathways leading out of the cavern, not including the ledge we dropped down from. One of them has to lead us out. With a body to carry, the ledge isn't our best option.

"They'll come through this one," I say, indicating the second tunnel from the left, the widest tunnel, naturally, where the growling sounds are the loudest. "Can you see anything down the other tunnels?"

The group disperses, trying the other surrounding tunnels.

"Captain!" Mandsy shouts. "I can feel a breeze down this one!"

The inhuman growls grow louder, uncomfortably close to us now.

"Run!"

Chapter 13

WE RACE FOR OUR lives down the tunnel Mandsy found. Eventually, a small light appears ahead. Sunlight. An exit.

I glance over my shoulder. The cannibals aren't in sight yet, but I'm sure it won't take them long to discover which way we went.

I slam into Riden's back. He turns and steadies me before I hit the ground, and I rub at my arms where I bumped him.

"Why are we stopped?" I shout at the same time I see the problem.

A cave-in. Sunlight filters through a small opening, not big enough for a person to fit through, not yet. The girls have their cutlasses out and are beating against the wall with their hilts.

Deros tries to find handholds on the rocks to move them out of the way.

"Keep at it!" I shout to them.

I wedge my torch into the ground in front of me, draw my sword, and prepare to greet the ravenous men. Riden stands at my side, ready to help. We barely fit side by side.

"Here," he says and hands me his sword while he reloads his pistol. "You weren't joking when you spoke of how much danger your crew gets into."

"We like to keep things interesting."

"And fatal."

The cannibals are within sight now, sprinting full speed.

Riden pours more gunpowder into his pistol, takes aim, and fires. The first cannibal in line falls, tripping those immediately behind. Some are smart enough to jump over the mess and keep running.

I toss Riden back his sword, and we begin to fend them off. Cannibals extend as far as my eyes can see in the scanty light.

The first cannibal who reaches me has bloodshot eyes, a scar on his forehead in the shape of a *K*, and long, matted hair. He swings his sword down at my head, and I raise my own to deflect it. Then he tries it again. He's quick, but after three times of this repetitious action, I sidestep as soon as he starts to move his arm downward and hack him at the elbow. His arm comes clean off, and a scream that makes me want to rip off my ears ensues. I silence it with a well-placed stab.

It takes me only one try to confirm my suspicions. The men

are unaffected by my voice. Their minds have already been charmed by sirens much more powerful than I.

There is very little left of the men they once were. They have no skill with a sword. Their strikes are imprecise, ill-timed, wild—like small children with toy clubs. They are desperate, quick, emergent. You'd think they were the ones fighting for their lives and not we.

But they are fresh and full of energy, unlike us.

"One of these days it would be nice to do something normal with you," Riden says as he punches a looming face, then stabs the cannibal in the stomach.

"I thought you were angry with me."

"I still am, I think, but it doesn't seem all that important when we're fighting for our lives."

Well, then. "What exactly did you have in mind?" I kick at my own assailant, right in the mouth. Must've knocked a few teeth loose.

"I don't know. We could share a meal together."

Share a meal? I don't know what he's going on about, but I say, "Oh, come now, this is far more fun."

We keep backing up as bodies pile up in front of us. The sounds of metal striking rock continue to pound at our backs.

"I will concede that I do feel more alive when I think I'm about to die," he says.

"You're not going to die," I tell him.

That's when one of them jumps me. I'd been fighting one cannibal, and the next one, instead of waiting his turn, launches himself over the first and flattens me onto my back as my sword goes flying from my hand.

The impact would have been painful enough without the bones on the ground digging into me. Sharklike teeth bite into my shoulder, and I let out my own sort of growl. I reach my left hand up around the cannibal's throat, squeezing and pushing those needles out of my skin. They've been filed down to points! They're gnashing, eager to pierce into my skin once more. His breath is rancid. I have to choke down my last meal.

Riden is busy blocking the tunnel by himself now while I grasp around frantically for my sword. Eventually my hand finds something hard and heavy. A human femur, I think. I bring it down on the cannibal's head, which knocks him out instantly.

I push and wiggle to get the dead weight off of me. Two seconds later I have my sword in hand again. I kill the man I'd just rendered unconscious—I don't want him waking up ever again—while Riden holds off the rest.

I'm bleeding now, and the cannibals become even more frenzied by it. Apparently their own bleeding companions lying around the cave floors have no allure for them. It is only the unenchanted sailors unfortunate enough to land on this island that whet their appetites.

One more *chink* and I hear rocks cascading behind me. Light bursts through the tunnel, temporarily blinding the cannibals in front of us.

"Run!" I shout again.

The light burns my eyes as I turn, and I run blindly at first, tripping over the rocks and forest floor. But I don't stop. My breath makes my raw throat ache, but I ignore the pain. I can only imagine how everyone else must be feeling if *I'm* getting tired.

They are only yards behind us. Deshel is slowed down by the body she carries, but no words would convince her to drop it. Nor would I dream of doing so. To not be buried at sea is to be damned for eternity, never finding rest with the stars.

Deros and I reach the beach first. Our strides never falter as we shove our strength into the single rowboat left for us, plunging it into the ocean. The others tumble in, and we are finally drifting off toward the ship. Toward safety.

The cannibals wade into the water. Deros and I row with every bit of strength we have left. But as soon as the cannibals get in over their heads, they falter, scrambling for purchase on the sand below, swallowing water—drowning.

They forgot how to be men long ago.

∝⌣

"What happened?" Niridia asks when we finally drag ourselves back onto the ship. "What beasts did this?" She stares in open horror at Lotiya's body.

"Men," Sorinda answers.

"Not just men," I say. "Bewitched men. They were pirates once. Men from my father's own crew."

"How is that possible?" Niridia asks.

"On his first voyage here, my father claimed they were set upon by sirens, but not all of his men made it off the island. It

180

would seem that those left for dead were enchanted to guard this place and feast on any who stopped on their way to the Isla de Canta."

"How do you know they were your father's men?" Riden asks. He stands near Deshel, who hasn't yet dropped Lotiya's body.

"Some of them bore Kalligan's mark. My father's men distinguish themselves by drawing the letter *K* on their foreheads. Years ago, those who wished to truly prove their loyalty would carve it into their flesh, letting the skin scar. Father's mostly done away with that, since it makes it difficult to hide them in a crowd or to send them out as spies."

"Just a moment," Enwen pipes up. "You're telling me you can bewitch men into cannibals?"

"No. I am merely half siren, and my abilities last only as long as I have song to fill a man's ears. As soon as my song fades, the enchantment ends. It would seem that full sirens are much more powerful than I."

Enwen sticks out his tongue in disgust, as though imagining his own life as a cannibal. Everyone else is silent as they take the new information in.

Deshel breaks it as she lets out a single laugh, one without any humor in it. "We risked our lives to save a siren. Who then left us to be hunted down by the king. And now we were almost eaten alive because of that siren's enchantments from long ago." Her gaze cuts to me like a knife. "I hope you feel her life was worth my sister's." She sets the body down.

A new kind of silence fills the ship, that of held breaths.

I'm already running at her. I have a fistful of her shirt in my hands as I slam her into the ship's railing and tilt her backward, so most of her weight is teetering off the side, held up only by my arms.

That kind of talk is tilting toward mutiny, and I won't have it. "Lotiya was family to me, not in the way she was to you, but still in all the ways that mattered."

I loosen my grip, set her weight back onto the ship. "I cannot undo what has been done. But remember, I gave everyone a choice to stay or leave before we set out on this voyage. And you have a choice to make now, Deshel. You can lay all the blame on me, let bitterness and resentment fill you until you're no longer able to sail with my crew. Or. You can accept that your sister knew the risks and decided to sail for adventure and treasure anyway.

"You will grieve for her. We all will, but we can keep fighting and living our lives as she would want. Now, go below and get yourself cleaned up. Take some time to adjust. Decide what you will do."

I release her. She has no words for me in return. Not yet. She slinks belowdecks.

"As for the rest of you—get this ship ready for sailing. The king could be only a day behind us now."

They've already started cutting and smoothing our new mast to shape, and Radita sets about ordering everyone back to the task.

It's probably overkill—I've already seen that the cannibals can't swim, and they don't seem intelligent enough to use boats, but after one is faced with the danger of being eaten alive, I don't think that really matters. Either way, I post watches while we're making repairs.

A hand gently grips my elbow.

"Come on," Riden says. "Let's get you cleaned up."

I realize now that I'm still covered in blood, and my shoulder needs to be cleaned. Likely with a whole bottle of rum.

"Mandsy," Riden says, "your healing kit."

"I'll go fetch it."

"And some water. Captain needs to clean up."

He leads me toward my quarters, now by the hand, and I let him. It gives me some time to think over the tongue lashing I'm about to give him. I tell him to stay above deck while I replenish my abilities and he goes below. I tell him to stay put in the cave with everyone else and he follows me. I can't have people on this ship I can't trust.

He closes the door to my quarters and has me sit on the bed. After examining my shoulder for a moment, he reaches down to his boot and pulls out a knife.

"Where did you get that?" I ask.

"Won it in a game of cards from Deros. He's always losing his knives to us." Riden doesn't look at me as he talks. Instead he keeps his attention on the knife, which he brings down near my shoulder.

"What are you doing?" I snap, pushing his hand away.

"Cutting at the sleeve of your corset. I need to get a proper view of the bite."

"And ruin my corset? Are you mad?"

"Alosa, it's already bloodstained. Give it a rest."

"Give what a rest?"

"The arguing."

"*You* are the one who needs to give the arguing a rest. It's becoming a habit—you disobeying and questioning orders."

"So punish me again," he says. "But right now we need to get you cleaned up."

I raise both my arms, possibly in an attempt to strangle him, but my shoulder burns, and I have to settle for yelling. "It's not about punishing you! It's about getting you to listen! I need sailors under my command who I can trust!"

Those brown eyes flash with hurt for an instant before they harden. "You can trust me."

"Can I? You wander belowdecks when you're ordered to stay above. You follow me into danger when you're told to stay behind."

"Apologies, Captain."

"Don't apologize to me unless you mean it. Do you intend to disobey orders again?"

He looks down at the ground for a moment, searching for the right words to say. He pierces me with that stare of his when he finds them.

"I can't help myself when it comes to you."

"What is that supposed to mean?"

"I used to be able to rationalize. When we were on the *Night Farer*, I could push feelings aside and focus on what was important. At the time, it was giving Draxen what he wanted. But that's not what's most important to me anymore."

I swallow loudly during his brief pause.

"I'm fascinated by you. I needed to see you when you were alone in the brig. I didn't like the thought of you being by yourself, and I couldn't help my curiosity. I had to see what you were like when you were . . . different. You have so much power. You tempted me with just one movement of your finger. And yet, when you're yourself, you treat this crew as though they're your family. You like to pretend you're so tough and nothing hurts you, but you care so deeply.

"And when we were in the cave, you ordered me to stay behind. You were trying to protect everyone again. You don't care one whit about putting yourself in danger if it's the trade-off for keeping everyone else alive."

He takes a step forward, and my heart beats faster at the proximity. "I do not value my life above yours, and I could not let you be in danger alone. I wanted to be a part of your crew so I could fight with you, not have you trying to save me from danger.

"I made myself a promise," he continues, "after we left Draxen at the supply post. I'm not going to follow orders blindly like I did as first mate of the *Night Farer*. I don't want to be the man who doesn't do what he believes is right because he's too busy following orders. I want to make my own choices. Especially where you are concerned."

I'm speechless, completely caught off guard by his reasoning. He continues still, reaching a hand out to stroke my hair, "You're beautiful, the most stunning person I've ever seen. You're fearless. You like danger. You like to make your friends laugh and your enemies cower. You have the power to obtain anything you want, yet you've worked hard for everything you have.

"So, no, Alosa, I cannot promise that I won't ignore orders again. Like I said, when it comes to you, I have no control over my actions."

I stand and move over to one of the portholes in the room to stare at the fading sunlight. I need to put distance between us so I don't do something embarrassing. Like spout off my feelings or lunge at him again.

I take deep breaths, trying to calm my heartbeat, trying to focus on the pain in my shoulder instead.

But then I feel his hand touch the base of my neck. I almost jump. I hadn't even heard him approach. When did I relax around Riden enough to no longer consider him a threat? My guard isn't up. And strangely, that realization doesn't bother me. His fingers slide up my neck and into my hair, raising the strands away from my skin.

My heart leaps as I feel his breath there.

"Your enchantments last long after your song fades." His voice takes on a huskier tone, and my senses sharpen with it. His lips brush my neck as he starts kissing his way up to my hairline. My body shudders, an uncontrollable reaction to him. He smiles against my skin, pleased by the response.

I swallow. "I thought we weren't supposed to be kissing anymore."

"We are not kissing," he whispers. "I'm kissing you." His free hand slides around my waist, pressing me into him. "Your skin tastes so good." His teeth nip at my neck, and an excited gasp leaves my mouth.

I'm about to round on him, possibly to demand a kiss or fifty from him, but then Mandsy arrives with her kit.

"I've got everything," she says brightly. "I'll have you patched up in no time."

Riden doesn't move. I'm still facing the window, so I can't begin to imagine the look on her face.

"Or I could come back later," she says in the same chipper tone of voice. Nothing fazes her.

"No," Riden says. "The captain needs treating now. I'll leave you to it." His warm arms leave me, and his footsteps retreat until they're cut off completely by the door shutting.

What the hell just happened?

Does he think I've forgotten how he reacted to my saving him from drowning? He can't just make everything disappear by touching me!

Although, apparently, he can, since I forgot completely about it in the moment.

I shake my head and turn toward Mandsy. She doesn't look as though she saw anything of note. She's smiling, but she always smiles.

"Have a seat, Captain." She points toward the bed.

I don't realize how warm I am until Mandsy touches a cool cloth to my blood-streaked face. Its weight is a comfort, unlike everything else.

Lotiya is dead. My father is almost upon us. My mother is probably swimming somewhere without a care in the world.

My muscles sag from the fighting and running and heavy lifting. And I can't even begin to figure Riden out.

It just keeps piling up, and I don't want to deal with any of it.

"What took you so long?" I ask Mandsy to distract myself.

"Took me a while to get a barrel of freshwater opened."

Her response is far too hasty. She's meddling again, and I narrow my eyes at her.

"Oh, all right. So I thought the two of you could have a nice moment together. The least he could have done was help you out of your clothes so I could better—"

"Mandsy!"

She holds up her hands in defense. "I'm just saying—"

"Well, stop just saying."

"Sure thing, Captain."

She stays silent, but a knowing smile won't leave her face.

Mandsy has me cleaned in no time. I didn't need stitches, although I'll likely have that man's canines printed into my flesh forever.

By the time I leave my rooms, the mast is cut to scale, and the crew carefully lowers it into the space left by the previous one. It's a balancing act, raising such a massive piece of wood without tipping over the ship. They've attached pulleys to the foremast and mizzenmast to get the trunk upright, and I jump in to help. After that's done, we have to attach the crossbeams and fasten Roslyn's crow's nest up top. The sails are attached next.

As soon as the mast is functional, we set sail again. Radita is a little put out at not being able to polish out all the flaws, but it's vital that we get sailing again. The crew whoops as the sails fill with wind. We begin moving at our usual quick pace once again. I look over my back at the horizon; no sign of the fleet yet.

At night we light the lanterns. We let the remains of Lotiya's body drift off to sea, buried with the fallen pirates before her. When her soul departs from her body, it will follow the lantern light and find the water's surface. From there, it will be able to see the stars and fly up to the heavens. Every soul parted from this world is a star in the sky. They live in peace, reunited with lost loved ones at last.

Deshel is silent through the whole affair, never taking her eyes off the water, as if willing her sister to return to life. My own heart aches at the loss. Deshel may blame me, but I blame the man who forced me into this course of action. My father is at fault. No one else.

∝

After another week at sea and no signs of the fleet, I relax. We've put some more distance between us, and I don't feel the need to look over my shoulder every hour.

My wound is healing nicely, and everyone is in better spirits. I finally have the time to deal with other things.

With Riden things.

I find him belowdecks, sitting in a bunk opposite Deshel, both of their faces somber. He puts a consoling hand on her shoulder. I wonder if he's feeling guilty for all the complaints he made against the sisters. Trying to make up for it somehow.

As I watch him comfort her, I'm struck with the thought of how *good* he is. I mock his attempts at being honorable, but in this moment, it's so easy to see that he truly is a generous and thoughtful person. I'm sure he imagines how he would feel if he were to lose his brother. He has so much kindness to offer a woman he usually can't stand.

And yet, when a woman he *does* like saves his life, he has nothing but contempt. And then he has the audacity to touch me, to whisper tantalizing thoughts in my ear, to kiss my skin. As though nothing happened.

The anger rippling through me could make the sea boil.

I approach the two.

"I forget she's gone sometimes," Deshel says. "I catch myself looking for her, calling out her name, even. And then I remember. . . . That's the worst part. Realizing it over and over again. There's a constant ache, too, but then it will really slam into me all of the sudden."

"There were times I would forget my father was dead," Riden says, "but I always felt relief when I remembered. I can't imagine what it would be like in your situation. I'm so sorry. I'm here whenever you'd like to talk."

"Thank you. I think I'd like to be alone now, though."

Deshel looks up, noticing me. "Captain." She stands, takes a step toward me. "About before, I'm sorry for what I said. I do not blame you. I was hurting—am hurting—more than I ever have before."

"It's already forgotten," I tell her.

She nods once before lying back down in her bunk.

"I need to see you in my quarters," I say to Riden.

"Is something wrong?" he asks.

I don't answer him. I turn for the stairs leading above, expecting him to follow. I relax slightly when I hear his steps behind me. But I'm still worried over the conversation ahead. I don't know how it will go. If it will only make things worse.

Riden shuts the door behind himself as he steps into my rooms. Natural light pours in from the portholes, illuminating his even features.

He leans against a wall, crossing his arms lazily over his chest. "What have I done?"

"I'm ready for your apology," I tell him.

He blinks, stands up straighter. "What am I sorry for?"

I make sure my words are clear and do my best not to raise my voice. "You don't get to decide how to treat me based on what your mood is. I don't care about your gratitude; I don't need it. You're a member of my crew, and I would try to save anyone who fell overboard during a storm. But your reaction was completely unwarranted. Yes, I broke a promise, but I saved you and everything was okay."

His crossed arms rise as his muscles tighten, but I press on. "You pouted in your self-righteous anger until our lives were in danger. 'It doesn't seem all that important when we're fighting for our lives'?" I quote back at him as a question.

"Alosa—"

"I'm not finished."

He snaps his mouth shut.

"You're not allowed to turn me away when I'm at the height of vulnerability, then be furious at me for rescuing you, then touch and kiss me and spout off your feelings when it suits you. I want answers for why you behaved the way you did. And I want my damned apology, and I want it now!"

He uncrosses his arms. "May I speak now?"

I nod at him so I don't plunge into another tirade.

"I've been selfish," he says, "but so have you."

Through bared teeth: "That's not how an apology sounds."

"You had your chance to talk. Now it's my turn. Throwing yourself at me when your world comes crashing down around you? Selfish. You were trying to use me. I wanted more from you than that."

It doesn't escape my notice that he said *wanted*. Past tense.

"I meant what I said on the cannibal island. When we were fighting for our lives, I realized I didn't want to be angry with you. You might say my response to that realization was . . . hasty."

The memory of his lips on the back of my neck surfaces.

"But before," he says, "after you rescued me from the sea, you might say *I* was at the height of vulnerability. I needed time to sort out my own past and come to terms with it."

I'm silent, hoping he'll offer me an explanation without my prompting. When he doesn't, I ask, "What happened?" as gently as I can so as not to scare him off.

"I spent much of my early years not having control over anything." He closes his eyes, perhaps trying to block out the memories. When he opens them again, he says, "My father dictated when I could eat, when I could sleep, when I could piss—it didn't matter how hard I begged or pleaded. He hated me and did whatever he could to show it, preferring to make me suffer than kill me. There were times—few though they were—when I would do something that pleased him. He'd promise never to strike me again. Of course, those were lies.

"I won't get into the details of everything he did to me. Suffice it to say, Jeskor was a bastard. I still carry those scars. The fears of a little boy trying to trust his own father not to hurt him. When you used your abilities on me, when I specifically asked you not to, I was reminded of that time. Those scars came to the surface. I remembered broken promises. Beatings, lashings, starvation. I remembered it all, felt manipulated all over again. I'm sorry for what I said and how I behaved. I just needed time to remember you're not him. You didn't save me to be cruel."

"Of course not," I say.

"Then why did you save me?" he asks.

The question is so bizarre, I almost don't answer him. "Because you're part of my crew. I watch after my own."

He's quiet, staring me down. "Is that all?"

There are words he wants me to say. Words I should say. But

I can't allow myself to think them, let alone say them. My mind is as blank as my mouth is dry.

"That's twice I've been honest with you, Alosa. Twice I've made myself vulnerable to you. That's supposed to go both ways."

When I still can't say anything, he leaves.

Chapter 14

THE WIND STOPS, completely locking us in place after another few days of sailing. The weather can be like that. Wild and deadly one day. Nonexistent the next. In many ways, it's even worse than being caught in a storm, especially when one is racing against the deadliest man on the sea. Just like that, the lead we've obtained after fixing the mast starts to dissipate.

I give the crew chores so none can dwell on our dire straits. I send them below to clean their bunks. Trianne takes a few of the girls to help her tidy up the galley, and the deck is in desperate need of swabbing after the storm. Radita finally has the chance to fix up the mast just the way she would like it.

But it doesn't take more than a day to clean the ship to perfection. I'm itching out of my skin.

"Kearan! Why aren't you at the helm? Get over to the aftercastle."

"And do what? Spin us in circles?"

"Just try to look busy!"

He is busy, though. He spends his time doing more push-ups and stretches. He does heavy lifting around the ship, and I've even seen him traversing up and down the stairs leading belowdecks. Not because he's going anywhere, but because he's strengthening his legs. Before, he was grizzly-looking with a wild beard, had lazy fat rolls, and had the stench of a drunk permeating off him. Now he actually looks his age: nineteen.

He's not handsome—nothing could fix that—but he's healthy, sturdy. His eyes are still too far apart, his nose still broken and badly set. But every bulge on his skin is now muscle. The crew can stand to be within ten feet of him, and he's clearheaded in a way that makes him even more useful. I thought maybe the changes would cause him to stare at Sorinda less, but there is no change there.

Deshel comes up top through the hatch. Alone. And all I can think about is how she was always in the company of her sister, the two of them giggling at some private joke.

I lost a crew member on this voyage, and I will probably lose more before it is over. My own father is hunting me, and I'm not entirely sure what he will do if he catches me. My crew I know he will kill. Slowly. And me? Will he try to persuade me to his side again? Or will he even bother? Maybe my neck is already marked for a noose.

I'm fleeing one parent and returning to another, but what kind of reception will I receive from my mother? I doubt she knows me anymore. She is back in the water, and all humans will be prey to her. I may be her daughter, but will that matter if she is a mindless sea beast?

And then Riden—

No, I am not going to think of Riden.

The next morning, the skies are still empty of wind, but a fog fills the space instead. Roslyn can barely see the deck of the ship from up in the crow's nest. The ocean itself is against us now.

Enwen spouts off surefire ways to get rid of the fog.

"Toss three coins into the sea, Captain. One for the stars, one for the sky, and one for the ocean," he says.

"What need have they for money?"

"It's not about need, it's about showing reverence."

I'm usually patient with him, but I don't have it in me today. "By all means, Enwen, waste your money, but if you step one foot into my treasury, I'll toss you overboard."

Mandsy sits cross-legged on the deck with some fabric in her lap. Looks like she's working on a dress. Mandsy appreciates fancy things as much as I do. Niridia crouches next to her, chatting lightly.

Kearan rolls a barrel full of freshwater across the deck as a morning exercise. Sorinda sits in the shade made by the aftercastle, watching the crew on deck. I'm bored out of my mind, so I sidle up next to her.

"Kearan looks better," I say.

"I hadn't noticed."

"Maybe you should talk to him."

She turns her head to look at me fully. Sorinda often reminds me of a cat with the sleek way she moves. "Whatever for?"

"He's not a drunk anymore. He has things to say."

"I don't."

"You don't ever talk to anyone. Maybe it's time you started."

She turns away from me, peers over at Kearan again. "Talking isn't necessary for me to do my job."

"No, but you might enjoy it if you tried." I move to stand. No one can change Sorinda's mind. She follows orders better than anyone else on the ship, but when it comes to her personal life, she's as closed off as a clam.

"Captain." She halts me with a word. "I see everything on this ship. Instead of trying to engage me in conversation, you might consider talking to the person who you really desire to."

Her line of sight changes.

To where Riden is chatting with Wallov and Deros near the bow.

"That is none of your concern," I say, but Sorinda has already disappeared. I turn my gaze back to Riden.

"Ships in the distance!" Roslyn cries from the railing near the men. Though she's not up in the crow's nest, she's clearly been keeping a lookout better than anyone else.

Heads turn toward the starboard side. Fingers point. Hands cover open mouths. Wallov rushes Roslyn over to the crow's nest, so she can hide in the false bottom of her post.

The pirate king's fleet has found us.

The fog has started to clear, and in the distance are twenty ships, the *Dragon's Skull* at their head.

The air is deathly silent with not even a breeze to stir it.

I dare to hope they haven't spotted us, but then a ship pulls forward, separating itself from the fleet, using sweeps to sail right for us.

"Battle stations!" I shout. "Prepare the cannons! Gunmen, to your posts! Load every musket and pistol on this ship! Move, move, move!"

Quick-running feet thud over wood. Muskets are passed around. Barriers are fashioned out of barrels, crates, and spare rowboats to provide protection from gunshots. Below, Philoria, Bayla, Wallov, Deros, and the others will be hauling out the gunpowder and cannonballs.

Niridia and I set up a station just behind the companionway. We have five muskets and five pistols between the two of us, all laid out on the ground. Ammo and gunpowder are within reach for reloading. Niridia is there to reload me and dole out orders when I give them.

Riden tucks himself into the space with us. "I'm a good shot. You'll want me here—unless you have other plans for me?"

As the newest member of the ship, he hasn't been given a station for battle.

Part of me wants to send him away just to be petty, but I remember the first time we met, when he used his pistol to shoot my own from my hand. He does have good aim.

"You can stay," I say.

It's Tylon's ship, *Death's Secret*, that approaches us. I find myself wishing that my own ship was equipped with sweep oars, but the *Ava-lee* was not built for carrying them. We've no way to run. Nothing to do but wait.

"Do we fire on them while they approach?" Niridia asks.

"No. Father would just retreat and then order the whole fleet to fire upon us. If one ship is coming forward, it's because he wants to talk first. The rest of the fleet won't fire to risk hitting their own ship, and I like our odds better when it's one-on-one."

"Talk *first?*" she asks.

"If the pirate king had only talking in mind, he would have sent *his* ship forward. Because this will turn into a fight and he doesn't want to risk damage to his own vessel, he's coming over on another."

It's at least a little satisfying knowing it's Tylon's ship I'll be putting holes in.

Death's Secret ceases its rowing when it's perhaps fifty yards from us, angling itself so the starboard side lines up with ours, cannons to cannons.

My father is not hard to spot. He strides down from the aftercastle to stand on the main deck, as close to me as he can get. He has a belt slung over one shoulder, four pistols strapped across his back. A massive cutlass that would be a detriment to a normal man is sheathed at his side. He could take a head off with it.

My father enjoys looking fierce. As do I. Fortunately, I'd woken up in a bad mood today, and it shows in my clothes. My corset is black with a bloodred blouse underneath. I've tied my hair out of my face and wrapped a matching red bandanna over the top of my head. I look ready for a fight.

I stand opposite my father, nothing but water separating us.

"Where is she?" he says slowly, as though he's barely keeping his temper in check.

"I missed you, too, Father," I say in response.

"You will bring her over to this ship, lay down your arms, and surrender to my men."

"I don't have her. She swam away as soon as she was free of you. You can search this ship from top to bottom, but you will see I'm telling the truth."

He nods to himself, as though he'd been preparing for this answer. "Then command your men to lay down their arms and surrender the ship."

"And if I don't?" I ask.

"Then my ship will tear yours to ribbons!" Tylon shouts. My father turns his head on him, irritated by the interruption.

"Tylon," I say. "I hadn't noticed you in my father's shadow."

His fair complexion takes on a reddish hue.

"You're my daughter," Father continues. "Surrender the ship and we'll talk."

I'm surprised by the offer. Of course, I know there will be nothing but a slow death in store for my crew if I order them to surrender. I can see it in his eyes. But the fact that he would try this when everyone on Tylon's ship can hear him—it could be interpreted as a sign of weakness. I hadn't realized how much my father depended on me and my abilities. He thinks he can break me if he gets his hands on me, force me to do his bidding once again. He doesn't want to kill me, not yet.

But I will not fall into his hands again, and I sure as hell won't let him get ahold of my crew.

Better to strike than to dodge. It's one of the first lessons Father ever taught me.

I put a hand over my mouth and chin, as if I'm pondering his offer. "Niridia," I say quietly. "Tell the crew below to fire the cannons."

"Aye." She disappears casually through the hatch.

I make a show of thinking over Father's offer, but all I can think is that I never really knew this man. I thought I did. I thought I knew just how fierce and cruel he was, thought I was all right with it, since that cruelty was mostly directed at our enemies. But now that it's directed at my crew, it is something I cannot forgive.

"Let me tell you what I think of your offer," I say.

That's when the first cannons fire.

The *Ava-lee* rocks from the blasts. Wood rips open in the opposite ship. I have only four cannons below. Two were aimed at the deck of the opposing ship, one blowing apart a group of men huddled together while the other nicked the mizzen-mast. The other two cannons tear holes through the starboard side, one lodging into the wood while the other cuts clean through.

Father turns and bellows orders to Tylon's men. I smile at the little weasel's put-out face as my father takes control of his men, and dole out orders to my own crew.

"Fire the muskets!" I shout. "Aim for the gun ports. Take out the men at the cannons!"

Tylon's ship has more than double the cannon fire of mine. If we don't focus fire on the men operating the cannons, they'll obliterate us in no time.

Niridia appears back at my side. "Musket," I say, holding out my hand, and she places the gun in it. I sight one of the gun ports, narrow my gaze on the man loading the ball into the cannon, and fire. He goes down, and Niridia trades me a loaded musket for an empty one.

Riden veers around me to take his own shot, aiming for the gun ports as ordered. His mark goes down.

"Very nice," I tell him.

He grins before trading muskets.

Gunfire ripples through the air on both sides. My girls are well protected behind their barrels, crates, rowboats, and other hiding places, but the men on Tylon's ship fall like hail from the sky, some tumbling off the edges of their ship, hitting the water.

I only get out one more shot before the first cannon fire reaches us. The ship lurches back from the force of it, but there's no time to assess the damage.

Instead I reach out with my voice. I know that if Father is hurtling out orders, his men must not have their ears covered.

I find three men at a cannon, pull them under my spell. It's not hard to project a new image into their minds, make them think the bottom of their own ship is actually mine. They start to pull the cannon away from the gun port, aim it at the base of their own ship.

But then I lose one. He was killed by his own men once they noticed what he was up to. I grab another man, have him help with the task. One finally manages to clean out the carriage, another reaches for a cannonball, but I lose all three of them. Someone is putting up a good fight over there. Luckily, though, it's pulling the rest of the gunmen away from their own cannons as they try to stop their fellow men from blowing holes in their ship. I keep them busy, seeking out live men when the previous ones die, just like I did at Vordan's inn.

Sorinda races toward me, ducking behind the barrier we've fashioned. With four of us, we're all pressed shoulder to shoulder.

"Acura eels have surfaced," she says.

I smile. "How many?"

"At least two. One is enormous."

"Perfect."

I switch tactics, singing to the men on the top deck, enchanting them to jump into the water. As soon as they leap, I release them, searching for men still aboard the ship with my voice.

"Keep firing," I tell Riden and Niridia. I grab another loaded musket and an extra pistol, then race with Sorinda over to her previous position, blocked from attack by barrels storing freshwater.

I peer into the sea.

Men shriek as the eels circle them. The eels like to toy with their food first. It's when they dive below the surface that one needs to worry. That's when they're readying to charge. They're deadly carnivores that spend most of their time on the sea bottom, sensing for disturbances in the water.

Their nostrils stand out prominently, giving them an even fiercer look. They're navy blue on the top half, white on the bottom: the perfect camouflage, not that they need it.

Acura eels are far worse than sharks. Sharks only kill when they're hungry. But eels—they don't leave anything alive, whether hungry or not.

One of the eels currently in the water must be at least twelve feet, teeth twice the length of a finger. Tylon's men swim desperately for the ship, clinging to its sides—before they're dragged under.

I can't sing and fire at the same time, and the men at the gun ports are back to loading the cannons. I reach for them with my song once more, and I finally enchant one of the men to light the fuse at the cannon pointed downward.

I hear the blast seconds later, and it brings a smile to my face. That'll keep the gunmen busy as they try to stopper the hole.

My father is visible from this vantage point. His voice bellows over the sounds of my ship's cannons firing again.

I spot one of Tylon's men right next to him. With my song, I promise him riches lie in the water if he'll only jump. My father watches as the man tosses himself overboard.

An eel circles him, spinning the current around him, before diving. Seconds later it drags his scream under the water.

Kalligan searches my ship. When his eyes land on me, they narrow.

I wish I could take Father out, but he's too skilled of a fighter. He'd only be momentarily distracted if I sent men to fight him. And it would take all of my focus just to keep him busy.

A breeze ripples across my forehead as I utter one last note, sending three more men overboard, and my song officially runs out.

But my father doesn't know that yet, and I hear one word rise out of the chaos.

"Retreat!"

He's done playing with us. Now we'll face the fleet as soon as he and Tylon's ship are out of the way.

I wipe the sweat from my forehead, shoot my musket at another man through a gun port, just as another comforting breeze wafts over my heated skin.

The breeze . . .

"Riggers! Get those sails down!" I shout.

The girls leave their safe places to race for the masts. Riden hurries to join them.

"Not you, Riden! Keep shooting!" I tell him.

We're taking as many of those bastards down as we can.

"Aye-aye!" He dives back behind the companionway with Niridia. Sorinda fires her own musket from beside me, and I raise a newly loaded gun.

Something launches over the distance between our two ships, striking my deck, ripping up the wood, before catching against the railing. Another soon joins it. Then another and another.

The harpoons.

Father must have changed his mind as soon as the breeze picked up. He knows we can outdistance him now.

"Cut those lines!" I shout to the crew. Niridia, Teniri, Athella, Sorinda, and Deshel rush to the railing and lean precariously off the deck to reach the ropes tied to the harpoons. Cutlasses hack and saw at the taut lines. Two go down, but another three harpoons quickly replace them.

Damn it!

I cease aiming my musket toward the men at the harpoon guns to join the girls.

Shots rain down on us, now that the men aren't afraid I'll pick them off. Riden continues shooting, but several enemy shots hit their marks.

I hear a scream and thud as one of the girls up in the rigging falls. Mandsy is already ducking out of her hiding place to reach whoever it is. Teniri hisses through her teeth as a shot skims her arm, but she doesn't stop sawing at the rope in front of her.

And then Niridia—

Niridia falls into the water.

Time seems to slow as my mind tries to work through so many things at once. Even if we get the sails down, we're locked in place by the lines connecting us to the other ship. The shooters are picking us off. And I'm sure it won't be long before the men are back at the cannons. If they manage to reel us in with the harpoons, the men will outnumber us at least two to one. My abilities are drained. We've faced worse odds, but my father is on that ship.

He's as good as ten men. Not a single person on this ship could take him, save perhaps me. When I've sparred with my father in the past, I only win about half the time. We're too evenly matched.

But Niridia.

She's going to die if I don't get her out of the water.

One of my girls goes for a rope, but an eel near Tylon's ship breaks away to investigate the disturbance near ours.

The *Ava-lee* jerks to the side so violently, I barely catch myself on the railing, but Teniri, Deshel, and Athella fall into the water. Only Sorinda manages to keep her hold.

The harpoons have started to reel us in.

My mind spins. I need to go after them. Sorinda needs to tie me with a rope. I'll need a dagger if I'm to face an eel. But if I have something sharp, the siren will cut through the rope and follow her own agenda.

They'll die, and I'll be lost to the sea.

Unless . . .

Riden fires off yet another shot.

Every time I've managed to keep myself in control of the siren, Riden has been there. Somehow, he keeps me human. I don't know why. I don't know how, but I need him if I'm to do this.

I rush at him as iron balls pelt around me. He releases another shot just as he notices me.

"Come with me now!" I tell him. I grab him firmly by the upper arm. He doesn't hesitate to listen, though he can't have any idea what I intend.

"Run!" I tell him, so I'm not dragging him quite so much.

He does, until he realizes we're heading for the edge of the ship. He tries to stop, but by that point, there's already enough momentum for the two of us to go over.

My grip on him is like a vise as we fall. I cling to him as though he's the key to my survival. In a way, he is. If this doesn't work, my girls are dead, and I will be a mindless beast forever. Every muscle in my body tenses at the splash, and I really hope my grip doesn't break Riden's arm—

All fear and tension drain away. It's like waking from a good night's sleep, fully rested. Full of energy. Full of power. Ready to sing the day away.

But my ocean is full of disturbances.

Men scream from far away, their cries cut off by eels tearing into them. What wonderful beasts. Another comes pelting in this direction, after the women whose legs kick to keep them above the surface. One of them is bleeding, sending the eel into a frenzy. I stay right where I am, ready to watch the show. Until something kicks me.

I hadn't even noticed I was holding on to a man. Though the salt water must sting his eyes, he manages to glower at me thoroughly.

I laugh at the silly creature. Watch him struggle against me. We're below the water's surface. It won't be long before his lungs give up. But then, he stops fighting. He can't have drowned so quickly. No, he draws himself nearer, places his forehead against mine, noses bumping.

The heat from him—

This sensation. This lack of fighting. It's—

It's—

A memory pushes itself to the surface, words fluttering into my mind on wings. *Your enchantments last long after your song fades,* he said before he kissed my skin.

Suddenly, peace and eagerness are gone, replaced once more by fear and urgency. I throw Riden toward the ocean's surface before launching myself toward the oncoming eel. The largest one yet, perhaps fifteen feet—all teeth and muscle. Its tail rippling through the water so quickly I can barely see it.

But I'm faster.

I may not have been born in the sea, but I was born to rule it.

I am the daughter of the siren queen.

The eel has already finished its circling of Niridia and the others. It's far below us now, surging up, up, up, mouth gaping.

I reach for the dagger in my boot, launching myself at the eel from the side. Dagger connects first, then my legs wrap around the creature's body, just barely long enough for my feet to connect on the other side of the massive water beast.

It wriggles at the pain, sending us shooting in random directions. I pull out the dagger and drive it in again. And again and again. Finally the creature stills, and I release it. A quick glance shows me that someone lowered a rope for the girls and Riden.

But *Death's Secret* still pulls us in.

A harpoon dislodges from my ship; one of the girls must have tossed it over after cutting the line. An idea hits me, and

I grab the harpoon before it can sink to the ocean's bottom. I swim down, down, down—as far as I can get while still traveling toward the opposing ship.

Then I propel myself toward the enemy ship, all muscles straining, swimming as fast as my siren nature will carry me, angling the harpoon so the tip will hit first.

It pierces the wood, and I rip it back out. I pull at the boards in the opening, widening it as water gushes into the hole. They must have patched up the cannon hole I made the men launch into their own ship.

Let's see them patch this up.

I repeat the action, swimming down and then striking the ship with the harpoon three times more.

Death's Secret is rapidly sinking.

I am underwater, fully in control of my mind, and the ship holding my father is sinking. I should be a mindless beast right now, lost to the sea forever, my crew and ship disappearing into the deep.

Instead I am more powerful than I've ever been before in my life.

The realization is intoxicating.

I don't want to leave the water. As soon as I do, I know I will have the same weaknesses as before. Unable to replenish my abilities without losing my mind, useless to everyone.

But what is the alternative? To stay underwater with my human mind forever? Never living life as a siren or human. Trapped somewhere in between.

I swim back toward my own ship, watching the lines from

the harpoons fall into the sea. The *Ava-lee* is free, beginning to sail away.

I don't breach the water's surface until I'm on the port side, where the fleet can't see me.

I don't want my father knowing I beat his ship by destroying it from under the water's surface. This will not be the last time I see him or his fleet, and I don't want him knowing I've found an advantage.

Chapter 15

"ROPE!" I SHOUT UP from the water.

Sorinda peeks over the edge of the ship once before tossing me one. I haul myself up with her help.

The ships in the distance fire their cannons, now that Tylon's ship has gone down. Holes ripple in the water near us, but we'll soon be out of range.

We need to get our lead back.

It's too much to hope my father went down with the ship. He would have been the first one off it.

I expel some of my song so I can absorb the water drenching my clothes. Once I am dry, I will no longer be able to restock without losing myself. I know this, somehow. I can feel the siren part of me just waiting to come back out.

I plant myself on the aftercastle with Kearan. He steers us while I keep my eyes on the fleet. I can't see the faces of the men from this distance, but there is one figure—bigger than all the others—that stands out. The king. He will be furious. His men will be terrified of him.

They must already be exhausted from rowing all this way, because they are unable to keep pace with us.

I stay up top with Kearan for maybe an hour, just long enough to determine we are still gaining a lead and are long out of range. The fleet is still in sight. It will be a while before we no longer see them on the horizon. But it is safe enough to check on other things.

My first stop is the infirmary. I find Mandsy wrapping Niridia's hand in gauze. My first mate is covered in a large blanket, water pooling below her on the floor.

"How bad is it?" I ask.

"The ball went clean through the middle of her hand. It's hard to say how the bones will heal."

"It's my left hand," Niridia mumbles. "I'll still have a sword hand. Nothing to worry about."

"I've tried to give her something for the pain, but she won't take it."

I raise a brow at Niridia.

"You need me sharp. Our enemies are far too close."

I place a hand on her shoulder. "I need you well. We're okay for now. Get healed up. You're to take whatever Mandsy gives you. That's an order."

Niridia purses her lips, but she doesn't refuse the bottle Mandsy passes her.

"Niridia is the last to be patched up," Mandsy says. "I've taken care of the others. They're already resting below. A few of the girls took balls to the legs and arms. Mostly nicks as they were veering around their hiding places to take shots."

"I heard someone fall from the mast as I ordered the sails unfurled," I say. "No concussions?"

Mandsy's face turns grave. "No, a casualty, Captain."

I swallow. "Who?"

"Haeli. She took a bullet to the back. I tried to stop the bleeding, but it was too late. I left her on the deck so we can put her to rest as soon as we have enough of a lead on the fleet."

Haeli. One of my best riggers. I picked her up off Calpoon— one of the Seventeen Isles. She was in a traveling band of performers. Half the time she played the lute during performances, the other she was out in the audience, stealing from their pockets. I was one of her marks. After she robbed me, I offered her a job. Told her I paid better than thieving.

Now she's lifeless out on my deck.

I force a deep breath through my nose. "Any other casualties?"

"No."

"Good."

I leave them. The weight of this journey presses down on my shoulders, physically exhausting me, despite the nourishment I've just received from the ocean. How many of us will be left once we reach the siren island? How many of my loved ones will I be forced to lose in order to make the rest safe?

I can't stand the pressure of my own thoughts. I need to keep busy.

I seek out Radita belowdecks.

"She took a few hits, Captain," she says once I ask after the status of the ship. "A cannon struck through the galley. It took out most of the water storage, and all the water barrels on the deck were riddled with holes during the battle. We've lost most of our drinkable water."

"How much do we have left?"

"A single barrel."

"Only one!"

She nods. "The one we've already opened and started drinking from."

I cover my face with my hands. Our days are numbered. I'll order Trianne to start rationing the water. Even then, I don't see how we can make it to the siren island with what's left. Then there's the return journey. . . .

"Can you see to the ship's repairs?" I ask.

"I already have some of the girls on it."

"Thank you."

"It's my job, Captain, but you're welcome."

When I pass by the bunks, Roslyn is fretting over Wallov's injuries.

"It's a scratch, sweet," he tells her.

"No, it was a shard of wood to your shoulder. Now lie back down."

"I'm *fine*," he says, emphasizing the last word.

"In that case, there's no reason to halt my dagger lessons."

I manage a grin as I close the hatch behind me, heading now for my rooms. But my amused expression disappears as soon as I get inside.

Somebody is already here, waiting for me.

"What are you doing? You're not allowed in here unless I invite you in."

"I have a bone to pick with my captain," Riden says. His body is rigid with fury, and I wonder how he manages such an even tone. "I thought it best to do so in private so you don't hold me over the edge of the ship for mutiny."

"You're not the only one with problems," I snap. "My own father blew holes in my ship. A third of the crew is injured. One of our own is dead. So unless your issues are bigger than those, I suggest you leave because I don't need more added on to my load."

His calm tone vanishes. "It was very nearly more than one casualty! What the hell were you thinking yanking me into the ocean with you?"

"I was thinking I had girls in the water and I needed to save them! I didn't exactly have time to ask for your permission before eels would be upon them."

"And I was what? Bait? An expendable body while you were off saving your real crew members?"

"My *real* crew members? You can be so thick sometimes! I took a calculated risk. I had no choice but to involve you."

His nostrils widen as he takes in another labored breath.

"I needed you," I spit out. "Without you, I turn into a monster beneath the water. But you—you keep me human. You are what I needed to remember myself. I hate it, but I realized that something about you, *only* you, keeps me human when my siren nature tries to take over."

That brings him up short. "Why?"

"Hell if I know. I wasn't about to let four girls under my protection die as I paused to figure that out."

He raises his gaze from mine, pondering something. "You weren't yourself at first. You were dangerous. You were the siren, and then—I knew what to do somehow. I knew that if I didn't struggle, if I just got close to you, you wouldn't drown me."

"In the story my father always told me about how he met my mother, he said instead of fighting the siren trying to drown him, he didn't resist. That's what stopped her, made her bring him up on land instead."

It can't be that simple, can it? An unresisting man causing a siren's nature to be replaced with humanity? Whatever it is, I need to learn to control the siren, and Riden is the first chance I have at doing that.

"What is it?" Riden asks. He's looking at me once more.

"I need your help. I was able to take out a ship from under the water. If I could learn to control myself, so I could go underwater anytime without fear . . . It's not just a want. It's a need. I need this in order to protect my crew. I need to learn to restock my abilities without losing my mind. I need to submerge myself in water without turning into a mindless beast. I need you to help me."

Some of the fight leaves him at the look on my face. I don't know what he sees there.

"Alosa, there is very little I wouldn't do for you, but what exactly are you asking of me?"

"I need you to be with me when I replenish my abilities. I need you to bring me back. Over and over and over again. Until I can do it on my own."

He scoffs. "I came in here to tell you *not* to drag me underwater with you, and you're asking me to do just that?"

"Riden, we need this."

"You *promised* you wouldn't use your abilities on me. You broke it once to save my life. And now . . ." He shudders.

"This is different. I'm asking for your permission ahead of time."

"And if I say no?"

"Then I'll respect that."

"Good. I'm saying no."

I hadn't expected him to answer so quickly. He could have at least pretended to consider it.

Part of me is relieved. The siren terrifies me every time I have to stock up. But the other part of me is disappointed. Doesn't he know what this could mean for the crew, for our chances of survival?

It doesn't matter. Riden won't cooperate. That means I'll figure something else out.

"Then on your way," I say, pointing to the door.

Kearan, Niridia, and I are back in front of the maps. I've already explained the water situation to the crew. Now the three of us need to find a solution.

"There's this large island on the Allemos map," Kearan says, pointing to it. "It's likely to have freshwater. We could stop."

"The last island we stopped at had siren-made cannibals," Niridia says. "Devil knows what's on this one."

"The question is whether we'd rather die of thirst," I say, "or risk running into danger on another island."

Niridia considers this. "Dying of thirst is assured if we don't stop. Dying on this second island is only a possibility at this point."

"Agreed," Kearan says.

I'm thinking the same thing. "Good. Kearan, set a course."

∾

My eyes trail along the horizon, as they have for the last several days, but there is no sign of the fleet. Roslyn hasn't shouted out anything from her better vantage point in the crow's nest, either, so I decide to give it a rest.

A pod of whales swims a few hundred feet to our right. They leap from the water and splash back down. Roslyn laughs from the railing, straining as close as she can get, trying to catch the sea spray with her fingers.

The water is startlingly clear out here. Bright fish in reds and blues and yellows swim in the shallows as we pass by more isles along the way. They're barren plots of sand without more than a palm tree or two sprouting up. We've passed nothing yet containing a freshwater source.

Today I find myself observing the crew at their chores. Radita walks around, checking the rigging, making sure the new fixes hold. Some of the gals swab the deck. Others drape down on the outside of the ship, suspended by ropes to pick off barnacles and other unwanted creatures trying to hitch a ride.

The temperature has warmed even more, making us thirstier with the new rationing. The girls wear their sleeves rolled up and their hair up and off their necks.

Riden is up in the rigging, fiddling with the sails. He's barefoot, shirtless, and he's gone a few days without shaving.

Holy hell.

I'm staring. I know it, but I can't seem to stop.

"I could get used to warm weather," Niridia says from next to me. "Won't exactly make everyone smell nice, but the view is vastly improved."

I should have a clever response, but all I can manage is "Aye."

We stare a few beats longer, until he's about to turn around and we'll be caught for sure.

"What's going on there?" Niridia asks.

"What do you mean?"

"I mean, why don't I see him waltzing out of your quarters every morning with a spring in his step?"

I laugh. "Because there is *nothing* going on there."

"Why not?"

I dare a glance back up at him, watch the purposeful way he moves, watch his muscles tense as he pulls on a line. "He can't handle what I can do. My abilities terrify him."

"Any person with sense is terrified by what you can do. That doesn't mean we don't all love you."

"Thanks, but it's different with him. He has a history with people trying to control him. The fact that I can literally make him do things takes his mind back to a darker time."

"He'll get over it," Niridia says with a certainty that surprises me.

"How do you know?"

"Because he's not an idiot."

I take a deep breath. "I made things worse."

"What did you do?"

"The few times that I've been able to control myself underwater—it's always been because of Riden. I wanted to get a better handle on my abilities, so I asked him to help me. I asked him to make himself vulnerable like that over and over again."

"And he said *no*?" she asks in astonishment.

"Of course he did. I shouldn't have asked it of him. It was wrong—"

"No, Alosa. What's wrong is you not trying to do everything in your power to protect your crew. You did the right thing. He'll see that it's right, too."

"There's no way he'll come around."

"Well, not on his own," she says. "Men can be so thick sometimes. They need help every once in a while."

I smile. I'd said as much to Riden's face, but when Niridia starts walking off, the smile drops. "What are you doing?"

"Helping."

"Niridia!"

"Riden!" she shouts.

He looks down, his eyes roving until they spot her. "Aye?"

"Come down for a moment, please."

He leaps for the netting and begins to crawl his way down.

"Niridia, he already said no. Leave him alone."

"Just let me try something. You do trust me, don't you?"

"Of course."

"Then let me do my job on this ship."

Riden drops into a crouch as his bare feet hit the deck. He straightens, notices me next to Niridia, but focuses on her.

"Do you consider yourself a selfish person, Riden?" she asks brazenly.

If he's at all uncomfortable with the question, he doesn't show it. "I can be," he says.

"I'm the first mate of this ship, which means I see everything that happens. I see you comforting Deshel, see you softening every time Roslyn is around, see you laughing with Wallov and Deros. You've grown fond of us, haven't you?"

"Aye."

"Good. Now the captain tells me you could be invaluable in helping her control her abilities, thereby helping us survive the pirate king. Do you think she's right about that?"

He closes himself off, his face turning away slightly.

I'm shocked when a weak "Yes" comes out of him.

"You risked your life for Roslyn once already. You very nearly died for her. Tell me, if the pirate king catches up to us, do you think he will spare her because she is a child?"

His head whips back around. "No," he says, stronger.

"No one is ordering you to do anything. I just think it's important for you to see things exactly as they are. You could tilt the odds in our favor, Riden. Remember that when you're trying to sleep at night."

And then she just walks off. Leaving me to deal with Riden. With shirtless Riden.

"I swear I didn't put her up to that," I say. "I told her to leave you alone. I was just venting to her, and she got it into her head—"

"It's all right."

"Is it?"

"You will recall I was once a first mate. We can be a stubborn bunch."

He scratches a spot on his arm, and I focus on that instead of his abdomen.

"She's right," he says suddenly, drawing my gaze to his face. "I don't like it, and I can't promise that I won't lash out afterward—but we need to do this."

"If there were any other way for me to do this, I wouldn't have asked. I've tried my whole life to control this. My father put me through all kinds of—never mind. That's not important. I'm just saying that if the pirate king ruled it out as a lost cause, then I know you really are my last option."

"Hmm" is all he says.

"When should we start?" I ask tentatively.

"Probably the sooner, the better."

"Probably." A pause. "So . . . now?" I venture.

"Yes."

I nod. "Let me make some arrangements."

It takes a quarter of an hour to get things ready—and only that long because I took my time. I am in no hurry to use my abilities in front of Riden again. To see his disgust and anger. If we succeed, it will make an insurmountable difference in the battle against my father. But if something should go wrong, if I should hurt anyone while lost to the siren—

I'm walking a very fine line.

When I reappear at Riden's side, he says nothing, only follows me belowdecks. All the other men have been ordered to cover their ears with wax by a smug Niridia. Sorinda is waiting for us in the brig, outside my cushioned cell.

"Doesn't Mandsy usually help you with this?" Riden asks, surprised at seeing the assassin.

"Should things get out of hand, Sorinda is here to put a stop to them."

Calmly, he asks, "You mean she's here to put me down if I'm pulled under your control?"

"No," I say, horrified at his accepting tone, that he would think I'd allow such a thing. "She's here to make sure I don't hurt you." *You imbecile.* My eyes dart down before immediately returning to his face. "Go put on a shirt before we start."

"It's hot," he says, and I can guess what he's thinking. *This is going to be miserable. The least you can do is let me be as comfortable as possible.*

I have two choices. I can let him think I'm being unreasonably cruel, or I can explain things. He insists I never open up to him.

Fine. I'll explain things.

"Sirens want two things from men. Gold and pleasure. Do you have any gold on you?"

"No," he breathes.

"The siren in me would have you moaning in pleasure as she whittled holes into you with a knife. She'd strip you naked and watch you dance until your feet peeled away to the bone. Once you bore her in life, she'll enjoy dancing with your corpse under the sea. Do you want me to tell you how much that thought delights her? She's thought it about you before."

Shattering silence is all he has in response.

"I thought not. Put on your shirt. Let's not make her hungrier than she needs to be."

He leaves the brig, and when he returns, he has a sterner expression on his face. But at least his top half is covered now, too.

I step into my cushioned cell, handing Sorinda my weapons, my corset, my boots. Anything containing metal, everything sharp. All the things the siren can use to try to escape.

She locks me in, then does the same thing for Riden, making him hand over his weapons, and locks him into the cell across from me, where I cannot reach him.

But I will be able to hear him.

"On the island with Vordan," I say, "when he put me in that cage and forced me to sing to you, you kept me sane enough to do as I was told, so he wouldn't kill you. You should have died. I've never stayed human so close after replenishing my abilities. Those pirates poured water onto me, forcing me to take it in over and over again. But just by speaking to me, you kept my head clear. It took some effort. But I think toward the end of our stay on the island, it was easier.

"Stocking up my power is different from being submerged under the sea with all that power endlessly flowing through me. But we'll start small and work our way up. If there's any progress to be had," I add.

"And provided I don't die," he says.

Sorinda pulls her rapier from its sheath. "You're not going to die. Not on my watch."

"I promise this isn't going to be any more fun for me than it is for you," I say.

Right now my power is at its fullest, so I sing to expel some of it. I'm not enchanting anyone. My song doesn't have to be a command. Riden flinches anyway. I pretend not to notice.

When I've depleted it some, I dip a finger into the water. I almost ask Riden whether or not he's ready, but I realize neither he nor I will ever be ready for this.

I pull the water through my skin, let it fill me. It's like taking a cool drink of water into a parched throat. The way the drained abilities within me crave strength and power. Crave the water.

I take in my surroundings with new eyes. Eyes that can

see the individual fibers of wood on the walls, the stains on the floor, the flecks of gold in the human man's eyes across from me.

The humans have trapped me again, but this time they were kind enough to leave me someone to play with.

"Alosa," he says firmly, as though it is a command. Worthless human. No creature commands me.

"Alosa." He says it again, but this time it's different. It's soft, pleading.

Where before there was just another human, now there is Riden. My Riden.

Mine.

The siren still pushes to the front. She is ruthless and brutal. Hungry for her own enjoyment. Hungry for power. But I place a cage in my mind, put her behind it. I don't need her now.

"It's me," I say.

Riden lets out a long breath.

I am used to the siren after dealing with her all these years. It's so strange. Because I am her. When I take in the water, I become a creature with no knowledge of my human existence, no knowledge of those I care about or my human aspirations. I become what I would have been if I'd never known life above the sea.

It's terrifying to know I could lose myself to her. But it won't happen here. Not in an environment that I control. I take comfort in the *Ava-lee*'s familiar surroundings.

But what I'm most concerned about right now is Riden. He appears all right, despite what I've just put him through. I dare to speak.

"Before," I say, "when I was replenishing my abilities and you disobeyed orders by coming to *observe* me, you didn't speak. And I didn't come to my senses. I remained a siren the entire time. I wonder if it's your voice, somehow, that does it?"

"What about when you're underwater?" Riden asks. "I can't speak to you then, but you've still managed to come to your senses three different times."

"You're right. Those times, you . . ."

"Kissed you," he fills in.

Sorinda remains as apathetic as always as Riden continues talking. "When you saved us from Vordan, you held me under the water. I thought I was going to die, and the last thought I remember having was that I wanted to kiss you one more time before that happened."

He's never told me that before. . . .

"That's when I came to," I say, remembering. "And when you fell into the water during the storm, you were drowning again. The siren put her lips to yours to give you some air, so you wouldn't die before she could have her fun. That's when I was myself again."

"And then during the battle," Riden says, "I put my forehead to yours. Not quite a kiss, but it was close."

I stare at him through the bars. "Why did you do that? You couldn't have known what I was trying."

"Somehow, I just thought that if I could get closer to you, maybe we wouldn't die."

It is not only the siren who reacts to Riden, then. He somehow knows how to handle her, too.

"Let's go again," I say, dipping my finger in the water once more.

Riden doesn't object, so I draw it in.

Riden and I practice for hours. Each time, all he has to do is say my name, and I'm me again.

I can't explain it. Riden is not the only one who has spoken to me while I was the siren. In the past, my father kept me contained while I was stocking up on my abilities. His voice didn't bring me to. Tylon has seen me as a siren, tried speaking with me. That did nothing for me, either. Wallov and Deros have done it. A few other captains at the keep.

Nothing.

It's Riden. Only Riden.

Chapter 16

That was close, wasn't it? When next we meet, Alosa,
you will face the full force of the Dragon's Skull *and*
my fleet. Things will go differently then.

ANY PROGRESS I thought I'd made with Riden the previous
day feels insignificant when reminded of the sheer size of the
fleet. So what if I can keep my mind while restocking my abilities? What am I to do against twenty ships? With the thirty
more that may already be following behind them? Without the
siren treasure to bribe my father's men away from him, I don't
like our odds.

Only a few hours later, another note arrives.

I see you.

I climb the rigging all the way up to the crow's nest. Even then, I have to squint to see the brown line on the horizon. There must be a good current back there, helping the fleet along. It sets my heart to pounding to see them so close.

I climb back down as quickly as possible.

"Go find me Radita," I say to Niridia.

My father must be working his men into the ground, rotating them at the sweeps. They'll be exhausted by the time they reach the Isla de Canta. But I don't think that's my father's current goal. He only needs to catch me. Then they can rest before continuing on.

When Niridia returns with Radita in tow, I can't get the words out fast enough.

"He's gaining on us. Now that he has us in his sights, he won't slow. What can we do to build speed?"

Radita's answer is immediate. "We can't do anything to the ship itself, but we could lighten her. The most effective way would be to throw the cannons overboard."

"We can't do that," Niridia says. "Then if he catches us again, we have no way to fight!"

I don't have solutions for anything. There's sense in lightening the load and sense in keeping the cannons. It's impossible to know which is the smarter choice right now.

"All right," I say. "We don't do anything yet. Roslyn!"

The lass isn't on duty, but I need to quickly change that.

"Yes, Captain?" she asks, strolling over from where she was chatting with a group of the girls.

"I need you up top. You report to me immediately if the ships in the distance get larger. Understand?"

"Aye." She scurries up.

"Search the ship, Radita," I say. "See if there's anything else we can toss over that will make a difference."

"There isn't any—"

"Just check, please!"

She shares a look with Niridia before going below.

"I'm not being unreasonable. Maybe she's overlooking something. He can't catch us, Niridia."

"We beat him once," she says, "we can do it again."

"He won't face us one-on-one this time. We can't take on twenty ships."

"That's true," she says. "But there's nothing you can do to help the situation yet. Focus on practicing with Riden. I'll oversee everything out here."

∞

I'd wanted to give Riden a break after what we accomplished yesterday. Being around me while I'm using my abilities isn't easy on him. But the need to figure things out has become more urgent than ever.

I sigh in relief when Riden doesn't give me any snark after I tell him we need to begin practicing again immediately.

He must be able to tell I'm on edge, though, because once we get to the brig he asks, "What's wrong?"

"We can see the fleet from the crow's nest. Father is pushing his men to the breaking point to catch us."

"Then we'd better be ready for him."

Under Sorinda's watch, we spend the rest of the day learning the extent of my control over the siren in me.

Riden tries leaving the room—with his ears covered, of course—to see if distance affects the response the siren has to him. It does. He needs to be in my line of sight, or the siren blocks out his shouts.

He tries calling to me more and more quietly, until he doesn't say anything at all, with the hopes that eventually just looking at him will be enough. But that doesn't keep the siren at bay.

It's his voice while he's in my sights.

Nothing less.

I'd so hoped that maybe with practice, I could learn to control the siren on my own.

But after three more days with the same results, I'm forced to give up that notion. Still, so long as Riden is near, I can replenish my abilities and regain my senses immediately.

The next time I face my father in battle, I will not have to worry about what I will do when my abilities run out. I can restock without fear of the siren taking over as long as I can hear Riden—until my strength fails or every one of my father's men is dead. Whichever happens first. Still, it is too easy for our enemies to cover their ears. It isn't enough.

This is only the first step. The real challenge will be staying myself while surrounded by ocean water.

I need to be in the sea and still be me.

The fleet disappears beyond the horizon, and I can't decide if it's better or worse not knowing where they are. Still, not being able to see them means we've gained more ground.

Perhaps that's why I delay taking the next step in learning the new control I can master over my abilities with Riden.

It's more than the fleet, I tell myself. *I can't push Riden too far too fast. He needs time to cope.*

It's a lie I tell myself. Riden actually appears to be getting more and more comfortable with the siren the longer he spends with her. And while, of course, I'm taking his feelings into consideration, the truth is—being in the water terrifies me. There's so much harm the siren can do. So many people she can hurt on this ship.

I'm absolutely petrified of being her and being at risk of losing myself to the sea forever.

But as the threat of dehydration looms ever closer over our heads, I'm running out of excuses.

Kearan thinks we should be upon the island any day now.

Out on the deck, he and Enwen hang off the railing, staring longingly at the flat expanse of water.

"It looks better than it tastes," I tell them.

"Why, oh why, does the sea contain salt?" Enwen asks.

"To drive us mad," Kearan says.

"Stop looking at it," I tell them. "Go distract yourselves."

As if they'd coordinated it ahead of time, the two turn around and slump to the deck simultaneously.

We might not survive to reach that island.

I head for the kitchens, seeking out Trianne. She's got that last water barrel under lock and key in one of the storage rooms. I trust my crew not to steal more than their share when it comes to gold. But water is an entirely different matter. The lack of it messes with a person's mind.

"How much is left?" I ask her.

She knows immediately what I mean. "If we continue at these portions? Five days."

Five.

"Start serving the rum with dinner in place of water," I tell her. Not only will it give us longer on the sea, but it'll help the crew sleep at night with thirsty bellies.

"That'll buy us an extra week, maybe. Stars be thanked, Kearan cut himself off. Else we'd be out by now."

"That's the truth."

I clap her on the shoulder before leaving the galley.

"They're back!"

The shout is quiet from down here, but I know it's Roslyn. She must mean the ships.

The fleet.

Is he playing with me? I wouldn't put it past my father to give his men a break long enough for me to feel safe just to speed them up again to throw me off.

Father likes games, and at this point, the only advantage I have over him is being able to restock my abilities without having to incarcerate myself and wait a night.

It's not enough.

I know this. I know what I need to do next.

My limbs shake just thinking about it, but I force myself to take the necessary steps. I locate Sorinda first and give her orders. Then I go to my rooms to change. Finally, I seek out Riden.

He is chatting with Wallov in the brig when I find him. They are probably too far below to have heard the shout, and when I start to catch the topic of their conversation, I decide not to interrupt right away.

"Caring after a child is hard work," Wallov says, "especially when they're too little to walk on their own. But I wouldn't trade Roslyn for all the gold in the world."

"Is it ever awkward being a father to a daughter?" Riden asks.

"It hasn't been yet, but I'm dreading the conversations we'll have when she gets a bit older."

"Fear not, Wallov," I say, alerting the two men to my presence. "There's a whole crew of women to help with that."

"Good," he says, the relief evident in his voice. "I was really hoping for that."

"Sorry to interrupt," I say, my voice taking on a more urgent tone, "but I need Riden."

Riden cocks his head to the side, and I hurry to add more to my statement.

"The fleet is back. It's time to take the next step."

The lighthearted expressions on their faces falter. Wallov hurries up top to be near his daughter while she does her job.

"Follow me," I say to Riden.

When he sees me go for the stairs, he asks, "Above? We won't be in the brig?"

"Not today."

He follows without any more questions, and I find myself thinking back on his conversation with Wallov, despite the looming threat the fleet presents.

"Are you planning on having children anytime soon?" I ask him once we're up top and headed for my quarters. Niridia gives me a calculated look, nodding in approval when she sees I'm with Riden. Her injured hand is held up by a sling around her neck.

"Not soon," he says, "but someday. I hadn't thought it possible with this life before. But here, on this ship, a child would be safe. Well, probably not quite as safe as on land, but safe enough with this crew around."

My mind is turning at this reveal. Riden fathering a child? I can't quite wrap my head around it, and my mind is having a harder time than usual with my father in our sights.

"Wouldn't you like to have a child someday?" he asks.

The question puts Roslyn and my father in the same space of thought in my head, and I shudder before finding a response. "I've honestly never thought about it."

"Never?"

"No. I already look after a whole crew. I don't see how a child would fit into the mix."

"I can picture a fiery-haired child running amok on this ship, locking her dolls in the brig when they misbehave."

I laugh.

"You can probably only have daughters, right? No sons?"

I suppose I hadn't really thought of that, either. "Probably. But would they be like me? Or would they be . . . human?" I almost said *normal*.

"Does it matter?" he asks.

Confusion tears through me. He begrudgingly allows himself to be in the siren's presence. Why wouldn't he worry that a child I bore would have a siren in her, too?

The lack of water is getting to his head. He's delusional.

Sorinda is already waiting for us in my bathing chamber.

Riden takes one look at the tub full of salt water. "Are you serious?"

"Very."

"What is the plan, exactly?"

"I get in the bath, go full siren, and you try to bring me back."

"You're not contained," he says.

"The bath is bolted to the floor. I can't move it to the brig."

He must sense how nervous I am, how much I really *don't* want to do this, because he says next, "It's fine. Get in the water."

I take off my boots and any other dangerous items. I stand only in a black blouse and leggings. I decided it best not to wear white since I knew I would be getting wet. In front of Riden.

I step into the tub, every muscle in my body tensing at the onslaught. The water is cool, causing bumps to prickle along my skin. My own mind turns traitorous, begging me to take in the water, aching for the power and surety and revitalization that come with it.

I know that as soon as I allow myself to sit down, the water will consume me, and I will be helpless to take it in. To be the siren is to never be afraid. To never hunger or thirst. Never doubt or worry. Never fear. It is an existence unlike any other. Carefree and wondrous. Sometimes I crave it, but I also know that with it comes the lack of all things human. Causes me to forget all the humans I love so dearly.

I don't want to forget, but I need the siren to beat my father. I'm sure of it in a way that I can't explain. If only I can merge the two halves of myself to achieve it.

I let myself sink into the water. My worry morphs into confidence. Weariness turns to strength. I lie down, letting power envelop me. I raise my arms to stretch, to swim, but they crash against metal.

What the—

This is a container. Not the sea. No, I can feel my precious ocean below me, separated from me by meters of wood.

Clawing my way downward isn't an option. I have to leave the water in order to reach my real home.

A voice calls to me from above. "Alosa, get out of the water."

The voice is male. The same male from before. The pretty one. The one I've still failed to turn into a corpse.

I raise my head out of the water, peer at him through eyes that see so much better under the sea.

"No human commands me!"

I wait for him to cower, to shrink away. But if anything, he holds himself taller.

"Part of you is human, too. Let it out."

I stand, my eyes landing on the exit. The human is between me and it. I raise my first finger, examining the pointed claw at the end. "I think I'll draw a line across your throat. You'd like that, wouldn't you?" My tongue curls around a sweet note, letting my will become this man's as well.

"Yes," he says eagerly, extending his neck toward me.

I could draw the prettiest red pictures all over you, I sing. I delight in deciding where to start. With that muscled torso? On his lean legs?

But being away from the sea is like having an uncomfortable itch; I need to hurry back to her.

I suppose I'll just have to take him along with me. I step out of the tub.

And hiss through my teeth as red hot pain slices into my arm.

There's another human in the room. A woman hidden from my sight until now. Her sword drips with my blood. I'll tear off the arm holding that sword.

But before I can move, a body presses against my back. One arm clamps around my waist, the other bars across my shoulders and chest. A chin rests against my shoulder, pressing a scruffy cheek next to mine.

"You will not harm those you love, Alosa," Riden says. "Not while I still breathe."

My legs lose their strength. I'd tumble to the floor if Riden weren't still holding me. Tears prick at my eyes, but do not fall. My stomach turns at the thought of what I almost did. To Riden. To Sorinda. To the rest of the crew.

I could have killed all of them.

"I'm me," I say quietly, trembling. The movement is shaking Riden, too. I absorb the water still clinging to my clothes, thinking perhaps I'm only cold.

But the shaking doesn't cease.

"We're done for now," I say to Sorinda. "You can go."

"I'll send for Mandsy," she says, nodding to the cut she gave me.

"No, I'll tend to it. I think I need to . . . to properly process."

She doesn't argue. I love that about Sorinda. She leaves silently. I don't even hear the door close behind her.

"You can go, too," I say to Riden, who still has himself tucked behind me.

"Not yet," he says, holding me as I wait for the shaking to subside. When it does, I say, "We are never doing that again."

He loosens his hold on me, letting one of his hands rub circles into my back. "Yes, we are."

I turn on him, breaking his hold on me completely. "How can you say that? You haven't liked any of this from the beginning. You only did it because you're too damn selfless for your own good."

"I care about this crew. So do you. That's why we have to try again. Until we get a handle on this, just as we have with restocking your abilities."

"I was overconfident. I thought it would be easier because we'd practiced so much beforehand. But this was different. I nearly killed you and Sorinda. Then I would have been loose on this ship. I don't even want to imagine the damage I could have done."

"But you didn't," he says, trying to reach for me.

"Why are you trying to touch me!" I scream at him, losing my composure. "I disgust you. My powers terrify you. You can't stand to be near me. You don't have to pretend."

Riden freezes in place. "Is that what you think?"

"It's what I know, Riden."

"And I suppose you know my mind better than I do?"

"It's fine, Riden. I can handle the truth."

He pulls a hand down his face, as though trying to erase the tension there. "I don't hate you or your abilities, Alosa. I only needed time to adjust to them. To get over everything that happened to me in the past."

I'm quiet for a moment. The horror of what I almost did still swirls inside me, like a storm waiting to be unleashed. There's just too much that I'm feeling right now. Too much for me to be silent.

"I can't get over the way you acted when I saved you," I say. "You made it seem like I sing to men for sheer enjoyment—as if they're toys for me to play with. You should know by now that the *only* time I use my voice is when I need to protect my crew. That includes you. When you fell in the sea, I didn't think, Riden. I didn't remember our deal. The only thing I could think about was the fact that you were in danger. I acted. I jumped."

My voice gains strength as I talk, as I fill the words with meaning, with emotion. The way humans do, not sirens.

"But even if I had stopped to remember," I continue, "I would have made the same choice. I couldn't help myself. When it comes to you, I have no control over my actions." Those are the same words he said to me after we escaped the cannibal island. I can see by his face that he remembers, too.

"I know that," he says. "I know that you never use your abilities for your own amusement. It's just not the way you are. In the moment, I couldn't see that. It was easier to believe you were manipulating me just like my father used to than to think you were saving me because you actually cared. I can't take back the way I acted after you saved me. But honestly, this"—he gestures to the salt water in the tub—"these moments where we work on controlling your abilities, they've helped me grow as much as you.

"You are perfect just the way you are," he continues, "and I wouldn't change a single thing about you."

I want to pull his face down to mine. Kiss him until I can't breathe. His eyes intensify, and I can tell he's thinking the same thing. It sends a searing heat all the way down to my toes.

Riden breathes in deeply. "You're doing it again, Alosa. You're furious at yourself this time. You feel guilty for what could have happened. And you're looking for a distraction."

So what! I want to snap. How does he read me so damn well? Why does he keep the siren at bay? What is it about this blasted man?

Before I can say anything, his eyes land on my arm.

Where Sorinda cut me.

"Can I help you with that?" he asks.

If he expects me to keep my hands to myself, then no. "I've got it. Would you tell Niridia to send someone in here to get the water out of my tub?"

"Of course," he says.

He leaves.

I head for my wardrobe and bandage my wound alone.

Chapter 17

I REQUIRE CONSTANT UPDATES on the fleet now. They're drawing closer and closer. It occupies my mind at all hours of the day. That and the havoc I almost unleashed on my own ship.

On top of that is the guilt I feel at my parched crew. It's so strong, I find myself taking my meals later than most, just so I don't have to watch them drain their meager rations.

I sit down to my dinner a few days later, the galley nearly empty. Kearan and Enwen are at a table together, Enwen doing all the talking, of course. Kearan slumps in his seat, the rationing affecting him more than the others. He's refused to drink rum with his dinner.

"What you need, Kearan, is to take your mind off things," Enwen says.

"How am I supposed to do that?"

"Want to hear a joke?"

"No."

"A pirate at sea has a peg leg, a hook for a hand, and an eye patch. One of his companions asks him how he lost his leg."

"Please stop," Kearan begs.

"He answers, 'A cannonball.' Then his companion asks how he lost his hand. He answers, 'A sword.'"

"Enwen, I will knock you unconscious," Kearan threatens, but I can tell he doesn't have the energy to carry it out.

"When the companion asks how he lost his eye, the man says, 'A spray of the sea.'"

Kearan stares at Enwen. "That doesn't even make any sense."

"It was his first day with the hook."

Kearan groans and leans his head down on the table.

I grin at the two of them, if only to mask the guilt building within my chest. I wish my abilities included extracting salt from water.

Across the galley, only one other duo is seated: Wallov and Roslyn. Roslyn upturns her cup over her mouth, trying to get the last drops. She sets the cup down, looks at her father, whispers something to him.

He hands her his own cup.

I stand so quickly the bench behind me tips over.

"Wallov," I say, perhaps too sharply, "don't."

Kearan and Enwen's bickering instantly quiets, their attention now drawn to the scene I'm making.

"She's so thirsty, Captain," Wallov says.

"We're all thirsty. But no one will die under the current rationing. If you start giving your shares to her, you *will* die. She won't thank you then."

I turn my attention to little Roslyn next. "You are never to accept his portions. Do you understand? It will be hard, and your throat and belly will hurt, but you will lose your papa if you take his water."

She swallows, never breaking eye contact with me. "I understand, Captain. He won't hear any complaints from me again."

Such conviction from someone so small. I believe her.

"We'll be upon that island soon," I say. "Then we can all drink our fill."

The two nod at me.

When I take my empty plate and cup up to Trianne, I tell her, "You watch those two."

"Aye, Captain."

I'm still thinking over the exchange when I get back up top. I'm forcing a father to watch his daughter wilt away in front of him.

Niridia rushes to me, pulling me from my thoughts. "We have a problem."

"What is it?"

"We can see them now."

My gaze turns toward the horizon behind us, where that brown line is darker than ever. From the crow's nest, one can see miles farther than on the deck. If I can see the fleet now with my naked eye—

"He's taunting us," I bite out. Keeping himself in our sights, now. He'll keep at it for days if he wants. Not drawing closer, just invoking fear.

It's what he excels at.

My suspicions about his brutal games are confirmed just a few days later. He's grown closer, but not by much.

Radita has brought me no new ideas for how we can make the ship lighter. It's the cannons or nothing at all.

I can count the days we have left before we're completely out of water on my fingers. The fleet is right there.

Half the crew is staring over the railing behind us, watching the fleet draw closer. And closer.

"Land ho!"

A few cheers float up on the air, but they're only half-hearted; the stamina of my crew is at an all-time low.

But we have a bigger problem.

We cannot stop with the king on our heels. If we do, he'll catch us for sure. It could take us hours trekking on the new island before we find water. Then more time still to haul it back to the ship.

Time is the very thing we don't have right now.

Kearan and I take turns looking through the telescope and examining the Allemos map. In the end, our findings are in agreement. It's the large island from the map. We're so close to the Isla de Canta. It's just past this island we're approaching now. And through the telescope we can make out a junglelike terrain. So green. So full of water.

My stomach drops at our salvation right ahead of us, our doom right behind us. We cannot have one without the other.

Those who were staring behind us at the fleet now turn their gazes toward the bow. Toward their hope.

"How many should go ashore, Captain?" Niridia asks.

So many hands go up into the air.

"You need me," Athella says.

"I will not be left behind," Deshel says defiantly.

"Please take me this time." That comes from little Roslyn.

So many hopeful faces, so many bodies desperate to go ashore and find water first.

"None," I croak.

So many eyes widen. So many thirsty mouths swallow. So many of them stare at me as though I've suddenly sprouted a tail.

"None?" Niridia asks. "Captain, I was speaking of the island. The very green island that's sure to have water."

"I know. I didn't misunderstand. We cannot stop."

"We're dying!" Deshel insists.

I point emphatically at the fleet behind us. "If we stop, they catch us. We're dead."

"If we don't stop, we die of thirst!"

Sorinda appears on the deck, where everyone can actually see her. "I'm with the captain. We should keep going."

Mandsy speaks up. "I've had too many bodies resting in the shade of the infirmary from heat exhaustion. Captain, we *have* to stop. We won't make it otherwise."

"Alosa—" Niridia starts.

"No, don't *Alosa* me. I said we're not stopping."

Kearan looks apologetically at Sorinda before saying,

"I don't know how much longer I can continue like this. I'm probably the biggest body on the ship and the most dehydrated. I don't know that I can get us to the Isla de Canta if I don't get more water soon."

"The captain gave her orders," Sorinda bites out. "We're not stopping."

Riden, I notice, is over at the side of the ship, saying nothing. Does he not have an opinion?

"But, Captain—" It's Roslyn again. "We're so thirsty."

"If we don't stop, we'll die of thirst," Niridia says. "I think that's a worse way to go than in the hands of the pirate king."

I can't handle this. Cannot handle seeing their distraught faces. Cannot handle not being able to protect them this time.

And I snap.

"That's because you've never suffered at his hands before!" I look around at all the bodies on the deck, watch the wind chafe at their dry skin. Watch their ragged breathing with open mouths. "You've seen him at a distance because I've kept all of you out of his clutches. But *I've been there*. I've been beaten until I blacked out. I've been starved until I wanted to eat the skin off my own bones. I've been chained up in that dungeon so dark and cold for months on end that I forgot the way the sun felt on my skin."

I take a steadying breath, trying to pull my mind back out of those dark times. "You must trust me when I say, it is *far worse* to die at the hands of that man. We. Don't. Stop."

They're silent now. No one has a response to that.

"If anyone tries to leave this ship, I will personally drag you back and lock you in the brig." And with that being said, I lock myself in my rooms.

I am not at all surprised when the knock comes later.

I debate for a minute whether or not I will let him in. I can't handle anyone arguing with me.

"Alosa, I'm not here to argue with you," Riden says.

So he can read my mind on top of keeping the siren at bay? Has he really come to know me so well?

I let him in.

Then I go back to leaning against the mountain of pillows on my bed, crossing my arms, and staring at the royal-red goose-feathered comforter.

"Don't hate yourself," he says, taking a seat on the edge of the bed. "This is out of your control."

"I know that. I hate that I can't save them, but I don't hate myself for it."

I can tell he picks up on my meaning immediately. "Why do you hate yourself right now, then?"

This little secret has become a burden of its own. I've pushed it from my mind ever since we ran low on water.

"Because I'm not thirsty."

He cocks a brow.

"Riden, the sea nourishes me. Every time I stock up on my abilities, it's like eating or drinking. I'm. Not. Thirsty. And my entire crew is suffering. And I just told them that we couldn't stop, when I'm not feeling what they're feeling. I'm selfish and horrible." I draw my knees up to my body, rest my crossed arms on top of them.

He puts a hand on my arm. "You are not selfish and horrible. You are what you are. There is no changing that. If anything, this is a good thing. It keeps you clearheaded, allows you to make the decisions necessary to keep the rest of us safe."

"Half of them don't believe me. They don't see the threat that my father is. They have no idea what he's capable of."

"They trust you; it's just harder when the pain of thirst is clouding their own minds."

"And what about you?"

He bends his head down so his eyes are level with mine. "I trust you, too. Alosa, if it were my own father behind us, soon to catch us, I would make the exact same choice you are making right now."

I take some comfort in that, in knowing I'm not the only one who would have made this decision.

"How did we turn out the way we did when such horrible men raised us?" I wonder aloud.

"Because we are not our fathers. We saw what evil looked like, and we knew we wanted to be different."

I stare at the hand on my arm, thinking over his words. I may not be my father, but that doesn't mean I always know the right choice to make.

And right now I'm terrified, desperate for someone to confide in. It can't be Niridia when she's at odds with me over this.

"Am I going to be forced to watch everyone I care about slowly fade away?" I say. "Will I be the only one left on this ship? The only one my father catches? It feels like my only choices are to be lost to the sea or to be lost to him. I'm not sure which is worse."

"Neither of those is going to happen." He says it with such confidence, like the cocky bastard I've always taken him for.

"And how's that?"

"You're going to master yourself underwater."

I scoff. "So I can save myself?"

"No, so you can save all of us."

I shake my head. "It won't happen. The siren can't be tamed when she's in her natural habitat. I almost slit your throat last time. I don't think you realize how close you were to death."

"And I don't want you to be at risk of losing yourself. What if you fall in the water after the *Ava-lee* takes her next hit? Just like that you'd be lost to us. Unable to save anyone. Isn't it worth it to try again?"

"Not if it means I'll kill the entire crew."

"Alosa, we're already surrounded by death on all sides. We need to take this risk."

My mind is so exhausted. All those disappointed faces . . .

"You said you didn't come here to argue with me. I want to be alone now."

He takes his arm back, watching me carefully. "You're running out of options. And we're running out of time."

The next day, the entire crew watches as the island approaches.

And we pass it by.

Niridia can barely stand to talk to me or dole out my orders she's so furious. Mandsy is in the infirmary with more exhausted patients. Sorinda stays by my side, in the shade, but close nonetheless. A physical support.

It's too much to hope for rain. There's not a cloud in the sky. Water won't be coming that way.

We have days left. Only days.

Niridia approaches me another day later, when the island is at our backs near the fleet.

"Niridia—"

"Quiet," she snaps.

I level her with a warning glare.

"No, Alosa," she says. "I'm going to talk. I seem to be the only voice of reason on this ship these days. Riden tells me you're refusing to practice with your abilities underwater."

"Of course I'm refusing! I nearly killed everyone last time."

She grabs me roughly by the arm and drags me toward the stern. The crew watches, and I try to decide how I can put her in her place without lowering morale further. The crew can't see its first mate and captain at odds.

But she releases me before I can think of anything to say or do.

She points a finger in front of us. "Fleet! Right there! We're out of options!"

I take a step back from her.

"Our choices are death, death, or death," she says. "Go make yourself useful! We need the siren! At worst, she gives all the women a quick death. At best, you use your newfound control to find us a way out of this mess. You've made stopping for water impossible now. This is our only choice."

I growl. "Damn, Riden."

"He is the only thing that has kept us alive so far. I owe him my life thanks to what he does to the siren. Now we need her again."

With everyone looking on, I realize I have no choice. I'm going to have to risk killing them all and hating myself afterward. I have to risk it for them.

∝

"You ratted me out," I say to Riden when I find him belowdecks.

"You did the same to me last time."

"I don't see how the two of you expect different results from last time! Bad things are going to happen!"

I feel myself close to hysterics. There is no happy ending I see for any of us.

"I've already thought of that," he says.

I look sharply at him.

"If you hadn't kicked me out of your room last night, I would have had time to explain."

I want to snap at him, but I clamp my mouth shut, ready to listen.

"I'll stay close to you the whole time," he says. "Last time, all I had to do was touch you, put my face next to yours, and you returned to yourself. This time, I'll keep you close while you submerge. You won't hurt anyone. And you yourself won't get hurt."

It's—

A good idea.

The fear is still there. I'm absolutely terrified that I will hurt someone. But we are also desperate. And Riden seems so sure that he can help me this time.

And I trust him.

That realization is such a shock, and I find myself giving in.

Sorinda and Mandsy fill the tub. I prepare myself, both mentally and physically. No metal. No laces. No pins or hair ornaments. Breathe in. Breathe out. Try not to kill anyone.

Mandsy stays after the tub is full to help keep me in line should things go south. This time I decide two girls prepared to act if something should go wrong are better than one. I worry that Mandsy won't be brutal enough to injure me (or more) if need be. I know I can count on Sorinda to do what needs done, but anyone else might hesitate. And a moment's hesitation is all I need to do some serious damage. The next time, the siren may not be in a playful mood. Maybe she'll go for the kill right away.

I climb into the tub, my bare toes curling from the promise of power caressing them.

I nearly jump when Riden climbs in with me.

I know this was the plan, but what if it doesn't work? What if I drown him? Or snap his neck?

I'm edgy, uncomfortable, drained from all the external pressures. He must sense this.

"Relax," he says.

"You relax," I snap. "You're the one who is about to die."

He shakes his head. "Come here." Before I can listen, he pulls me to him in an embrace. "Just stay right next to me. Now sit."

It's awkward trying to do it with him clinging to me, but we manage. Each inch we descend, the water becomes more and more irresistible. I'm so anxious, so tired of everything—the water promises relief from all of it.

When it reaches my waist, I cannot help it anymore.

I let it in.

And with Riden's face right next to mine, the siren doesn't even surface. She stays far away, just where I want her. I let my head sink under the water, and Riden, as though sensing that it's me the whole time, lets me go.

After maybe a minute of resting on the tub's base, I return to the surface, step from the tub, pull the water into myself, and smile.

"Again."

After a few more tries with the same results, Mandsy and Sorinda leave the room. I don't need them. Riden is the key.

I dry myself off again after the fifth time and toss Riden a towel. He tousles his hair with it, wrings his clothes out over the tub.

"All this time," I say as I lace back on a corset, "I just needed you to come along and keep me human."

"Why do you think that is?"

I don't know yet. Maybe I'm not ready to know yet. Not with danger looming so close.

Danger so close.

The fleet is close.

The fleet will have water.

"Riden, I have an idea."

Chapter 18

I TALK WITH NIRIDIA and Riden in private. "I don't want to get anyone's hopes up in case this doesn't work."

"The crew needs hope right now," Niridia says. "How about if I tell them after you've gone?"

She knows that I don't want to face them. Not after I took away their chance at water. I don't want to offer a new one. How much will they hate me if it doesn't work?

"All right," I answer. Then I turn to Riden. "Are you comfortable with this?"

"I'm willing to try if you are," he says.

"Then let's be off."

The two of us approach the gap in the railing, the one used

for climbing down to board the rowboats. We step up to the edge, peer down into that blue abyss. Probably thousands of feet deep. It is such a scary mystery, the ocean.

I look at Riden nervously.

"It'll be the same as in the tub," he says.

"It had better be."

Behind us, the crew must be watching, curious as to what we're up to.

"This is your last chance to—" I start.

He wraps his arms around me, and we fall.

Warm salt water encompasses us after the splash. Riden has both arms and legs wrapped round me tightly, the side of his face pressed firmly against my own.

The siren is nowhere to be found. Not with him here.

The most profound sigh of relief escapes my lips as I kick us both to the surface. The power of the ocean floods me, soothing my guilt, my fears. They're still there, in the back of my mind to pull out and process should I wish to. But right now those things will not be helpful.

I feel Riden's breathing against my ear. It tickles my wet skin. His arms and legs grasp me so tightly, as though he's afraid I might leave—be lost forever.

"Riden, I'll swim more easily if you loosen up."

He pulls back then, stares at my face. "It's you."

"It's me."

We just stare at each other, water dripping down our faces, holding on to each other.

Every time I've been in the water with him, danger was riding on our heels. But now, there's no immediate threat, even if we have a job to do.

So I take just a moment to enjoy this. Feeling empowered by the ocean. Having Riden pressed so close to me, trusting me to keep him afloat, to not hurt him.

Swimming is as easy as walking for me. And Riden's weight does very little to slow me down. I could stay with him like this forever.

Whispers float down to us from above. I look to see most of the crew staring over the lip of the ship at us.

"We'll be back," I say.

Then I start to swim.

I don't know how fast I can swim. I've never had the opportunity to figure it out. But I know I am faster than a ship. Much faster. And when I am in the water, with all its power rushing to me, I won't tire. I can maintain this speed forever if I need to.

The water is warm—the ship has taken us into a tropical climate. A good thing, too, otherwise Riden would freeze.

He is silent as I swim. I'm careful to keep his head above the water as my arms and legs make silent strokes through the sea. It's almost nightfall, and I hope to reach the ships just as darkness takes over. We cannot risk them spotting us in the water, and I cannot swim under it when I have Riden with me.

When the sky finally darkens completely, we are upon the fleet. The lookouts won't be able to spot us, not that they'd know to look for us anyway.

I select one of the smaller ships, a vessel along the edges of the fleet formation. Fewer chances for us to be seen, this way. And should we get caught, there will be a smaller crew for us to battle.

The *Serpent* is the perfect choice. Lanterns are lit on its decks, but there is little movement. The majority of the crew must be below, hopefully already asleep.

I find a handhold on the ship, a line tied down along the side. Riden reaches an arm up and begins climbing first, water running down his body, trickling into my eyes as I follow after him.

He stops at one of the gun ports and pokes his head inside. After a few breaths, he hauls himself through, and I follow after.

The gun deck is empty, but not quiet. We can hear voices below us, trickling up from the open stairway at the opposite end of the ship.

The water from my clothes pools onto the floor. I whisper a song to expel some of the power before absorbing the water and drying myself.

Riden huffs out a breath before pointing to himself.

We won't make it far with his boots squeaking or the sound of water dripping.

Without saying a word, I press him back against the empty wall between two cannons, and cover his body with mine. More words float on the air from my mouth, much too quiet to be heard by anyone other than Riden. Then I start to draw the water from him.

He lets out a little gasp as he starts to dry. Of fear or awe or something else entirely, I'm not sure. My head is over his shoulder, my hands roaming his hair, his back, drawing every last drop into me.

"My backside is still wet," he teases.

"Deal with it."

I smack his shoulder and glimpse his amused face before turning away. I realize now that I'd been touching, well, *a lot* of him. Something I haven't done since the last time we kissed.

A time that seems forever ago.

But there's no time for those kinds of thoughts. Thirsty crew. I have a thirsty crew.

The galley is one deck above us. We take the stairs carefully, watching the lower decks to make sure no one looks up. I can see two heads of hair from up here. A couple of men sit on the stairs, laughing loudly at some joke a person I can't see said.

We veer around tables and benches to reach the storage rooms in the back. Drying meats hang from the ceiling in the kitchen. The stove is full of nothing but soot and ash. The dishes from their dinner are already clean and put away.

A locked door provides us little trouble. I didn't bring my lockpicks with me, but I use a knife to pull apart the hinges.

A light scraping noise is all the sound I make. We freeze, but no one comes running. Not with all of the chatter below to mask what we're doing.

Inside, we find an assortment of foods: breads, pickled vegetables, flour, sugar, and other cooking ingredients.

And in the back: water barrels.

Riden cracks one open, sticks his whole head in, and drinks.

"Careful, you'll make yourself sick," I say.

"I don't care," he says and dips his head in again.

When he's done, we carry the barrels (one at a time, the two of us using our combined strength) down the stairs, back to the gun deck. From there, we tie them together with rope found on the ship. Then we toss them out the gun ports.

Riden starts to climb through the hole, but I halt him.

"Just a moment."

I open the storage rooms off the gun deck, these ones unlocked, smiling when I find what I'm looking for.

I sling an ax through the belt around my corset.

Riden eyes it, but doesn't ask any questions before holding me again as we fall back into the water. When we surface, we're both smiling at our success.

"Can you wait here for a moment?" I ask him.

"Where are you going?"

"To slow down the fleet."

"With an ax?"

I grin wider before dunking my head below the surface. I swim far below the ships, sizing up the hulls, until I find the largest of them at the head of the fleet.

And just like I did with the harpoon during the sea battle, I swim like a shot for the *Dragon's Skull*, the ax held out in front of me with two hands, angled so the honed blade will hit first. It connects with the rudder, sending a sharp reverberation up my arms. The whole ship must jerk at the contact. I wonder what my father will make of it.

I brace my feet on the base of the ship, tugging at the break until the rudder comes clean off. With my work done, I return for Riden and the barrels.

The swim back is the best swim of my life.

I'm me, fully in control. I'm towing the water that will save my crew's lives right behind me. Four glorious barrels' worth. And the best part is, if we need more, Riden and I can make the trip again to another ship.

It's nearly dawn when we catch back up to the *Ava-lee*.

"Toss down a hook and line!" I shout.

The call is obeyed, and I place the hook around a section of rope looping the barrels together.

"Tug!"

They pull the barrels from the water. I hear them bounce onto the deck. Another line is thrown down to help Riden and me up.

As we step onto the deck, we're met with the sounds of slurping, swallowing, laughing. *Laughing.*

They take turns, sharing freely, passing cups around.

And when they're done, they have me surrounded. Hugging me, clapping me on the back, murmuring *sorry*s and *thank you*s.

"I couldn't have done it without Riden," I say, and then they leave me to surround him.

Niridia catches my eye, and I stride over to her. She scratches at the bandage over her left hand.

"Captain, I apologize," she says. "I shouldn't have argued with you in front of the crew. I shouldn't have spoken so directly, I—"

"Don't you go calling me 'captain.' Not right now," I say, hugging her.

She lifts her head from my shoulder, looking behind us. "The fleet is gone."

I grin. "That's because I took out the *Dragon Skull*'s rudder before Riden and I left."

"Of course you did."

I would love to stay and celebrate with the rest of them, but I've been up all night. "I'm going to sleep. Keep things running out here?"

"Of course."

∞

I hear them out on the deck, their laughter and singing. Someone else must pull out Haeli's lute and strike up a song. It makes my heart warm to think of how they're honoring her. By keeping what she loved most alive.

I'm so tired, still fully dressed in my corset and boots. I take off the latter and pad over to my wardrobe.

Knocking.

I hope Niridia doesn't have bad news for me.

"Come in," I say, searching for some nightclothes.

I stop when I see not Niridia, but Riden enter my bedroom.

"Aren't you tired?" I ask him. I've had the sea nourish me for hours today, so if I'm sleepy, he must be exhausted.

"I don't think I could sleep right now," he says.

"Why not?" I step away from the wardrobe, face him.

"I can't stop thinking about what we've been doing together.

All the practicing. Can't stop wondering why it's me that keeps you human."

My heart pounds heavier in my chest, but I shrug. "One of life's mysteries," I say.

I turn my attention back to the clothing in front of me, but his footsteps grow closer.

He stops before me, putting himself between me and the view of my clothes. Suddenly, any desire for sleep vanishes.

"I think you have an idea," he says. "Why won't you share it with me?"

"I don't know why," I whisper.

But it's a lie. Such a lie.

"Why me?" he whispers back, so gently. So invitingly.

Unbidden, the truth rises to my mind.

Because you love me, I realize, but don't say aloud. That's why. That special relationship—the one more powerful than anything else. The most *human* thing there is. That's what does it.

"Alosa?" he prompts.

"I have a—different relationship with you than I do anyone else."

"Different," he repeats, amused. "Different how?"

"You know."

"I want to hear you say it."

Maybe it's the thrill of being able to stay myself while under the water. Maybe it's the realization of why he is able to keep me human. Or the realization that whether or not I call it what it is, that relationship between us is there. I only need to choose whether or not I want it.

He's been so open with me. If I want to take this jump with him, it's my turn.

"I think you love me," I say.

"I do."

"And I think I love you."

"You think?"

"I know."

He steps even closer to me. One hand slides up my arm from my wrist to my shoulder. He grabs a strand of my hair and twirls it around one of his fingers before bringing it up to his lips.

"What are you thinking about right now?" he asks.

"Just you." Not anything that's worrying me or frustrating me. There is only Riden.

He slides his hand to the back of my head to bring my lips to his. He kisses me softly, languorously, savoring every time our lips connect. I melt under that pressure, but manage to yank at his still damp shirt. He helps me take it off. I run my hands over his smooth chest. A torso as perfect as Riden's should never be covered.

His lips slide down to my throat, and I tilt my head back. He supports me with his hands at the small of my back.

"And what about that girly fellow?" he asks.

"Hmm?"

"Your lover."

"Oh, I lied about that. I can't stand Tylon."

He pulls away just enough to look me in the eye. "Why would you do that?"

"You were being cruel, and I wanted to make you jealous."

"I think we could argue about who was being more cruel at the time."

I smile and bring my lips to his shoulder. "Are you saying it worked?"

Instead of answering, he picks me up with a hand under each thigh and braces me against the wall. His lips are on mine again, hard and unrelenting this time. I connect my legs behind his back. My arms tighten around his neck.

I can barely breathe, and I don't care one bit. Air isn't what I need to live. It's him. It's always been him. Why did it take me so long to realize?

Riden sets me back on my feet so he can roam my body with his hands. They slide up my sides, into my hair, down my back.

This is usually the part where I talk myself out of what I'm doing. Not this time. There is no reason not to kiss Riden. There is no reason not to let him in. No reason not to trust him. He's what I want.

I spin him around, planting him against the wall. I nip at his lips, trace them with my tongue, listen to his breathing hitch and feel his muscles tighten.

Without breaking the kiss, I start to pull him backward with me, toward my bed. I must have been moving too slowly, though, because he picks me up again and carries me the rest of the way.

He sets me down, lays himself on top of me, but the pressure of his lips never softens, never stills, and I don't want it to.

I realize my corset is loosening. His fingers, so adept and

featherlight, pull at the strings, slipping them from one hole after the next. When he finally gets it open, he splays his fingers across my stomach, which is now covered only by a thin blouse.

His lips leave mine. I'm about to protest when I feel them where his hands once were. They inch lower, and I feel my blouse slowly rise. I shut my eyes, awash in sensation.

Riden pauses with his lips at my navel.

And he sits up.

"What are you doing?" I ask. "Get back here."

He doesn't look at me. Instead he starts for the door.

"Riden—"

That's when I hear it.

Singing.

Oh hell.

Chapter 19

I GRAB RIDEN BY the shoulder and pin his face against the nearest wall in the room.

"Riden, come out of it."

He strains against me, swings an arm, pushes off the wall with his feet.

"Damn it, Riden. Stop!"

He jerks his head backward, connects with my nose. Blood runs down into my mouth. I wipe it off my face with my arm.

All right, that does it.

I grab the nearest sturdy object within reach, a pretty glass jar from the island of Naula that holds my hairpins.

What a shame, I think as I bring it down on his head.

It shatters, and he goes limp. I rummage through my things until I find the wax I brought for the men. I shove some into Riden's ears before hurrying outside.

Sorinda has Kearan flat on his back, her sword pommel ready to strike again if the first hit didn't do the trick.

"Here," I say, tossing her the wax.

Mandsy and Niridia have Enwen's arms pinned behind his back as he squirms against the ground. I rush over to help them get his ears covered. Deros is already unconscious on the ground near them, and Niridia approaches him next with a ball of wax.

Then that leaves—

"Papa! Come back here."

Wallov.

I dash down the stairs, collide with Wallov in his rush to get above deck. The two of us roll head over heels all the way down the steps.

I groan as I rub my head, but Wallov is already back on his feet, ignoring the pain as he tries for the stairs again.

Roslyn races ahead of me and launches herself at Wallov, wrapping her tiny arms around his legs. She gets her legs around him, too, and squeezes with all her might.

It sends him to the ground again, which gives me the time I need to reach them. I dig a knee into his back, force the wax into his ears.

He stills.

"It's okay, Roslyn," I say. "You can let go now."

She does and lets out a long breath. "That was close."

"You did great," I tell her.

Wallov stands, rubs at his side, which he must have hit on our tumble down the stairs.

I point to my own ears. He reaches for his, feels the wax. Realization shows in his eyes. Roslyn puts an arm around him. He nods to me.

I leave the two of them, returning up top.

"How are they doing?" I ask Niridia.

"Enwen's back to himself. Riden, Kearan, and Deros are passed out cold. We tied them to the mast, lest they try to unplug their ears first thing upon waking. Sorinda is keeping an eye on them."

"Good. The island isn't even in view yet," I say.

"I know. Perhaps the sirens are taking a swim away from its shores?"

"Or their song reaches farther than we realized."

Niridia's eyes widen. "You really think so?"

"No way to know."

"It's probably too much to hope that the king will be caught unawares like we were."

I snort. "He'll probably send a ship far ahead of his to test out the waters first."

Niridia grimaces.

My father's cruelty really knows no bounds.

"I want to know the second the island comes into view," I say.

"Aye."

The singing comes and goes as we sail, but we dare not allow the men to uncover their ears. Not for an instant.

It's a full week before the Isla de Canta comes into view. A full week without talking to our men. A full week without being able to talk to Riden.

I observe the isle now through my telescope. Trees cover the place, making it impossible to see anything else. Another jungle like the island we passed by in our search for water.

On a piece of parchment, I write, *See if you can find somewhere out of sight to drop anchor.*

Kearan reads it and nods.

Riden stands by my side on the aftercastle. He doesn't speak; he couldn't hear my response if he tried. But his presence is a comfort. The closer we approach the island, the louder the singing becomes.

The singing that interrupted me and Riden.

I suppose I could have pulled him back to bed with me when he came to. He certainly doesn't need his ears for it, but I don't want to take that step with him when he doesn't have use of all of his senses. Not for the first time.

I go warm just thinking about it, and I quickly turn my thoughts back to the island ahead.

But that only heightens my anxiety.

Is my mother nearby? I equally dread and relish the idea of speaking to her again. I want to ask her—no, demand of her why she left me. I want to know what's become of her. Is she still fragile and weak? Does she remember our meeting at the keep at all? Or is she now a senseless monster with nothing but a need to kill men?

No one dares to speak as we sail. Several of the girls lean over the ship's edge, peering into the water, looking for sightings of sirens.

Despite the fact that they must know we're here, they're staying out of sight.

Kearan finds the perfect spot to drop anchor.

The beach curves, making a little nook blocked by trees and other greenery. It's far enough from the main shore for comfort's sake and gives us some shelter from anyone heading this way. It also blocks our view of the sea, but I'm not worried now. My trick with the rudder should have had the fleet stopped for hours. Maybe even a full day.

"Shall I give the order to go ashore?" Niridia asks.

"No. We're not going ashore. Not yet, anyway." Not when the last island we stopped at housed such horrors. "I want to take a look below the surface first."

She raises a brow. "You're going into the sea alone?"

"If this legendary treasure has been hoarded by sirens, it's probably better accessed by the sea. Besides, we need to know what we're up against. It's better that I go alone. I'm less likely to be noticed." Not to mention it's impossible for anyone else to follow.

"Keep a sharp eye out," I say. "One on the sea and one on the island. Under no circumstances is anyone to go ashore."

I lighten my load, removing my boots and corset. I don't

want to be weighed down, and I have no use for them where I'm going. I strap a knife to my ankle, but otherwise, I'm going unarmed. A sword and pistol have no use below water.

I grab Riden's hand and pull him over to the ship's edge with me. I jerk my neck toward the ocean, indicating what I want.

He shakes his head fiercely. He knows that this is what we've been practicing for, but he also knows there are sirens in the water right now.

I understand his hesitation, but I gesture around the ship. *I need to do this to keep everyone safe.*

His eyes are still hard, but he steps over the railing with me, giving in.

Trusting me.

He wraps his arms around me, and the two of us jump.

I hit the water; all that power rushes in, and—

I'm still me.

I can do anything right now.

I could sing forever. My limbs are strengthened. I can move faster underwater than I can on land. I was already the perfect killing device as a pirate.

But now—

It's hard to remind myself I'm not invincible when I feel the opposite.

I search the ocean's depths: no sirens in sight, though their singing has become even louder now that I'm underwater.

I swim with Riden up to the ocean's surface. A rope is thrown down. He gives me a parting glance as he grabs it and mouths two words.

Be safe.

I watch him until he disappears back over the ship's edge. I won't be able to go on until I know he's safe. Then I dive back down.

The water has never been more beautiful. So clear and clean, untouched by humans. The light filters through the water, spots dancing on the sandy bottom. A school of fish with bright blue and red stripes swims by. A turtle sets its fins on a large rock resting on the ocean's bottom. A young shark barely bigger than my arm meanders around.

I swim farther out to sea, then follow the shoreline around the island, following the singing. More and more critters surface. Crabs skitter sideways across the sand. A jellyfish flows with the waves moving toward the shore. Shells, both broken and whole, turn over the sand as they're pushed toward the island.

But no sirens, not yet.

At first I'm perplexed by the lack of sentries, of people on lookout. Wouldn't they wish to be alerted to any threats?

But then I realize, there is no threat to them when they're under the water's surface. Nothing can harm them. No man can survive under the water. What need have sirens to watch for approaching ships?

But my thoughts fall away as I focus on the singing.

Voices intertwine in melodies so complex, no mortal could write them down on paper. They pull me in as the tide does the water. Like calling to like. I have sung alone all my life. And always with a purpose. Singing was never something I did for enjoyment alone, especially when those around me feared I was enchanting them. Not my crew, of course, but my father's men.

I follow the sound, savoring every note. But there is a chord missing. A place in the melody that needs to be filled. Before I consciously make the decision, my voice is filling the gap, throwing out a line of notes that fit perfectly with the voices of the others.

My muscles hum at the synchronization. The music grows louder as I approach, rounding a coral reef.

And there they are. Hundreds of them, but I can hardly process it until my throat lets out the last note, holding it, letting it fill the space around me.

Like a flame doused in water, the music cuts off. Heads turn in my direction, long, luscious hair swirling at the movement. Creamy brown. Sun-darted yellow. Inky black.

And then, in the center, one rises above the rest with hair the color of flame.

At last, you've come home, Mother says.

∝

Were I above the water, I might find it strange that they wear no clothing. But it makes perfect sense down here. The water does not chill us. There is no harsh weather or extreme temperatures to be shielded from. There is no one to hide their nakedness from.

The older sirens, my mother included, have shells strung through their hair like beads. My mother, I notice, has the most. The mature sirens don't have lines near their eyes or any other indications of age, but there is something about them that marks them as older. Something that I can sense rather than see.

Siren children—I'd never even considered their existence before—stay near the ocean's bottom. They skip through the sand, roll in it, reminding me of human children playing in mud puddles. One sees me and immediately swims for the siren I assume is her mother. They both have the same golden locks.

My mother is so different from when I beheld her on land. Where before she was sunken, weak, barely able to stand, now her muscles are toned, her skin smooth and unblemished. She is a creature of power and beauty that is unlike the rest. Their queen.

When she sees my eyes return to hers, she says, *There was always a piece missing. We are complete now that you're here to fill it.*

She swims past the others, using both arms and legs to propel herself toward me. When she's there, right in front of me, she extends her arms out to me. *What took you so long? I missed you terribly.*

I want to be wary of her. Of all of them. Sirens are beasts. They're mindless monsters that care for nothing and no one but themselves.

But I can't.

Not after what I felt while singing. There was always a place for me here. My mother left an opening in the song just for me, hoping—no, desperate—for me to come and fill it.

I don't understand, I tell her. *You left me. You abandoned me after I freed you. Why?*

Her brows lift in a perfect arch. *I had to get back to my sisters. I am their queen. They needed me. You were told to follow. Why did you not listen?*

Because I couldn't. I become something else when I am in the water. I'm not myself. I've only recently found a way to control it.

There is a rippling in the water, as I feel those around us shifting uncomfortably.

My mother closes her eyes, taking in my words, thinking through them. *Of course*, she says. *You are land-born. Your natures fight together for dominance. One stronger on land, one under the sea. But it would seem the human in you has won.*

Almost imperceptibly, every siren in the water drifts back an inch. All save my mother.

Is that a bad thing? I ask.

Not to me, she says softly, so only I can hear.

And everyone else? I ask just as quietly.

It may take them longer to warm up. But never mind that for now. I want to show you something.

This time, instead of swimming ahead without me, she takes my hand. I had every intention of following, but I enjoy the contact. I know what it means. This time, she is not giving me a chance to become separated from her.

We swim around the group of sirens, who start chatting among themselves.

What is that covering her skin?

She smells like a human.

Why does the queen welcome her?

She's an outsider.

My mother halts, turns, and sings one booming note all in the same movement.

Enough! the song commands. Every mouth closes, as though forced shut with a hand at the top of their heads and under their chins.

With my hand still in hers, she pulls me closer to land.

Do the sirens have to obey your song? I ask.

Yes, but it's not the same as when we sing to men. I am their queen. My voice moves the charm.

The charm?

The entirety of our people together is called a charm. I say where we swim, what we do, and the charm follows. It is in our nature. It's different from the magic that compels men.

Like a queen bee commanding her swarm.

It doesn't work on me, though, I say, knowing this somehow. She can't command me.

No. It is in you to become a queen. You are my daughter. You are meant to rule when my soul passes.

That halts me in place. Rule the sirens? My mind has always been set on ruling the sea. I have a crew to care for and command. I can't take over the charm.

But I shake the thought from my head and continue to swim after her. It's not something that needs addressing now.

I know it's a lot to take in. You'll fit in and understand. Just wait until you see!

The ocean bed grows rocky as we approach a new side of the shore. A series of rocks opens into an underground cave. Mother swims through, holding my hand the entire way. The path grows darker, but we can still see. Urchins and starfish cling to the rocks. Barnacles open as the current moves through the cave. But the current is no deterrent for Mother and me. We push right on through it.

Eventually, the cave widens into a cavern. It's very deep, the bottom some fifty feet below. And resting atop it . . .

So much gold and silver.

In coins, jewelry, goblets, and dishes. Encasing precious stones and gems.

I could purchase the entire world five times over with the amount contained in here.

My mother swims down to it, picks up a handful of coins, lets them slide through her fingers.

It's been in the family for generations, Mother says, *but we've all added to it.* She finds a silver ring with a diamond in the center. She strokes her finger across it. *I took this off a sailor who fell overboard during a storm. The sea swallowed his cries as I pried it from his pocket. I think he was saving it for a sweetheart back home.*

And this, she continues, pulling up a gold plate and fork, *fell off a vessel near your Seventeen Isles. As soon as we knew there was treasure aboard, we sang to the rest of the men, demanding they throw everything valuable overboard. When they were done, we had them toss themselves in afterward. So we could enjoy them.*

I keep my face carefully neutral, but she asks, *Does that trouble you?*

What she's revealed is disturbing. It's wrong by my code of ethics. By my human nature. But I can also see it from the point of the siren in me. It's natural. The way of sirens. Would one blame a tiger for hunting a human as its prey?

I have killed many men, I say.

But do you enjoy them first?

No, I only enjoy *the men I like. Not the ones I intend to kill.*

She turns back toward the treasure. *He took you from me. Someday, I will add his gold to this pile, and I will think with pleasure on how he died.*

I hope that time comes soon, I say. *I hate that he kept us apart. But I like being who I am. My human side may disgust you, but I wouldn't have it any other way.*

But just look *at you,* she says. Her hand goes to my sleeve, pulls it up to reveal all the scars there. *You must be covered in these. He did this to you, didn't he?*

It was part of my training.

She lets out a sound so inhuman, I don't even have the words to describe it. *You were meant to be with me, not to suffer! You were meant to swim with the charm, add memories to this pile of gold. To hunt for colorful shells, dance in the currents. To observe the sea life, to sing with your family, to explore every hidden crevice the ocean possesses. Our existence is a full and happy one. You were not meant to be beaten!*

She composes herself, pulls me toward her in another embrace. *My dear girl, he will not harm you again. Stay with me, and I will protect you.*

As much as I want to believe her, to let her, even, I know I cannot. *I cannot. I have those I must protect.*

Your crew.

Yes.

A pause. *You're not here for me at all. You're here for the treasure.*

I want to say no, but I don't think she would believe me. *I thought you abandoned me. I thought you used me so I would free you, faked your concern for me. After I freed you, the pirate king came after me. He's hunting me. He can't be too far behind my ship. I thought if I could get my hands on the treasure, I could bribe his men away from him, set myself up as the pirate queen. I came here to survive. Not because I wanted to steal from you. Although, when I thought you used me, stealing from you didn't seem like such a bad thing.*

Her face softens at my words. *I do not have concern for you. I love you, Alosa-lina.* The way she sings the last part of my name, it fills the room with truth, with power. It's impossible for me to doubt. *Mere concern is nothing compared to what I feel for my own flesh and blood. You are mine. Mine to protect and care for. I already know you are fierce and powerful, and I cannot wait to get to know you better.*

My limbs tremble as she holds me, knowing every word she speaks is true.

But first, she says, *you must make yourself and your friends safe. Take as much gold as you need from here. Go set up your regime. I will wait for you.*

My relief sags through me. *Thank you.*

The charm will not harm you nor your crew.

Even the men? I ask.

Even them. Now go. Bring your ship to this position. The charm will help you carry the gold that isn't claimed by living sirens.

It's almost too good to be true, but I cannot doubt her words. Not the way she speaks them.

To go from such hate and disgust toward my mother, to suddenly being filled with love and understanding. It nearly undoes me. I cannot believe all that has happened.

Yet there is still so much to do.

I will come back after I and my crew are safe. I promise, I tell her. *Good. Now go. The sooner you leave, the sooner you can return.*

I wish there were more time. My mother is no mindless beast. She is a siren, true to her nature, but that does not make her a monster. She is deadly and ruthless, but so am I. A new future opens up before me. One in which I know my mother. I visit her. We are different, and I can never abandon my human nature, but there is something for us. Where before there was nothing, now there is hope.

And my fury toward my father burns only brighter for his keeping her from me. But beneath that fury, there is still fear. He's right behind us, could come upon us at any moment. My ship has kept a lead, but he has those sweep oars. For all I know he's worked his men half to death to catch up.

I swim back for my ship. For the *Ava-lee*. I suppose there is no need to rename her after all.

Niridia's left a rope for me. It hangs down into the water. I grab it and effortlessly hoist myself onto the ship, taking in the water as I go.

When I reach the deck, I find it empty.

My heart plummets. I told them not to go ashore. Made that perfectly clear. And I told them to keep watch. The ship is *never* unattended. Something is very wrong.

The railing is chipped and broken in places on the port side. Grappling hooks? I search the water on that side, opposite from the way I came. Wood scraps float on the water's surface. Blown-apart rowboats? Did something come aboard from the island and run off with my entire crew? I didn't even think to ask my mother what lived on this island in all the emotions of seeing her again.

I don't have any weapons except my dagger. I go to my rooms first.

He's waiting for me there.

"Alosa."

The voice is deep and curt, swift and piercing all at once. It is the voice of pain, the voice of violence, the voice of terror.

My father's voice.

Chapter 20

DREAD SEIZES EVERY MUSCLE in my body for a full second.

"Where have you been hiding?" Father asks. "My men searched the ship thoroughly."

My mind races. Did he see me in the water? Is he trying to get me to admit something? Where is my crew? What has he done to them?

"I went ashore," I lie smoothly.

"Good, you can show us where the treasure is."

Several of his men stand behind him, hands resting against their sword hilts. Tylon is among them.

"Don't bother trying to sing. Their ears are covered," Father says. I'm only mildly surprised he would risk himself by not covering his own ears. But then I attribute it to his own arrogance.

As soon as he is done with me, he will cover them and move on with his plans. It's probably too much to hope for the charm to start singing again.

"I'm giving Tylon your ship, since you ruined his."

"Ruined? I sank it. Where is my crew?"

"They're below, waiting for you. Why don't we go see them?" His tone replaces the blood in my veins with ice. What has he done to them?

Tylon's men draw their swords at some unheard command. There are over ten of them crammed into my modestly sized room. Were my father not here, I might attempt to fight my way through them. But with him here, I know I don't stand a chance.

And I *need* to see my crew. Horrid images flash in my mind. Images of them already bloodied and dead. It would be like him to kill them all and lock me up in the brig with nothing but corpses of all my loved ones for company.

But when we get down there, I am not met with death. My crew is safe for now, but locked in the cells, with even more of my father's men stationed to watch them.

"Captain," Niridia says with relief. Mandsy is in the cell with her. Sorinda, Riden, Kearan, Enwen, and the others are spread throughout all the cells in the brig.

"Quiet," my father barks out before turning to me. "Where's the treasure, Alosa?"

"I didn't find it."

My father draws his pistol and points it at me. I stare at it, unblinking.

"I don't care what you do to me."

"I thought not," he says, and rotates his arm slightly to the right, to one of the other cells.

Before I can scream, he pulls the trigger. Niridia's leg buckles, forcing her to the ground, blood seeping through a hole in the leggings over her knee.

I stare at the red spreading across the floor, trying to make sense of it, pressing myself against my father's men to reach her.

Another shot fires.

My gaze snaps back up to my father. He has out a new pistol, smoke coalescing from it. Reona, one of my riggers, jerks to the right and falls.

Father pulls out a third pistol.

"Father, stop it!"

He ignores me. A change is coming over him. Maiming them isn't enough now. He's angrier with me than I've ever seen him. I know that the next shot will claim a life.

"Please!" I shout as I try throwing my father's men off me. There are too many of them.

It's Deros who takes the shot through the heart. Deros who sinks to the ground with lifeless eyes. Deros who I'll never see again.

I want to run until my legs fail me. Yell until my voice runs dry. Pound at my father's head until it flattens into a puddle on the ground.

But none of those things would change the fact that he's gone.

"You cannot get to the treasure from the island!" I scream at him. "It's under the water, where only sirens can reach it."

The fourth pistol he'd drawn lowers slightly. "How do you know this?"

I can barely see through the water that's gathered at my eyes, but I somehow manage a quick lie. "I'm unaffected by the siren's song, but I still hear it. They sing about it. I heard them singing as they counted their coins and moved about under the water. The only way to that treasure is below the surface."

Father is silent. I can tell he thinks over the words very carefully, deciding whether or not to believe them. I'm desperate for him to believe the lie.

"Then we'll have to deal with the beasts first," he says, "before we go exploring underwater with our diving bell."

"No!"

"You care what happens to the sirens now? Good. You can watch from the porthole." He grabs me by the arm, and it takes him and three others to restrain me, but I don't go without a fight. I get a good kick in between the legs of one of the pirates, then take a fist to my jaw. My nails rake down the face of another man.

In the end, they wrestle me into my own cushioned cell. The one with a tiny porthole, too small to shimmy through, were I to knock out the glass.

"You don't have a say anymore," Father says. "You're going to stay locked up until you've learned your lesson and watched every member of your crew suffer and die."

I scream at him, rattle the bars, but I know there is no escaping from these cells. They were built *for* me, so I could stock up my abilities. I know there is no getting out of them.

No running to my bleeding crew members who are still alive. Mandsy is already at Niridia's side to help her. She shouts orders to Sorinda, who is in the cell with Reona, trying to staunch the bleeding wound.

I can't even warn the sirens about what's coming for them. They are too far away for me to sing to them. Were I under the water, I could do it, but like this, trapped above it—I'm useless.

Father exits the brig, satisfied by my temporary punishment. He leaves Tylon and several of his men to guard us, now that my ship is his. As if. Not while I draw breath. The *Ava-lee* is *mine*.

Tylon offers me several sneering, preening looks before saying, "Thank you, Alosa," much too loudly with the wax in his ears. Only when he's satisfied with his own gloating does he leave me and my crew belowdecks.

I kick at the bars and hiss profanities in his direction.

When he is out of sight, there's nothing I can dwell on but the bleeding girls in the brig. On Deros's body. Wallov closes his friend's eyes and sits on the floor next to him.

"Push harder, Sorinda!" Mandsy says. "It will hurt her, but it's better than her dying! Wallov, toss her your shirt!"

Mandsy has already tied a tourniquet above Niridia's knee. She focuses now on directing Sorinda.

"She's having a hard time breathing," Sorinda says.

Her voice less urgent, Mandsy asks, "Is blood coming out of her mouth?"

"Yes."

Mandsy blinks slowly. "Let go of the wound, Sorinda. Hold her hand and talk to her."

"What is it, Mandsy?" I ask.

"The ball must have struck a lung. It's kinder to let her bleed out than choke on her own blood."

Every breath I take seems to fuel my hatred for my father.

"It will be all right," Sorinda says, her voice taking on a soft tone. I didn't think she knew how to be soft. "The pain will stop soon, Reona. Close your eyes. Just listen to my voice."

I cannot take this. I cannot stand being trapped in here and unable to do anything while my crew dies around me!

"Athella?" I call out.

"They searched me too well, Captain," she answers. "I haven't so much as a hairpin on me."

"Sorinda, do you have any weapons hidden on you?"

"No."

Reona lets out her last breath. Sorinda releases her hand, setting it gently at her side.

For several seconds, I can do nothing but blink. "We'll find a way out of this. Everyone think."

I refuse to give up, even when my own mind tries to tell me it's useless. Tylon has the keys. He will keep them close. He won't let anything go wrong. Not now that he thinks he's so close to getting what he's always wanted.

Thank you, Alosa, he said. For betraying my father. For taking myself out of the running. For making him look good. He thinks my father's legacy will go to him now. I curse Tylon's name.

"How's Niridia?" I dare to ask.

"I'm fine," she says. Her grunts are audible now that Reona's gurgling gasps have ceased.

"She'll be okay," Mandsy says, "so long as I can get to my kit soon. I need to dig the ball out of her knee."

What I need is to get Tylon back down here. I can't get us out of here unless I can reach something useful.

"Are you all right?"

Riden is in the cell next to mine. I haven't been able to spare him a glance with everything else happening.

"I'm fine," I say. But it's not true. Not with the two bodies in the brig.

"What happened after you left?"

It clears my head to focus on something other than the deaths around me. I tell them about meeting my mother again and what she offered us.

"We were that close to beating him?" Niridia asks.

"Stop talking," Mandsy tells her.

"It distracts me from the pain!"

"We've been in tough situations before," Riden says, "and we made it out alive. We'll do it again."

"Are you working on another brilliant plan?" I ask.

"Not yet. But I'm sure I'll think of something. And this time, I'm going to avoid getting shot."

The situation is too dire for me to laugh, but I appreciate Riden's efforts at lightening it. I stare at the porthole in my cell. It offers a torturing glimpse of freedom while being utterly useless.

Through it, I see the fleet move farther out to sea, and my ship moves with them just a ways. Just enough for me to get a view of the fight that's about to happen, I realize. The ship is moving for my benefit.

Though my father's men all have their ears covered, it won't stop them from communicating. The fleet already has signals in place. My father has different flags he hoists up in the air, each one with a different meaning. They can still coordinate an attack.

My focus is no longer on me and my crew, but my mother and the sirens. They won't come to the surface, will they? Not when they can see the hulls of all those ships. They must know they are at a disadvantage. But how could they know their voices won't work on the men? They'll think themselves invulnerable when pitted against them.

"Stay under the water," I whisper. I did not come all this way just to lose my mother to death.

At first nothing happens. The ships anchor themselves and wait.

Until a man is thrown overboard.

I didn't see it happen, but I heard the splash and then spotted the man in the water. Did they draw straws? Or did Father pick some unknowing victim, lure him over to the side of his ship, and push?

All is silent for a moment. Nothing but the pirate stirs in the water.

And then a song can be heard, faint at first. Then overpowering. I assume the poor sod in the water can't hear it, because he doesn't dive down toward it. Instead I watch as graceful arms grasp onto him before pulling him below.

The water stills once again, but not for long. Several more songs rise to the surface—the most beautiful, glorious songs I have ever heard. They're all different, coming from many sirens at once, but somehow the melodies do not clash. They rise and fall together in cadences that pierce my heart.

My men are unaffected. Their ears are uncovered, the wax probably stolen by my father during the attack, but it is of no matter. True to my mother's promise, the sirens are not pulling the four men left in my crew under their spell.

They sing to all the other pirates, inviting them to join them in the invigorating water, promising them love and warmth and acceptance. Heads full of luscious hair breach the water's surface, mouths open in song. They move tantalizingly, trying to entice the men into the water.

It's odd how clear the sound is amidst the exploding of gunpowder.

Battle cries carry to us on the wind. Sirens shriek and hiss.

Many men hold harpoons, waiting until the right moment to fling them into the sea at targets I can't see clearly. Others point cannons or muskets directly into the water, firing and reloading as quickly as possible.

The water turns rapidly in multiple currents—the currents

of swimming sirens. Luminescent bodies float on the surface of the water in a tangle of rich hair and blood-stained skin. And some of the sirens turn to songs of grief instead of those of seduction.

While the men on the ships remain unharmed, some do not get to fight from safe heights. Many are forced into rowboats to fling harpoons from a shorter distance. Others on the boats point their guns at the water, but they cannot reload them quickly enough. As soon as they've deposited one round into the water, arms in glistening hues, from ivory to golden-brown to midnight black, break the surface and drag men under. One siren flings herself out of the water, leaping over the boat as a dolphin might, and plummets into an unsuspecting pirate, knocking him into the sea below with her.

She had a beauty that was almost painful to look at with hair the color of white starlight, strung with pearls and shells. It clung to her body as she thrust herself out of the water, reaching clear down to her knees.

The sirens look so very similar to human women. If it weren't for their sharpened nails and teeth, and exquisite beauty, one wouldn't be able to tell the difference.

Even without the lull of the sirens' songs, the pirates stare, mesmerized, at the water. It costs many of them their lives.

It's a strange thing for me to see firsthand the brutality and beauty of my own kind. So much of what I am makes sense. The ruthless killer in me might be part of my nature, rather than my upbringing.

A head of red hair appears above the ocean's surface.

"No! Get down!" I scream the words as loud as I can, but they cannot be heard over the distance that separates us, over the cannon fire and gunshots.

There's pointing and shuffling in the ship nearest my mother. Guns are immediately replaced with nets.

It takes some time; the siren queen is a formidable creature. At least a dozen men lose their lives.

But they catch her. I watch as she's transported to the *Dragon's Skull*. Watch as the rest of the sirens left alive retreat to below the surface. Now that their queen is gone, there is nothing they can do without her direction.

He will question her. Torture her, until he has all the information he wants.

And I can do nothing while stuck in yet another cell.

The ocean returns to calmness, as though a fight never happened. Night hits the water, and the pirates go to sleep.

∝

I try shouting for Tylon. Maybe now that the sirens lost the battle, the men won't have their ears covered.

But as the night goes on, I'm forced to accept that none of them can hear a damned thing. They don't respond to my yelling. They don't venture down to the brig. They're probably sleeping in our bunks over on the other side of the ship.

I slump to the floor, arms resting atop my bent knees. What can I try next?

Riden moves around in the cell next to mine. He presses against the bars, where he can get a good look at me.

"Come here," he says.

I edge as close to the bars as I can get. Several quiet conversations have broken out over the crew. Ours probably won't be overheard.

"I want to tell you something."

"What's that?" I whisper.

"Sailing with you and your crew was the first time I ever enjoyed being a pirate."

I laugh, the sound loud and awkward. "Don't try to make me feel better. I lost two friends today, and Niridia is injured. I don't want to laugh."

"You need to keep your spirits up. We'll find a way out of this. He hasn't won yet."

But the longer we sit here quietly in the dark, the more I start to think that he *has* won. We're trapped. He has my mother. It's only a matter of time before he has the treasure, too. We're locked in this brig with two corpses. My heart is breaking from how much I've lost on this journey. More death and torture are all that await us once we get back to the keep.

I don't see how anything will change with time.

"Captain?" A whisper floats through the brig—and not from one of the cells.

Chapter 21

"ROSLYN!" I WHIRL AT her tiny voice.

Her grin exposes a loose tooth bent slightly out of place. "I've got something for you." She holds up a ring of keys.

"I knew you'd save us," Wallov says, a father's pride glinting in his eyes.

How could I have forgotten little Roslyn? Stowed away all this time in her hidey-hole up in the crow's nest. "How did you get the keys?"

"I had to wait for the girly-looking fellow to fall asleep," she says apologetically. Riden gives me a look that says, *Didn't I tell you?* "It was a good thing his ears were covered the whole time because the keys jangle so."

"Sneaky little thief," I exclaim proudly.

She steps in front of her father's cell. "The next time you're cross with me, Papa, I want you to remember this moment." She inserts the key into the lock. "Oh, and Captain?"

"Yes?"

"I want to fight with the crew in six years' time." Her voice changes slightly, as though she's trying for a more adult tone. She could never mask the chirp of a six-year-old girl, but it's something adorable watching her try.

I raise a brow at her, achieving what I hope is a slightly stern look.

She bites the inside of her cheek, but waits to twist the key.

I look behind her at Wallov, who is trying to keep from laughing.

"Seven," I say.

"Done," she says, flicking her wrist. An excited smile nearly splits her face in half.

A gunshot explodes through the mostly quiet brig. Every head turns toward the entrance where Tylon has appeared, a furious scowl spread across his face.

A cloud of smoke overtakes his features for a moment.

My eyes drift down to where he has his pistol extended in front of him.

I follow its line of progress to where Roslyn stands.

Blood spurts wildly from her head.

And she falls.

A wailing scream fills the sudden quiet. I think I might be the source, but I realize a moment later it's Wallov.

My eyes rivet to Tylon, and I say the only words that make sense when the impossible lies before me. "You're mine."

"No, he isn't." Wallov has the door to his cell open before anyone else can move. He launches himself at Tylon, who was only halfway through unsheathing his sword. More pirates barge into the brig behind Tylon. The girls start billowing out of the unlocked cell, following Wallov's lead.

My eyes return to my fallen crewman. To little Roslyn, who hasn't moved since she fell. Despite the yelling and grunting, I can't focus on anything else.

Eventually I find my voice. "Toss the keys!"

I don't know who I'm speaking to. I don't know if anyone can hear me through the cacophony of battle cries.

But someone must have, because the keys clank against one of the bars to my cell and slide to the floor. I snatch them up and maneuver around to unlock my own cell. Before I can fit the key in, one of Tylon's men whips his cutlass at me. I pull both arms and keys back through the bars just in time, and the sword clangs against the metal, sending sparks to the ground. He eyes me, daring me to make a move, content to stand there until I get close enough for him to reach.

A sword point rips through the front of his stomach. A labored sigh escapes him as he stares down at the metal. Sorinda doesn't wait for him to drop before yanking her cutlass back through his gut and moving on to the next target.

A new sense of urgency overtakes me as a pool of blood forms near Roslyn.

I unlock my cell, toss the keys to Riden, and run to her, but Mandsy reaches her first, ripping off a section of her trousers to staunch the bleeding.

But I know how hard it is to survive a head wound. And for one so small.

Trembling fingers reach for her pulse.

It's still there. How is it still there?

"It skimmed her head, Captain," Mandsy says. "Knocked her out. There's a lot of blood, but I could see her skull intact underneath. If I can just get the bleeding under control—"

"Do what you can. I'm going after Tylon."

I throw myself into the fray, tossing enemy pirates around like they're rocks. I have metal bars at my disposal, so I ram heads into them in my search for Tylon. I finally catch sight of Wallov through the chaos. He's got Tylon by the shoulders, and he slams his head into the ground over and over. I don't know how long Tylon has been dead, but Wallov doesn't seem to notice anything at all.

I rush to him and pin his arms to his sides.

"Wallov, she's alive. Calm down."

It takes a moment for the words to sink in, but then instead of trying to go for Tylon, he's trying to get away from me. To go to Roslyn. I release him.

We outnumber the men on the ship. After depositing us in the brig, the majority of Tylon's men must have left to join the fight against the sirens. Those who remain go down quickly. We don't spare a single one.

By the time I reach Wallov and Roslyn, Mandsy has her kit. She stitches the head wound and wraps it. Then she moves on to Niridia.

Two of us hold her down while Mandsy digs the ball out of her leg.

"Pity you lot drank all the rum," Kearan says. "She could use it."

"I don't want rum!" she screams. "I want my sword, I'm going to—"

"You're not going anywhere," I tell her.

Mandsy wrenches the pliers deeper into Niridia's flesh. My first mate screams before blacking out.

"Got it!" Mandsy says. She begins cleaning and wrapping the wound. I sit back on my heels, grateful at least that Niridia isn't in pain anymore.

Now that we've finished taking care of those who are still alive, we tend to the dead. As I watch Reona's and Deros's bodies drift out to sea by lantern light, I vow that I will see justice done for the senseless way in which they died.

They didn't go down fighting, protecting what they held dear. They were caged. Like animals.

My gaze drifts up from the water. To the *Dragon's Skull*.

"I'm coming for you," I whisper.

∞

Back belowdecks, I survey what's left of my crew, take in all the faces and injuries. "We have two options now," I say to the group. "We can run or we can fight. I'm leaning toward option number two."

"As am I," Mandsy says, still wet with Roslyn's and Niridia's blood.

"I will kill all of them," Wallov says, clutching a slowly healing Roslyn toward his breast.

"No, Wallov," I say. "You will stay here and look after the wounded." With Niridia injured, Mandsy needs to fill the role as my second. "The rest of us will board the *Dragon's Skull*. Are there any objections?"

When I hear none, I tell them the plan.

Dead men are heavier than live ones.

We strip them of clothing that isn't too bloodied, then haul the corpses into one of the cells, piling them unceremoniously on top of one another. It's quicker than dumping them into the ocean.

There isn't enough clothing to go around, but we make do with what we have. The girls cover up their corsets with men's shirts. They stuff their hair under tricornes. From their bunks, they tear up sheets and stuff them into their leggings to make themselves look bigger, more masculine. Some even ask my permission to raid my cosmetics to draw facial hair under their noses and mouths. It won't do anything to mask them up close, but from a distance, it could work.

Tylon's body is the only one outside of the cell. I suspect no one is fond of the idea of touching him, even in death. But Riden moves toward him as if to put him with the others.

"No." I halt him. "We will need his carcass."

∝

Dawn hasn't yet made its approach. The stars in the sky reflect off the ocean below, trapping us in a world dotted with lights. The rowboats cut swaths through the water, rippling the illusion of peace.

We don't carry lanterns with us across the space between the *Ava-lee* and the *Dragon's Skull*. We need the absence of light to mask us. If we're to pass as men, we need to be as concealed as possible.

Though we don't call attention to ourselves, we also aren't trying to hide. We're there, floating in the dark. Easily spotted if someone should shine a light on us. Yet concealed until then.

Riden sits next to me in the rowboat. He rests his hand atop my knee, squeezes, and removes it.

"This will work," I tell him.

"I know. I'm reassuring you, not myself."

If we can reach the *Dragon's Skull* quietly and take out everyone on the ship, we can come out on top. The rest of the fleet will not unleash their cannons on the pirate king's ship. And once I can explain how I can get to the treasure, they won't care that their king is dead. They will rally to my side. That is the way of the pirate. I just need to kill my father first.

I've thought about it many times. Killing my father. When he'd hurt me. When I discovered he'd locked up my mother.

When he threatened my crew. Now I try to picture it, my cutlass sliding between his ribs to plant itself in his heart. The gasp that would float on his breath. The sightless look in his eyes.

I have killed hundreds of men. Why does my stomach sicken to think of killing this one? He is just a man. An admittedly powerful one, but still just a man.

But I have never killed my own flesh and blood. Why does it feel different? Should it feel different? Can I do what needs to be done in the end?

I must.

A light aboard the *Dragon's Skull* hovers at the edge of the ship, raises high into the air, shines on us.

We've been spotted.

It's time for these disguises to do their job.

Tylon's body is propped up against the front of the rowboat, his face pointing toward the men aboard the *Dragon's Skull*. Since half the back of his skull is gone, we have to keep him pointed straight ahead. I sit next to him, discreetly keeping his body upright. His glassy eyes are open, but thankfully the ship is too far for anyone to notice he doesn't blink.

Now there are two lanterns, but no alarm sounds.

We act calm, casual. A few of the girls offer gruff waves. Sorinda shields her eyes from the light and doesn't have to fake her irritable scowl.

Three lanterns gather together, watching our ship approach.

They lower us a rope ladder. They must have recognized Tylon.

Not a word is spoken on our end or theirs as we hoist

ourselves up the side of the ship. Through a porthole, I can see almost a hundred men sleeping in their bunks, undisturbed by our approach.

This will work.

I'm the first one over the lip of the ship. I size up the three men on watch. They don't say a word as they take in my disguise. I must pass the test, because they still don't attempt to speak. One of them hands his lantern to one of the others and pulls out a parchment and paper. He scribbles onto it while the rest of the girls join me aboard the ship.

When the pirate has finished, he shows me the paper.

Is your captain injured?

They're still blocking their ears as a precaution. They can't hear a thing. Their only means of communication is through the written word.

Just as I'd hoped.

I reach forward as if to grab the parchment. Instead I cut off the man's airway with a punch to the throat, then I reach for my cutlass to finish the job. Sorinda steps up beside me and rakes her rapier across another man's neck. Mandsy takes out the third.

They drop, dead at our feet, without making a sound, not that anyone could hear if they did.

"Sorinda," I say. "Find anyone else on watch above deck and dispose of them. Mandsy, lead the crew below and quietly take out the rest of the men on the ship. If you do not wake them, it should be as easy as butchering sheep. And keep your eyes open for the siren queen."

Enwen shudders from a few feet away. My men do not have their ears covered. I still trust my mother's promise.

"What about you?" Mandsy asks.

"I'm to face the pirate king."

"Not alone." Riden strides through the darkness and plants himself firmly next to me.

"I think this might be something I need to do alone."

"You need not do anything alone again if you don't want to."

It almost hurts to look into those golden-brown eyes. I know what he means by those words. He'll be by my side always, as long as I want him there.

It's so very tempting, but—"No. I need you below. We are vastly outnumbered. All hands need to take out those most loyal to the pirate king if we're to survive this. And stealth will be needed if I'm to sneak up on the king while he sleeps. One person in the room is best."

He nods, almost imperceptibly, but it is a nod, nonetheless. I kiss him for it, hating that I have to pull away so soon.

But what if it's the last time?

I pull him to me again. I don't care if it wastes time.

His arms come around me, crushing me, as if he means to permanently weld us together. His lips are frantic against mine, and they taste like salt. I wonder if he shed a few tears for Roslyn's injury when I wasn't looking.

Knowing that somehow makes me love him even more.

I pull back, even though it hurts, and turn to what's left of my crew. "I expect to see you all again soon."

"Whether in this life or the next," Sorinda says.

Chapter 22

THE *DRAGON'S SKULL* IS over three times the size of the *Ava-lee*. While my ship was designed for stealth, my father's was made for the complete opposite. Kalligan wants his victims to see him coming. He wants to invoke fear, to start attacking sailors' minds long before he reaches them.

His flag bears a dragon skull with its jaws open wide, readying to breathe fire on its enemies. Men on the sea have learned to fear that flag.

My father no doubt thinks of himself as the dragon—the biggest and most powerful creature of all. Dragons, however, are myths. My father is very real.

He is the dragon I must slay.

Everything about the ship is a message to those on board.

As I take the steps up the companionway, I can't help but stare at the skulls skewered through the pegs in the railing. Each of them is a man my father killed. Not a single peg on this ship is empty. The ropes are spotted with red, whether paint or actual blood, I couldn't say.

When I take the final step, a strangled cry interrupts the quiet, and a body falls from above. Sorinda must have killed another one of the night watches—someone up in the rigging. It's unlike Sorinda to allow her kills to be so loud, but everyone makes mistakes. Thank the stars no one aboard can hear.

I freeze with my hand on the door to my father's rooms. The reality of what I'm about to do hits me again.

Patricide.

No. Not that. Kalligan is a father in blood alone. What he's done—to me and my mother—that does not earn him such a title. He is only a name. Kalligan. A nobody.

There are different kinds of fathers, Riden once said. I ignored his words then. I didn't want to hear them. Kalligan was all I'd ever known. I didn't realize things could be different.

Or did I?

The image of little Roslyn's blood-streaked hair washes over me, a flare of pain and anger spreading through my otherwise numb limbs. I've seen Wallov with Roslyn hundreds of times. His kindness and compassion. His support and friendship. Yet his gentle discipline and direction.

I never realized that was what I should have had.

And because of Kalligan, Roslyn is fighting for her life back on my ship.

I meet no resistance when I push against the door latch. He must be inside if his rooms are unlocked. He always locks up when he leaves.

I shut the door gently behind me. I can't help but keep my steps light, my breathing soft, even though I know no matter how I approach, he won't hear me.

My pounding heart is the loudest sound as I walk through his sitting room. Chairs gather around a table. A storage of rum fills the wall with the finest vintages. His rooms are the only places on the ship that don't scream of death.

The study contains a neat desk with map pieces and notes on the journey next to them. I move past it all to hover outside his bed chamber.

Pressing my ear to the door, I hold my breath.

His deep breaths carry to me like beating wings on the wind.

I reach down and pause for a moment, wondering what my instrument of death will be. The cutlass? As tempting as shooting him from a distance is, the pistol can't be an option. I don't dare use something so loud. What if that could push through the wax-covered ears of the sleeping men below? Besides, this is personal. I should be right with him when I end his life.

I slide a hand into my boot, brushing my leggings, and pull out the dagger there. The hilt is small in my hands, but sturdy, the blade wickedly sharp. My fist closes over the smooth metal handle.

Everything is ready.

Everything except me.

I think of my crew once more for strength and open the door.

First, I spot my mother.

She is strapped to a chair with ropes. They bind her shoulders to the chair's back, her thighs to the seat, her ankles to the chair's legs. Her wrists are bound together behind her back. Her mouth is gagged, and her face is lightly swollen, starting to show the signs of the beating Kalligan no doubt gave her.

She looks up at my entrance, and her eyes widen.

I raise a finger to my lips, even though she's gagged.

She nods and watches me while I turn my attention to the bed. Kill him first. Then free her.

Kalligan lies on his stomach, his head twisted so it faces the door. And me. But his eyes are shut in slumber. One arm is tucked under his pillow. I know it grips a large dagger. He never sleeps without one near. Like a dangerous child with his doll.

I can give him no more thought. There is no time or room for guilt and indecision to set in. No emotion. Just action.

I tiptoe to the bed.

One quick swipe.

Now.

My wrist flicks outward. I force my eyes to remain open the whole time. No chance for error.

I tense just before the metal sinks into flesh—

Except it doesn't.

It meets metal.

The hand under the pillow arcs outward, catching the blow on the blade it holds.

"You should have gone with a pistol," he says.

That much is clear now.

He pushes back against my blade and rises in the same motion. Somehow, him standing makes everything easier. It's not difficult to fight someone who is also trying to take my life.

This changes everything. It's not about stealth anymore. It's about beating an opponent I lose to at swordplay as often as I win. Kalligan is immune to my song. We're matched in strength. I have him beat in speed, but he's trained me all my life. No one can anticipate my moves like he can.

"Put down your weapon, Alosa," he says. "Beg for my forgiveness. I might give it. After I'm satisfied with your punishment."

"I am not the one who needs forgiving."

"You would judge me? Because you're so pure? You're just like me. There isn't anything you wouldn't do to get what I have."

"That's not true. I wouldn't hurt innocents. I wouldn't . . ."

"Kill your own father?"

I switch the dagger to my left hand and draw my sword. "What we're about to do has nothing to do with power. It's about making things right." I have lost crew members because of this man.

He reaches for his own cutlass, a look of indifference upon his face. "You will accomplish nothing. I can assure you of that."

The ship rocks at the same time the boom of a cannon ignites on the air. The motion is slight, not enough to knock over either of us.

But it's surely enough to wake everyone on the ship.

Someone in his crew must have spotted the girls and fired a cannon to wake the rest.

"You're not as careful as you think," Kalligan says. "Everything you do, I am always one step ahead."

I realize then that we're conversing, which means he doesn't have his ears covered. Not like the rest of his men. He must have heard the dying call of the man Sorinda killed. It would have been slight in here, but enough to wake my father.

"The sirens will have you," I tell him, trying to hide my rage. I've doomed my whole crew. They can't have killed enough of Kalligan's sleeping men. If they even made it that far.

He grins, something born of triumph and greed. "The sirens can't touch me. I am immune."

I blink. I've always known *my* song doesn't affect him because of the blood we share, but he can't be immune to *all* sirens. But what does he gain by lying?

Nothing.

Shouts interrupt the quiet outside. Night is over. I can see the sun rising out the window now.

Our final battle has begun.

He makes the first move, a swipe meant to take off my head. I duck it and thrust at his gut. He tries to dodge it, but my sword catches him in the side. The tip of my sword comes back bloodied, like a spotted dog's tail.

I know better than to relish over the victory. My father does not weaken like a normal man after being struck. Pain fuels him, makes him stronger.

Makes him charge me.

I've already begun backing up, slamming the door to his bedroom in front of me. I do not turn my back to him. *Never give your back to an opponent.* Even now his training directs my movements.

BAM!

My arms barely shield my face in time. Wood splinters dig into my skin as the shattered door explodes in my direction. The blood lust is upon my father. His battle rage makes him forget pain. Forget reason. Rather than opening his door, he punched his weight through it.

It's a move meant to scare, intimidate.

And it works.

I falter a step, but manage to get the door to the deck open. I don't want to be enclosed in his quarters with him. Can't be. I need the dawning light from outside to capture him. To remind me he is only a man. If I avoid looking too hard at his face, I can forget it's one I've grown up seeing my whole life. One I actually loved.

I press my back into the outside wall to his rooms, right next to the door opening, and spare a glance at the scene below.

The girls are keeping themselves busy on the deck of the *Dragon's Skull*. They've come above from the sleeping quarters and are bottlenecking my father's men as they come up through the hatches.

Mandsy, you brilliant, brilliant woman.

Such a large ship has two hatches, one on either end, but she's already divided up the crew, half at each hatch, and they're cutting away my father's men before they can surround them and use their superior numbers to overpower.

I register this all in less than a second.

My cutlass is poised beside me, waiting to strike my father when he exposes his back by rushing through the door opening.

I lose my breath and sword when a bullet streaks through my right arm.

The muscle burns as I lower my arm, spreading fire all the way down to the tips of my fingers. I grit my teeth at the pain and my own folly.

Kalligan has once again predicted what I would do. He couldn't know exactly where I was standing, so he took his best guess. Maybe he's not as out of control as I originally thought. He only wanted to give off the appearance of having lost all reason. This was a calculated shot.

Though it's not lethal, it's cost me my sword arm and—very likely—the fight.

Part of Kalligan's endurance tests were making me practice fighting him with my left. I wonder if he's regretting how well he trained me now.

As I bend down to retrieve my sword with my left hand, Kalligan's boot comes careening around the corner, colliding with my chin, and sending me flying backward. I lose the dagger, now, too.

My eyes roll back into my head from the force of the kick. The pain is so maddening, I wonder if I were human if the kick would have taken my head clean off. My throat is stretched tight from the thick ache, my teeth are still ringing, and the ship wobbles for just a moment before I can collect myself, right my vision.

I make the mistake of attempting to use my injured arm to right myself. The slickness of my blood-drenched hand and the sharp pain lacing through my arm cause me to crumple to the deck.

Kalligan shouts something. I can't make out the words, but I think they're orders to his men. The words are much too loud to be meant for me. He's momentarily forgotten his men can't hear a thing.

Fortunately, his orders give me a chance to collect myself. I rise. But Kalligan still stands between me and my sword. I reach for my pistol, cock it back. Kalligan recognizes what I'm about to do and throws himself over the helm and off the aftercastle.

I miss the shot. The ball lodges into the deck, and I curse the stars in my vision, the unsteadiness of my left hand. But with him out of the way, I streak for my sword, grasp it firmly.

He waits for me on the main deck. As I jump the steps of the companionway, I spot Kalligan's pirates climbing onto the deck from over the sides of the ship. Some of them must have finally gotten the sense to haul themselves through the gun ports.

"Mandsy!" I shout when I land. "They're coming from the sides."

She turns and spots them, then shouts orders to the rest of

the crew. Bodies are layered next to the hatches. The men shove through their fallen companions to try and reach my crew. I see one fallen girl, her hair covering her face. It's Deshel, I think. Radita's gotten herself caught in a hold by one of the enemy. She brings her heel down hard on his instep before slamming a closed fist into his groin. Sorinda is already at the starboard side of the ship, slicing off the fingers of men trying to get a grip on the railing. Athella's perched up in the netting, launching herself at men who break through the forces of the girls at the stern hatch.

I see a flash of Riden before I have to return my attention to the pirate king.

Kalligan is bolting toward me again. I can't continue to let him take the offensive. I won't kill him that way. My right arm hangs uselessly against my side. I try not to jostle it as I deflect the king's next blow.

"You've already lost this fight," he says as he sends a volley of slashes at me.

"Not yet." As I block the next strike, I send my injured arm sailing toward his head, gritting my teeth at the murderous pain. I almost lose consciousness as black spots corner my vision.

It's worth it. He doesn't expect it, and I take my chance to fling my own strikes.

Nothing I do is light. With each swing I put forth all the force I have, all the speed I can muster. My arm throbs with agony. My ears are still ringing from the kick to the head I took.

One of my girls cries out. The men are gathering their forces. Superior numbers are encroaching on the deck. I need to finish this fight so I can help them.

Nothing I do gives me the advantage. The slice at my father's side barely bleeds. He fights as though he feels no pain. We will hammer and hack at each other until one of us collapses from exhaustion or makes a foolish mistake. Since I am the most injured, it will likely be me.

I don't let the fear of losing have any effect on me. I will see this fight through to the end, no matter the outcome.

Death pours into the air, a stench unique unto itself. I nearly trip over a fallen body, as Kalligan tries to press me back toward the stern of the ship. Shots no longer penetrate the air. Everyone has emptied their pistols. There's nothing but a stumbling of limbs and swords. Athella no longer sits up in the netting. She's on the ground trying to even out the odds. An enemy pirate comes up behind her and—

I look away before she goes down. A new urgency and rage fuels my fight with Kalligan.

"Surrender," he says.

"Getting tired?" I say through a heavy breath.

His chest heaves as well. I know better than to think he wants me to quit because he thinks he'll lose the fight. He wants to beat me. Both my body and mind. My giving up is as much of a victory for him. But by the way he pounds his sword and swings his fist, I know he wants to take my betrayal right out of my skin.

Surrendering is not an option.

"I'm tired of *you*," he answers. "Tired of your insolence and your weakness. I'm ready to be rid of you. But I'll save you for last. You can watch your crew suffer first."

"I will kill you before you can touch them," I bite out.

"They're being crushed like rodents underfoot now. My men might not spare any. Then I'll have only you to unleash my rage on."

"I'm not afraid of you."

"And what of your crew? Do you fear for them?" He sweeps his arms off to the side, and I dare to look.

Many have lost their weapons. They're being herded off to the side, tied with ropes. Mandsy and Sorinda are back-to-back fighting. I know neither will stop until they're dead. Riden, too, is still striking down opponents. He's drawing himself closer to me, trying to reach me.

I kick at empty air as Kalligan dodges.

"You think killing me will stop this?" he asks. "Look around you." I know he means for me to think of all the ships in his fleet. "Even if I were to die, you and your crew won't make it out alive. My men will finish what I started."

"They'll be too busy fighting each other to take your place to pay attention to me. They won't give your body a second glance. Your name will be forgotten. It will fade from memory, and any scrap of glory you've attained will be forgotten. No one will remember you. I certainly won't."

He doubles his efforts. He slices my already injured arm, bruises my ribs, swings my legs out from under me. I roll and roll and roll away from him. I don't stop until my back hits the railing at the starboard side. I come up on my feet, feebly hold my sword out in front of me.

I'm losing too much blood now that there are two openings.

He advances slowly. He knows I'm beaten. My crew is completely subdued. A third of them paint the deck red and lie at unnatural angles, unmoving. The rest are cowed into a corner.

And Riden—he's nearly upon me when three of my father's men tackle him to the deck and wrest his sword from him.

I look around for something—anything—to help me beat Kalligan. I'm useless. There's nothing Riden can do. There's nothing my crew can do. My mother is helpless back in my father's rooms. And the sirens—

What of the sirens?

They've already been beaten, have lost the fight in them now that their queen has been captured once again. They've probably already abandoned the area.

But what if they haven't? What if they are stirring below, just waiting for their queen to come to them?

I am not her, but I am the queen's daughter. They looked on me as an outsider, but could I call to them? Would they even listen?

Because it is the *only* option left to me, I sing. The song is a cloud of desperation and pleading. A cry for help, wrestling the wind, dropping into the water, searching its depths for anyone who can hear.

I can feel them, now that I'm calling to them. Hundreds and

hundreds of them. They cry beneath the waves. Fearing for their queen, weeping for their fallen, trembling for their lives. It's so . . .

Human of them.

Some quiet at my own song, listening. I can feel their attention shift to me. I am part of the royal line. It flows through my veins, rides on my song. They don't have listen to me, but if I can just say the right words . . .

I am Alosa-lina, daughter of Ava-lee. My mother is alive, but a prisoner on this ship. Will you not help? Will you fight against the pirates who have dared to breach your waters and steal what is yours?

They murmur among themselves. I feel it in their songs, in the way the water trembles around them.

The reply is faint, but one answers me. *Are you not one of the pirate scum? Did you not refuse the queen's call when she bid you home? Even now you stay on solid ground, refusing to join your sisters below.*

My father stares at me all the while, halting in front of me. "You're calling on the sirens? They fled, shrieking into the deep. You are a stranger to them. I made sure of that."

You outnumber the pirates, I explain. *My loyalty is not with them. I will help you beat them.*

Doubt sings to me from below. Emotions are songs of their own, pouring out of them without any effort, as if their voices cannot keep quiet.

No one will talk with me now. The sirens resume their wailing grief until my voice leaves me, and I can no longer hear them.

"Drop your sword," Kalligan says. His tone is clipped, final. He will not ask me again. His next strike will take a life.

"Alosa." This voice is quiet. It is from Riden. He stands so close by, all his limbs subdued.

I drop my sword as my father bids and turn toward Riden. With just a few well-aimed jabs from me, his captors release him.

I grab him, and the two of us leap from the ship.

Chapter 23

WATER ENVELOPS ME, cradles me, welcomes me home. My body shifts, stretches, relishes the new surroundings. My muscles feel refreshed, ready to get back in the fight.

Riden watches me, ascertains that I am myself, before giving me an encouraging nod and swimming for the surface.

My father's laugh reaches me, even down here. "Your captain has left you! She'd rather live her life as a senseless beast than go down with her ship and crew. I hadn't realized I'd raised a coward."

I feel nothing at the words. My crew knows how I've grown. They won't believe them. They must know I am here to save them, not to save myself.

For now, I swim far, far below, arcing down into the deep. It's clear as day to me where no human could see or bear the pressure.

I find them easily. The sisters I would have grown up with had I lived my life as a siren. They swim in circles or rest on the ocean's bottom, arms thrown over their faces in defeat. Limbs twisting and shifting uneasily, helpless, yet enraged.

I am here, I sing to them. *Now you can speak directly to my face. Tell me why you have abandoned your queen yet again.*

A group of older sirens looks away. Their hair obscures their faces as they shift uneasily. They were there when their queen was ripped from them the first time. They are ashamed—so much so they can't bear to look into my face.

The siren children are ethereal. Perfect pearls in this sea. They hang back behind their mothers—those that still have them. A girl with hair the color of sparkling sand huddles near a woman with night-black locks. The child, who can't be more than five, sings of her mother's death. She saw it with perfect clarity, the way the harpoon hit her mother, how her eyes rolled back, how she sank down to the ocean's bottom.

We need to make them pay for what they've done, I say.

How? the siren clutching the orphan asks. *The men cannot hear us. Their leader is immune.*

How is that possible?

He has lain with a siren and lived. Now the magic of our song does not affect him.

All this time I thought I couldn't control him because we

shared blood, but it is because of his relationship with my mother, not me, that he is immune.

And even if he weren't immune, she continues, *it would do us little good. Our voices do not work when we're completely out of the water as yours does.*

They don't need to. Do you not have arms and legs?

We are weak out of water. We will have no more strength than human women.

I smile at all of them. *I've been training human women to fight for years. A woman is not helpless when she knows what to do. And even a man is helpless when outnumbered ten to one.*

It's not a question of if you'll win, I continue. *The only question is whether you will choose to fight. Will you fight for your queen? Will you fight for your waters and treasure? Will you fight for your little ones?*

My song carries through the water, firm and unmistakable. A call to arms. A demand from their princess.

I am not your queen. You do not have to obey me as you do my mother. This is a choice you must make. A choice to avenge your lost ones, to save your queen, to protect your children. I am an outsider. The life I could have had with all of you was taken from me, but I am here now by choice. Will you not choose to rally with me now? I braved the ocean for you. Will you brave land for your queen?

All of their singing stops. The piercing chords of grief cease. The harsh thrums of anger relent.

In their place is conviction. A promise. As one they sing a song so powerful it brings tears to my eyes. It's a battle cry made of pure, heavenly song. The ships above shift from the force of it.

I show them their advantages over men—what they can do to subdue them—

And then we ascend.

∞

When my head breaks the water, I sing and pull the moisture into me, drying as I drag myself back up the side of the *Dragon's Skull*. I peek my head over the lip of the ship. My crew has been tied to the mainmast, bunched together under layers of rope. Some five men stand facing them, making sure no one leaves.

A soaked Riden is tied up with the others. He had no choice but to return to the ship and be taken captive once more until I returned. Sorinda, I can see, has already managed to free her hands without attracting the attention of the guards. Mandsy is opposite her, head slumped against the mast, only knocked out, I'm sure. Radita wriggles her shoulders, and a pirate advances on her with his sword raised.

"Stop that," he says, "or I'll run you through."

She gives him a look to say exactly where he can stick his sword.

He steps forward, catching a lock of her hair on his cutlass and holding it up to the light. "Captain says we can do what we want with you lot once we start sailing again, so long as you're all still alive once we reach the keep. I'm going to start with you." He puckers his lips at her and laughs, gliding his sword along her cheek now as though it's a caress.

No one lays a finger on my girls.

He's the first to go. With his back to me, he can't see me come up behind him, can't see me reach for his sword. With one hand at his wrist and the other just below his shoulder, I bring the whole arm down on my knee, ignoring the spasm of pain that erupts in my injured arm at the movement. The resulting crack is a fierce drum beat adding to the music of my sister sirens. I take his sword and rake it across his throat.

The struggle is enough to get the attention of the other guards. Before they can reach me, I toss the cutlass to Sorinda, who catches it easily and frees herself and the others.

One of my father's men rushes below for help. I start on the rest. Riden offers up a smile before leaping onto the nearest guard and taking his sword from him. I kick another's legs out from under him and stake him to the deck with his own cutlass through his chest.

By the time we've finished with the guards, my father has made an appearance once again, the massive forces of his men lined up behind him. His side is bandaged now; his hand holds his sword once more.

He doesn't appear surprised, only more enraged.

"You don't know when to quit, girl. You're just as outnumbered as before. This fight will not have a different outcome."

A scream rises in the air. First one, then another, and another. They're distant, traveling to us from other ships in the fleet. My father looks around, but he can see nothing from where he stands. His men still cannot hear a thing. They haven't a clue that anything is amiss.

Until the sirens pour onto the deck. Hundreds. As many as will fit.

Water falls off them in waves, dribbling down their long locks and smooth bodies, soaking the deck instantly. A line of sirens go down as my father's spooked men fire off shots, but they are helpless against the superior numbers. The sirens trample them underfoot. They force them off the edges of the ship and into the water. They fight alongside my crew, sending souls to the stars right and left.

I've never known Kalligan to run from danger, but he races for higher ground at the sight of all those sirens on his ship. He climbs the rigging, leaving his men to fend for themselves. And I realize then just how much he must fear death. He's been in a position of power and security for so long, I wonder if he'd forgotten what it was to be afraid. And now he has no need to worry about being seen as weak. None of his men will live to speak of it.

I leave him for now. My priority is my mother.

I cut a line through the masses, taking down the pirates in my path, assisting the sirens who need it. Eventually I make it to my father's rooms.

She is right where I left her.

First I take out the gag.

She coughs twice and swallows deeply. "You've saved me again."

"It's my fault he found you again. I'm the one who tracked down the map pieces for him." I use a borrowed cutlass to work at sawing through the thick ropes at her wrists.

"Is he dead?" she asks. It's the fiercest tone I've heard her voice take.

"Not yet. He's hiding from the fight."

The battle is over only minutes after it began. The sirens made quick work of the pirates. They've already taken back to the water by the time I get my mother out in the open air. I'm surprised she doesn't join them immediately. Instead, she stares purposefully at the mainmast, where Kalligan stands on the beam below the highest sail.

"You've lost," I shout up to him.

"I haven't lost until a sword plunges into my heart," he calls back.

"Mandsy, find me a saw," I say. "If our beloved king won't come down of his own free will, we'll have to hack down his throne."

A loud clang sounds. It's my father's sword hitting the deck. The purest sign of defeat.

He's no fool. He knows he's lost. He has no power over me. My crew and I are finally safe.

His feet follow, and everyone on the ship quiets, watching him. "Now what?" he asks as he rises to his full height. "Am I to face a firing squad? Be imprisoned till the day I die? You don't have—"

His words are stopped by a fiery-red blur crashing into him. They crack through the wooden railing and topple off the side of the ship, a tangle of limbs and hair and my father's shouts.

As soon as they hit the water, I know I will not see my father alive again.

The water churns violently as Kalligan tries to claw his way to the surface. There's a muffled, watery scream, a sound I've never heard him make before. My mother pulls him deeper. The water folds into place as their dark shadows fall away.

One,

two,

three bubbles.

And all is still.

The pirate king's reign has come to an end.

The cheering is ear-shattering. It mixes with the songs of hundreds of sirens, shaking the ship from under the water. The girls rush one another, tangling themselves in ferocious hugs. We're alive. We're still alive and the king is dead.

For one, brief moment, I mourn the man I thought my father to be. I mourn the rare embraces, the words of comfort and encouragement. I mourn the man who taught me to fight. Who set an example of leadership. Who showed me the joys to be had in a life on the sea.

I mourn him, and then I remember the ultimate choice he made. He wanted control and power. Nothing more. He did not know how to love, only to use what he had to get what he wanted.

So I mourn the man I once believed my father to be.

And then I let him go.

I throw myself at Mandsy, hugging her with as much strength as I dare without crushing her or jostling my own injured arm too much. Soon Enwen joins us, looping his arms around both of us. A relieved laugh escapes me as I look around at all the happy faces. Even Sorinda doesn't shrug away from the embraces that come her way. Until Kearan tries, that is.

As soon as Enwen and Mandsy leave me to celebrate with others, my eyes scan for the next closest person.

They land on Riden.

The look we share seems to crackle with its own energy. Suddenly he's not standing over there. He's here. Right in front of me. Until he's so close that I can't see him at all.

My eyes close as he presses his lips to mine. And though it is nowhere near our first kiss, it feels brand new. Neither of us is burdened down. Draxen is not here to keep us apart. My father cannot terrorize us. Even the threat of death doesn't hang over our heads.

This kiss feels honest. It feels real.

And I don't ever want it to feel differently.

Chapter 24

WON'T YOU STAY with me? my mother begs for the tenth time that hour. We've spent days together under the water, talking, singing. My aunt, Arianna-leren, stands next to her. Now that we're not under a time constraint, my mother made the introductions. Arianna-leren is a beauty with gold locks that pool around her in waves even thicker than mine.

The sirens no longer treat me as an outcast now that the pirates have been defeated.

You know I can't, I say. *I've stayed too long as it is.*

But Kalligan is dead. He is no longer a threat. I've added his gold to the hoard.

I look down at the sand.

The sirens have so few cares.

They do not need to eat. The ocean nourishes them. They do not need clothing or shelter. There is nothing that can harm them so long as they stay underwater. Time is not something they concern themselves with. Their lives last twice as long as a human's. While my mother has said I will likely keep my youthful appearance my whole life, my life span is likely to be as long as a human's, since I will spend most of my life living as one.

The sirens' way of life is a beautiful, carefree existence, spent constantly in the presence of loved ones. Had I never lived as a human, I'm sure I would think it perfect.

I try to find the right words to make her understand. *I have spent all seventeen years of my life above the ocean, save the few instances I've been forced into the water.*

I've seen more than perfection.

I've loved and lost crew members, I continue. *I've learned swordplay. I know the joy of climbing a mast and swinging on a rope. I've played the role of a teacher, a friend, a confidant.*

The sirens don't know the true value of these things, because they don't know anything other than peace among themselves. The only conflicts to be had are when they're luring men to their deaths.

I cannot live my life without the human experiences I cherish so much, I explain. *I promise to visit often, but I need to lead a different life from yours.*

Asta-reven will rule the charm when you are gone, sister, my aunt says. *You needn't fear for our sake.*

It is not for your sake that I am worried! Mother says. *I've finally met my daughter. My only daughter. I don't want her out of my sight again.*

I'm warmed by her words, but it doesn't change my mind. I say my good-byes before returning to my ship.

The bodies of the fallen have already been laid to rest in the sea. The *Ava-lee* was cleaned of blood and other refuse. We lit lanterns for the fallen, and the sirens gifted us with as much treasure as the *Ava-lee* can hold.

It is our gift to you, my mother said, *for saving us all.*

We set out on this voyage with thirty-four. Now there are twenty-two. It is plenty to sail us home and plenty to shred my heart. I will miss them terribly. Athella's clever lockpicking fingers, Deros's strength, Deshel's and Lotiya's laughter.

"Good visit?" Niridia asks at my return. Radita and Mandsy worked together to fashion a wooden crutch for her. She uses it to walk around the ship, despite Mandsy's efforts to keep her in bed. Roslyn, too, is on the mend. She's bedridden, but conscious now, her father never leaving her side.

"Yes. I could get used to having a mother fuss over me, but now I will miss her whenever I am away. It comes with both joy and pain."

"Perhaps she will come visit us."

I let out a guffaw. "You want to let the sirens roam the waters near wherever we establish our stronghold? I'd never rally more men to my cause."

"But it would keep the land king from ever looking for us," she points out.

"Very true. Perhaps I'll give it more thought. How are things looking here?"

"The ship is ready. What heading should I give Kearan?"

We can go anywhere. Do anything. My father no longer controls us.

"To the keep," I decide. "Let's see what's left of it after the land king swept through. We get rid of those who won't be loyal. We sail to the port cities and clean out the pirate quarters. We build. And we make it better than it ever was before. It's time to set up the reign of the pirate queen."

Niridia smiles her approval. "Kearan! Stop ogling Sorinda and get this ship pointed due northeast!"

I stand at the edge of the ship, peering around the aftercastle to get another look at the Isla de Canta before we go. Part of me will always miss it, I think. This place where my family resides. But I will be back when we can spare the time. When I've built up what I first started to destroy for my father.

"Having second thoughts?" Riden leans on his forearms at the railing, letting his skin touch mine.

"No. I am exactly where I want to be. I only wish I could have all the years back I missed with my mother."

"You could have them now," he says gently. "You could live your life among the sirens and leave this all behind you."

I smile and turn to him. "You and my mother are both missing one important thing."

"What's that?"

"I *love* being a pirate, and there's nothing I want to be more."

He relaxes considerably. "Thank the stars. I was trying so hard to be supportive and forget what I want most."

"And what's that?"

Those beautiful brown eyes glint. "You."

"Have you decided you want to be a permanent member of the crew, then?" I tease.

"Aye, Captain." He lifts the tricorne off my head and runs his fingers through my hair. "I'll sail with you anywhere. I don't care where we go or what we do as long as I'm with you."

"Could be dangerous."

"You'll protect me."

He leans in and kisses me. So slowly it's maddening.

When he pulls back, I say, "I run a tight ship, sailor. I expect the rules to be followed."

"What rules would those be?"

"All men are required to keep a couple days' worth of stubble on their chins. Makes them look more fearsome. Better pirates, you see."

He grins so widely, I can feel my heart melt. "I had no idea you liked it so much." He brings his lips to my ear. "You needn't make a rule and trouble the other men. I'll do it if you ask nicely."

His lips trail down my neck and I shiver. "Anything else?" he asks.

"I need to see you in my quarters for the rest."

"Aye-aye."

ACKNOWLEDGMENTS

I have heard other authors say that writing a second book in a series is so much harder than the first.

They were right.

I had fun with *DotSQ*, but it was a struggle, and I have so many people to thank for their help.

I have to mention my incredibly talented editor, Holly West, first. Holly, I can't tell you how much it meant to me for you to give so much care and attention to this book. It is 1,000% stronger for all of your insightful comments and brilliant suggestions. A thousand thank-yous for all the hard work you put into this manuscript.

Rachel, thank you for being so wonderful through another book. I love having you by my side during this process. You make it so fun with all your pirate gifs and pep talks. Thank you for championing this series. Here's to hoping we do many more together.

I'm so grateful to the entire team at Feiwel and Friends for all the various things they do for me and my books. Brittany, thank you for answering all my questions and helping get me and my book into new places. I couldn't have asked for a better publicist. Lauren, thanks for all the promotions you put together! I've had such fun with those. Thank you, Liz, for pimping out my covers! Thank you to Beka and Kaitlin for your copyediting expertise.

Thank you, Anna, for the mind-blowing blurb you gave *DotPK*! Thank you, Elly, for reading and blurbing *DotSQ*.

To Korrina, Cori, and everyone at OwlCrate, thank you. You helped my book reach so many new readers. The box you put together was beautiful.

Alisa, you were invaluable in helping me fix plot holes and talk out difficult scenes. I don't know what I would do without you. You are the best roommate.

I cannot forget Chersti Nieveen, Kate Coursey, Courtney Alameda, Taralyn Johnson, and Sarah Talley for giving me amazing feedback on such a rough draft of this book. Thank you for being so prompt and wonderful!

Thanks need to go to my mom and Tara for answering all of my medical questions so injuries were realistic.

Thank you, Emily King and Megan Gadd, for being awesome friends and a huge source of support. I know I can always count on you.

I also have to thank my aunts, Sue and Candace, for taking me on the vacation of a lifetime. Thank you for providing me with a way to get some hands-on experience in sailing. Love you both!

I don't know how I suddenly have so many writing friends, but you have all touched me as a writer. Huge thanks to Gwen Cole, Ash Poston, Mikki Kells, Kyra Nelson, Katie Purdie, Erin Summerill, Summer Spence, Nicole Castroman, Ilima Todd, Taffy Lovell, Brekke Felt, Veeda Bybee, Charlie Holmberg, and Caitlyn McFarland for all the writing nights and laughter.

Thank you to all the bloggers, bookstagrammers, and book clubs who have supported me and given the *Daughter of the Pirate King* duology extra love, especially Bridget at *Dark Faerie Tales*, AliBabaDeBooks, *Brittany's Book Rambles*, *FearYourEx*, Sara aka *Novel Novice*, the *Swoony Boys Podcast* group, Karina at 24hr yabookblog, Rachel at *A Perfection Called Books*, *Mundie Moms*, and *YA and Wine* (especially Krysti and Sarah).

Thank you, Tiff, Greg, Lucy, and Ruby, for being so patient with me as I adjusted to my new workload and travel schedule. I am so blessed for knowing you!

I have the best family in the world. Becki and Johnny, thank you for helping me get away from my computer by playing *Overwatch* with me. Mom and Dad, thank you for your continued support. Dad, your woodworking is astonishing, and I love it. Mom, you are such a talented seamstress. Thanks for making my pirate hat. Thank you to my grandparents and aunts and uncles for giving me places to stay on tour and for supporting me and my books. I love you all.

And, of course, thank you to my readers. Thanks for reaching out to me on social media. Your kind words keep me going and make all the hard parts of writing worth it.

Vordan's Map
Uncharted Waters
N
W
E
S
Isla de Canta
Seventeen
Teskoi's